RIG FOR SILENT RUNNING

Anthony Genualdi

BookLocker

To the submariners, of all navies and all wars,
who are on "eternal patrol."

CHAPTER ONE
15 AUGUST 1942

"Admiral, Commander Dominic Tomassi, commanding officer, U.S.S. *Eel*, reporting."

Rear Admiral Lockhart nodded to Tomassi, and the sub commander lowered his hand. "At ease, Commander," Lockhart said, "Have a seat."

"Thank you, sir." Tomassi removed his cap and sat down opposite his new commander, Commander, Submarines, Southwest Pacific (COMSUBSOWESPAC). The admiral's office was in Perth, Australia, north of the American base at Fremantle, in the building of a life insurance company.

"Let's hear about you, Tomassi. I mean, your record up to now with your boat."

Tomassi took a breath, then proceeded. "Well, sir, the *Eel* was commissioned on December 1st of '41. We got underway the next day for Pearl. We were off of Florida when we heard about the attack on Pearl. Then we heard the following week about Germany going to war with us, and as we passed Cuba, one of our planes came after us, and we had to dive to avoid attack. We got to Panama about Christmas time, and after passing through the canal, went up to San Diego to fuel up. We got to Pearl a week after New Year's.

"We went out on a patrol about a week later. We were sent to Hokkaido about mid-January, and we got there at the end of the month. We sighted a couple of freighters and fired at them, with no hits, and we got depth charged a couple of times. Our luck finally was good when, at the end of February, just before leaving the area, we sank an oil tanker with our torpedoes. She looked kind of small, so I set the torpedoes for a shallow run, and that seemed to do it. We went back to Pearl and got there, oh, about the end of April.

"After we got back to Pearl, we were sent at the end of May to patrol near Midway. We were part of the line of subs that was southeast of the island, between there and Hawaii. We didn't see a damn thing, of course. We heard about how our guys did on the radio, then we came home. We set out for here at the end of June. We were sent to patrol near Truk We spotted some merchant shipping and went after them, producing a hit on a freighter, but I only claim damage, since we had to go under right away to avoid attack. We later sank a sub chaser and shot down a Jap plane that was coming after us. I also managed to get a shot at *Luzon Maru #4.*"

"The ex-whaling ship?"

"Yes, sir. As you know, sir, she's now a tanker. Some 15,500 tons. I know I got a good shot with two torpedoes, but our sound reported them hitting the target without exploding."

"Damn," Lockhart said.

Tomassi nodded, "I said something to that effect, sir." Both men laughed.

"How much longer did you spend at Truk?"

"We were on patrol there for some twenty-five days, sir. Then we made the run here and arrived this morning. I came over as soon as I was presentable. I know whiskers are against regulations."

Lockhart nodded, "So they are. Well, what does that make altogether for your kills?"

Tomassi dropped his head for a moment, then said, "Well, sir, that would be two sunk and one damaged. The tanker off Japan was some 4,000 tons, and the sub chaser off Truk was some 300 tons, plus one patrol plane."

Lockhart was silent for a moment. "I suppose you're expecting a lecture now on fighting spirit and knowing how to handle your torpedoes."

Tomassi nodded, "Yes, sir."

"Well, put your mind at ease, Tomassi. While you were at Truk, we were conducting some experiments with the Mark 14 torpedo down at Albany. We find they're running eleven feet deeper than set. Try to remember that when you go out. We have skippers also reporting about duds and premature explosions. We're still working to correct all of that.

"Meanwhile, your boat is going to get a good going over here. She'll be ready in two weeks to go out again. Your crew will have their liberty here in Fremantle. By the beginning of September, you'll be back out at sea. Tell me about your exec."

"That would be Lt. Commander Davis Van Wert. He's a good man, and he's helped me keep the *Eel* running smooth."

"Would he be fit to take a command now?"

"No, sir, I don't think he would be good now. We've only had three patrols. I think I would give him a little longer."

"All right, Tomassi. You enjoy your leave. I have four hotels around town leased for our guys, including two on the ocean. I'll send a runner with the name of the hotel you and your men will go to."

"Thank you, sir. Um, also, I was wondering, and the men were too, about, um, female companionship. I mean, I've heard Aussie women are real friendly."

"Oh, I'd ask the staff of the hotel if I were you. They could steer you to, um, *those* kind of girls."

"Thank you, Admiral. The boys will be happy. They've only had each other to look at for months."

"You're welcome, Tomassi. Dismissed."

Tomassi stood up, put his cap on, and saluted. He stepped aside, did an about face, and left the office.

The driver who had brought him to the office now took Tomassi back across Perth harbor into Fremantle. They passed along the south edge of the big harbor, through Alfred Cove and Palmyra, past the Royal Fremantle Golf Club, and on to the gate of the base. They passed up the other boats docked alongside and went down to the submarine tender U.S.S. *Pisces*. The *Eel* was alongside her, away from the dock.

Tomassi got permission to come aboard the *Pisces*, crossed over the tender, then went down the gangway to the *Eel*.

As he went down, Tomassi looked over his boat. The *Eel* was one of the *Gato* class. She was a little over 300 feet long, some 27 feet wide at the conning tower, and had a draft of 15 feet. She had ten torpedo tubes, four at the stern and six at the bow. She also had two 20mm guns, fore and aft on the conning tower, and a 3 inch gun mounted forward. Tomassi smiled at this, since he'd seen boats with their deck gun mounted aft, and thought it silly, since it meant showing one's stern to the enemy to use the gun.

Her paint job could best be described as a sort of blackish gray. She had started out from New London painted black and got a gray paint job at Pearl before going on her third patrol. It didn't help with trying to hide in clear, shallow water.

As he got to the bottom of the gangway, a voice came from the bridge of the *Eel*. "Skipper?"

"Request permission to come aboard."

"Permission granted, sir." It was Van Wert, the exec. Tomassi snapped a salute toward the ensign, and turned to Van Wert.

"Well, Van," he said, "the admiral seems like an OK Joe."

"That's good."

As Tomassi climbed up the side of the conning tower to get to the bridge, he said, "Admiral Lockhart has four hotels locked up in town, and two along a beach. He's sending a runner later to tell us where we can have our liberty."

"Great, skipper. The men should be happy with that. They've been asking me about liberty."

As they headed below, Van Wert said, "I should tell you, skipper that the tender said they don't have enough torpedoes for us, and we might have to go out with mines."

Tomassi shook his head, "Lovely. Not enough torpedoes, and what they do have run too deep."

"Where'd you hear that, sir?"

"From the admiral. He told me they were testing torpedoes down south, at Albany. They run eleven feet deeper than set."

"Oh. And what about the duds we got when we went after *Luzon Maru*?"

"They're still working on that." Presently, the two men got to Tomassi's cabin. "Well, Van, this would be the time to write your folks and let them know you're OK."

"Yes, sir."

"Is your dad still sore at you for actually going to sea?"

"A little, sir. He wanted me to stay home, at least at the Navy Department, instead of going into action."

"He figured your place was at the Waldorf?"

"Yes, sir." Van Wert grinned a little. "I guess he figured only the little people should fight. But I said I wanted to go to Annapolis. He knew he couldn't talk me out of it. He tried to pull some strings to keep me in Washington, but I got around it, and went to the subs."

"Good for you."

"Thanks, skipper.

"I'm going to turn in, Van. Let me know when that runner gets here."

"Yes, skipper"

"Very well." Tomassi went into his cabin and lay down for a rest.

CHAPTER TWO
16 AUGUST 1942

Tomassi had gotten directions from the desk clerk at the hotel where the crew of the *Eel* was staying to Roe Street in Perth. This was the place with *those* girls. Not every house had a red light in the window, and the clerk had told Tomassi that some of the houses were home to various "reform" minded types who would probably tell him to not go into a "house of sin." But, Tomassi hadn't been with a woman since shoving off from New London, and that was more than nine months ago. He felt he needed this.

He walked up the steps of the third house from the corner. The man at the hotel told him this was a really good house, with many passionate women who would give him a great time. He knocked on the door. An older woman opened it.

"Yes."

"Hello, madam. A fellow at the hotel told me about this place and said something about Fiona."

She nodded, "Yes, Fiona always comes highly recommended. Tim rang me up about you. Come on in, Yank."

Tomassi removed his cap as he entered the parlor. "Make yourself at home," the madam said, "I'll go get her." Everything was done in red velvet. Even the walls were velvet. Tomassi sat down and noticed a young Chinese woman, about seventeen or eighteen years old. She had long, shiny black hair, a red corset, and fishnet stockings, with black high heeled shoes. She looked at him, and after a moment, Tomassi smiled at her. She managed a weak smile in return. No use being quiet, he thought.

"Hello."

She managed a nod and a soft "hello" in return.

"How are you?"

"All right, Yank. You here for good time, yes?"

"Yes. A fellow named Tim at the hotel told me about Fiona."

"Oh, yes," the Chinese girl nodded, "Everyone like Fiona. She is …a real tomato. That what you Yanks say?"

"Yeah, that's what we say."

She smiled. "All right, Yank."

Presently, the madam showed up with a stunning specimen of femininity. "Here's Fiona, Yank."

"Oh, my," Tomassi said as he stood to shake Fiona's hand. Fiona was about five-feet-eight, with long red hair, green eyes, and freckles. She had on a green bustier, green panties, black stockings, and a black feather boa.

"Pleased to meet you, Yank."

"It's Dom. Whaddaya say?"

"Dom?"

"Short for Dominic."

"Are you Italian?"

"Italian from Chicago, that's me."

Fiona looked over to the Chinese girl. "So, you've met 'Silly Lily?'"

Tomassi looked over. "Is that your name?"

Lily smiled and nodded.

The madam said, "OK, Yank, it's thirty pounds."

Tomassi looked at her. "I'm afraid I didn't get a chance to change money. How much is that in greenbacks?"

"What?"

"In dollars, Ruthie," Fiona said.

"Oh, well, you got thirty dollars?"

Tomassi looked in his wallet. "I sure do." He handed the money over to Ruthie."Have fun, you two."

Fiona took Tomassi's hand and said, "Come with me, love." They went upstairs and went into the first room on the right.

As Tomassi undressed, Fiona asked, "So, Dom, what are you up to tonight?"

"It's my birthday."

"Oh, really, love? Well, many happy returns. How many is this?"

"I'm thirty-five today."

Fiona smiled as she lay down on the bed, tossing off her shoes and dropping her boa on the floor. "You'll want to unwrap your present, then?"

Tomassi smiled, "Nice pretty present. But like all presents, nicer when it's unwrapped, and you play with it."

Fiona laughed. "Good one, Dom."

Now that he had undressed, Tomassi got on the bed with Fiona and did the unwrapping. The zipper for the bustier ran down the back, so he reached around and slowly pulled it down, to reveal Fiona's full, creamy breasts. He planted a kiss in her cleavage, then pulled down her panties. He kissed her neck while he pumped her. For her part, Fiona wrapped her left leg around Tomassi's waist, and moaned with delight.

After the big moment, Tomassi kissed Fiona's cheek and said, "Thank you, doll."

"Oh, you're welcome love."

He kept his arms around her and asked, "Can we talk a minute?"

"Sure, love."

"The Chinese girl, Lily."

"Silly Lily?"

"Yeah."

"What about her?"

"What's her story?"

Fiona thought for a moment, "Well, Ruthie brought her from China in '39. She's been here ever since."

"Really."

"Don't you trust her?"

"Well," Tomassi said, "if servicemen come in, and they go with her, how do we know she's not a Jap?"

"Oh, no, Dom. Ruthie brought her. We can trust her."

"How do I know Ruthie isn't a German spy?"

"No, love, nothing like that. I mean, I see why you'd say that. But, no. Ruthie's family is from England. All solid and loyal."

"The cops have checked on this?"

"The closest the law has touched us, was, I guess, last year, when the Manpower Inquiry came to see if there was anyone who could be released for war work. They asked Ruthie what she did, and she told them, 'Essential labor, madam of a brothel,' and they left her, and us, alone since."

Tomassi smiled at this. "All right! That's what I love about you Aussies; you just come out and tell it like it is.

Fiona smiled, "We are a straightforward people."

"Still, I'm not comfortable about Lily."

"What would you do?"

"Promise not to tell Ruthie?"

"I promise."

"I'll tell my guys about this place, and I'll tell them to give Lily a wide berth."

Fiona nodded, "I understand, and I promise not to tell Ruthie."

"That's a good girl." Tomassi kissed her cheek again and got up to get dressed.

CHAPTER THREE
30 AUGUST 1942

Dominic Tomassi didn't like to sit in his cabin and have his division chiefs come tell him they were ready for sea. He always felt it was better to come and look for himself.

He started, logically enough, with the after torpedo room and worked his way forward. On this day, Tomassi would see the Mark 12, Model 3 naval mines that were in the stern of his boat. The Chief Torpedoman's Mate, Chief Petty Officer (CPO) Barker, was there to supervise the handling of these mines.

"Hello, sir," Barker said.

"Hello, Chief." Tomassi glared at the cylindrical mines. "Do you have some loaded already, Chief?"

"No, sir, we were about to, though."

Tomassi looked at the mines for a moment. He'd had to give up carrying six torpedoes aft to make room for twenty-two of these evil eggs. "So, Chief, this means we only have two torpedoes for loading once the mines are all deployed?"

"Aye, sir."

Tomassi shook his head. "Oh, well. Proceed, Chief."

"Aye, sir. All right, you guys, load 'em up." The torpedo men loaded four of the eight and one-half foot long mines into the tubes and sealed them.

"Very well, Chief. The quicker we get rid of these, the happier we all will be."

"Except the Japs, right sir?"

Tomassi laughed, "Right, Chief. Carry on."

"Aye, sir."

Tomassi moved forward into the motor room, and then to the after engine room. Here was the Chief Engineman's Mate, CPO Grace. The ribbing he took for having a girl's name for a last name gave Chief Grace a quick tongue, but Tomassi never had to worry about it, for he knew Grace was the best at keeping the four diesels humming along.

"Hi, Chief."

"Hello, captain."

"Everything ready here for sea?"

"Aye, sir. Full allowance of fuel on board. Got all the spare parts we needed, too. We're ready for sea, sir."

"Very well, Chief. Carry on."

"Aye, sir."

Tomassi proceeded through the forward engine room, and into the crew quarters. Some of the men were relaxing with a poker game. One of them, Engineman Bellows, saw him and called, "Attention on deck."

"As you were. Is 'Doc' here?"

"Aye, sir. He's up there." Bellows pointed to an upper bunk on the starboard side. Tomassi looked up. "Doc?"

Pharmacist's Mate Matos, a Filipino, poked his head over the lip of his bunk. "Yes, sir?"

"Just seeing where you were, Doc. Get all the supplies from the tender you needed?"

"Aye, sir," Matos smiled. He had a great bedside manner, which made him perfect for his job. He may not have been a doctor, more like a medic, able to patch guys up without major work, but he'd make a great doctor one day.

"That's all. Carry on, men."

"Thank you, sir," Bellows replied.

Next on the list was the galley. "Cookie?"

The cook, Daniels, answered, "Yes, sir?"

"All ready for sea?"

"Aye, sir. Got plenty of steaks, and chops, and veggies. We've got milk, too, whole and canned."

"I look forward to the whole milk."

"Enjoy it while it lasts, sir."

"OK, Cookie, carry on."

"Aye, sir."

Forward of the galley was the radio room. "Sparks?"

The radio man, Boudreaux, answered with his Cajun drawl, "Aye, sir?"

"Ready for sea, Sparks?"

"Aye, sir. We got them new vacuum tubes in, and I can get any station you want. I guarantee."

"OK, Sparks. Carry on."

"Aye, sir."

Tomassi now went into the control room, where the sub could be made to maneuver underwater. He found Lieutenant (j.g.) Beck, the diving officer. "Mister Beck?"

"Aye, sir."

"Are you all squared away?"

"Yes, sir. The repair crew did a great job with fixing those stern plane controls. No problems getting her down now."

"Great. Carry on."

"Aye, sir."

Tomassi now passed forward through officer's country to get to the forward torpedo room. He entered the compartment just as the six tubes were being loaded. Torpedoman's Mate Marino saw him.

"Marino."

"Aye, sir."

"Loading up, I see."

"Aye, sir, just loading up."

"Got all the fish we need?"

"Aye, sir. Full allowance."

"OK, carry on."

"Aye, sir."

Tomassi turned back into the officer's quarters section of the boat when he came across Van Wert. "Van?"

"Aye, sir?"

"Do you have anything to report?"

"Aye, sir. We have a full load of ammo for the three-inch gun, all of which is stowed under the deck plates near the gun. We have a full load of 20mm ammo in the magazine, as well as .50-caliber ammo, and pistol ammo for the .45's and the two Tommy Guns, plus a crate of ammo for the carbine."

Tomassi shook his head. "That silly M1 Carbine. I don't know how they expect us to repel boarders with a carbine."

"Maybe we can throw it at them, skipper."

"That's the only way it could hurt them."

Van Wert smiled, "Yes, sir."

"Let's call the crew to quarters."

"Aye, sir." Both men proceeded to the conning tower. Van Wert got on the "squawk box," which was the PA system for the boat. One could address the whole crew, or only certain compartments, with a turn of the dial. Van Wert turned the dial to address all of the boat. "Crew, to your quarters. On the double."

Tomassi and Van Wert went out the hatch on the starboard side and went to the foredeck. The men and officers assembled as fast as they could. After a couple of minutes, the fifty-eight men and officers were on deck, and at attention. With the captain and exec standing in front of them, this made the whole ship's complement.

Van Wert turned to Tomassi and saluted. "Ship's company, U.S.S. *Eel*, all present and accounted for, sir."

Tomassi returned the salute. "Very well. When the men are dismissed, have the special sea section at their stations and prepare the ship to get underway."

"Aye, aye, sir." Van Wert saluted and Tomassi returned it. Van Wert did an about face and said, "Leave your quarters. Special sea section to your stations on the double. All hands prepare to get underway."

The men started below. Those who were to take in the lines went to their stations, and Tomassi and Van Wert went to the bridge.

Within half-an-hour, the *Eel* was ready to depart. Chief Barker informed the officers on the bridge, "All hands ready for departure. All connections with the tender are removed except mooring lines."

"Very well, Chief," Tomassi said. He turned to his exec, "Van, take her out."

"Aye, skipper." Van Wert cupped his hand to his mouth and yelled, first forward, then aft, "Take in two. Take in three." The men at their lines obeyed him and took in their lines. Tomassi looked up to the tender and motioned for them to haul up the gangway, which they did. An ensign on the deck of the *Pisces* saluted and waved. Tomassi returned the salute and waved back.

"Take in four," Van Wert yelled aft, whereupon the men on the stern mooring line took it in. He turned to the bow and yelled, "Take in one." The men at the bow line took it in from the tender. Van Wert then turned to the squawk box and said, "Helm, left ten degrees rudder."

"Helm, left ten degrees rudder, aye," came the answer from the quartermaster.

"Very well. Engine room, starboard ahead one-third."

"Starboard ahead one-third, aye," came the answer. The starboard engines came on and moved the boat away along with the turn of the rudder. After a moment, Van Wert said, "Engine room, port ahead one-third."

"Port ahead one-third, aye." Now the stern of the sub bubbled up fully as both screws turned to get the boat on her way.

"Helm, rudder amidships," said Van Wert.

"Helm, rudder amidships, aye," came the answer.

While this was happening, Lieutenant Odom, who was the Officer of the Deck (OOD), came up. Tomassi turned and acknowledged him, "Mr. Odom. Good to see you."

"Aye, sir," came the nervous reply.

"This is only your second patrol, isn't it?"

"Yes, sir."

"Well, this will get to be old hat soon enough."

"Yes, sir."

"You have the con, Mr. Odom."

"Aye, sir."

"Van, let's get below. I have something to show you."

"Aye, sir," Van Wert replied. The two of them went down the conning tower hatch, then down to the control room, where the chart table was laid out.

"We're going up the coast to top off our tanks," Tomassi said. He bent over and pointed to a spot up the coast from Fremantle. "Two days up the coast, we're going to reach Exmouth Gulf. Admiral

Lockhart told me before we shoved off about a new base we're establishing there. The code name of it is 'Potshot.'"

"OK, skipper."

"It'll be like Midway."

"Nice," Van Wert smiled.

"Well, not really. It'll be like Midway in that we'll be able to get fuel, and, the admiral hopes, one day we could have a tender there to give us torpedoes as well. Right now, there's only a dumb barge they towed up there with fuel in it."

"So, not really like Midway."

"Nope," Tomassi said. "Not like Midway. No bowling alley. No gooney birds. And –" he said as he straightened up, "– no beer."

Van Wert frowned at this.

CHAPTER FOUR
7 SEPTEMBER 1942

The orders for the *Eel* on her fourth war patrol took her to the waters off of Singapore. She was to plant her mines east of the island in the Strait of Johore, between the main island of Singapore and Ubin Island. After planting the mines, she was to patrol the mouth of the harbor for a few days, then proceed to the western side of the island to check the other entrance to the strait. She would patrol there until her fuel or ammo ran low, then come home to Fremantle.

Tomassi and Van Wert checked their charts to see how to proceed. Tomassi spoke first:

"I think it would be better to work from the big island toward Ubin. Don't you, Van?"

Van Wert stared at the chart for a moment. "I really don't like shallow water like this."

"Where are you looking?"

Van Wert pointed to the small strait on the north side of Ubin, separating the island from Malaysia. "There."

Tomassi shook his head. "No, Van, that's not where I mean." He pointed to the small island southwest of Ubin, called Serangoon. It ran parallel, from northwest to southeast, of the main island. "I'm talking about here, Van." Tomassi drew a line with his finger going up and to the right. "The orders say to mine this big channel. I'm putting the mines from the northwest tip of Serangoon to the northwest tip of Ubin."

"That's barely six-tenths of a mile, skipper."

"We're not going to run at flank speed. We'll be creeping along, and we'll have time to go someplace in case of trouble. This is a deeper channel that the other side of Ubin. No problem."

"OK, skipper. Now I'm clear."

Tomassi looked at his watch. "It'll be first light in a couple of hours. We'll get as close as we can to Serangoon before diving, then we can turn and make the run."

"Have you ever planted mines, skipper?"

"No. I never have, and I hope it'll be a long time before I do it again. I didn't go to sub school to be a minelayer." Tomassi looked at Van Wert and asked, "Did you?"

Van Wert shook his head. "No, sir. But, then, I'm just glad to be in combat."

As daybreak approached, the *Eel* moved along the eastern coast of Serangoon Island. Tomassi hoped no Japanese lookout on that little island was awake. Their luck had held. They had encountered no patrols on the strait up to this point.

The tip of the island was coming into view off the port bow. At this point, Tomassi and Van Wert were on the bridge. The lookouts in their perches were keeping their eyes open, scanning the horizon for anyone and everyone. Both officers had their binoculars as well, looking around to see anyone.

Van Wert was the first to say something. "Smoke off the starboard bow, captain." Tomassi looked to where Van Wert was pointing. Someone was coming down the strait. There was enough smoke for it to be two ships.

Tomassi called out, "Lookouts below." The men in their perches climbed down quickly to get down the hatch. "Can you figure a heading on that smoke, Van?"

"It looks like … zero-two-zero relative. We've got a few minutes, skipper. Should we wait for them to go by?"

"No. We'll try to get our mines in before they get here. Clear the bridge." The other men got down the hatch, with Van Wert behind them. Tomassi now stepped up to the squawk box and sounded the alarm. "Dive! Dive!"

As he got below, he closed the hatch behind him, and the quartermaster secured it. "Take her down to fifty feet," Tomassi called down the hatch to the control room.

"Fifty feet, aye," came the response from Lieutenant Beck.

"Helm, right full rudder, come right to course zero-four-zero."

"Helm, right full rudder, coming right to course zero-four-zero, sir," replied Seaman Lucas.

"Very well." Tomassi turned to Seaman Benton, the talker. Benton had his headset, with headphones and microphone, on. "Make ready stern tubes."

"Make ready stern tubes," repeated Benton.

Tomassi turned to Van Wert, "We're gonna try and get rid of these mines before whoever's up there gets here. Helm, ahead slow."

"Ahead slow, sir," Lucas answered.

Benton now spoke, "Stern tubes ready, sir."

"Stand by to fire."

Benton put his hand on the firing button.

"Leveled off at fifty feet, captain," Lieutenant Beck reported.

"Very well."

"Here goes," Van Wert said.

"Here goes." Tomassi turned to Benton. "Fire seven."

"Fire seven," Benton repeated into his headset as he pressed the button. The rush of air could be heard as the torpedo tube sent the mine on its way. "Seven's away, sir."

"Fire eight."

"Fire eight. Eight's away, sir."

"Fire nine."

"Fire nine. Nine's away, sir."

"Fire ten."

"Fire ten. Ten's away, sir."

"After torpedo, reload with mines."

"After torpedo, reload with mines," repeated Benton.

Tomassi now turned to the soundman, Marcus. "Marcus, what do you have? I need a true bearing."

"I have screws bearing two-six-five relative. Two sets." Marcus listened for a moment. "Bearing is three-zero-five true. It sounds like a freighter and an escort, sir."

"Do you mean a destroyer?"

"Negative, sir. It's more like a frigate."

"I hope they give us a minute," Van Wert said.

"Me too," Tomassi replied.

Benton now reported, "Stern tubes loaded with mines, sir."

"Very well," Tomassi said, "Stand by to fire."

"Stand by to fire," Benton said into the microphone.

"Fire seven."

"Fire seven. Seven's away, sir."

"Fire eight."

"Fire eight. Eight's away, sir."

"Fire nine."

"Fire nine. Nine's away, sir."

"Fire ten."

"Fire ten. Ten's away, sir."

"After torpedo, reload with mines."

"After torpedo, reload with mines," repeated Benton.

They went through this procedure three more times as they crossed the strait, getting closer to Ubin Island with each moment. Also with each moment, the soundman reported the two ships closing in.

"Give me a bearing on them, sound."

"Relative bearing two-three-zero, sir," Marcus reported as they got down to the last two mines.

Tomassi got on the squawk box and called, "After torpedo room."

"After torpedo room, aye."

"What do you have left?"

"Two mines and two torpedoes, sir."

"Load tubes seven and eight with mines, and tubes nine and ten with torpedoes."

"Aye, aye, sir."

Tomassi turned to Lucas at the helm. "Helm, ahead dead slow."

"Helm, ahead dead slow, aye."

"Very well." The sub slowed to almost the speed of a man walking. Tomassi knew the bottom had to be getting close. He turned to Marcus. "Give me a fathometer reading."

After a moment, Marcus replied, "Twelve fathoms, sir." That meant seventy-two feet, and that was below the keel, which was already fifty feet below surface.

"Come on, you guys," Van Wert muttered.

Benton reported, "After torpedo tubes loaded, sir."

Tomassi smiled, "Very well. Stand by tubes seven and eight."

"Stand by tubes seven and eight," Benton repeated. He put his hand on the firing button.

"Fire seven," Tomassi ordered.

"Fire seven. Seven's away, sir."

"Fire eight."

"Fire eight. Eight's away, sir."

"Helm, all ahead one-third. Right full rudder. Come right to course one-four-zero."

Lucas answered, "All ahead one-third, right full rudder, coming right to course one-four-zero, sir."

"Very well. Sound, are our friends still coming in?"

"Aye, sir. Still chugging along."

"Maybe we can get a look at them. Up periscope, Van."

Van Wert raised the periscope. Tomassi turned it to look back to the starboard quarter, where the enemy should be. There was a medium sized freighter and a sub chaser. Tomassi looked to the freighter. "She's coming into the string of mines! Oh, boy!"

Just after he said this, the freighter struck a mine. A great geyser of water went up, and the sound could be heard clearly throughout the boat. A cheer went up from everyone in the compartment. For his part, Tomassi beamed. "Look, Van."

Van Wert stepped up to the scope and smiled as he saw the freighter come to a stop. He turned to Tomassi and said, "The sub chaser is speeding up." Van Wert looked through the scope again, and after a moment, the boat felt another mine go off. "Skipper, now *he* struck a mine."

"Let me see, Van."

Van Wert stepped aside this time as Tomassi looked through the scope and saw both ships dead in the water. Laughter rang through the conning tower.

"I bet most minelayers don't get to see what they did, huh, sir," Benton asked.

"You bet they don't. Come look, everyone."

Each man in the con got to take a peek at the sight of the two ships starting to sink in the channel. Tomassi himself took the helm so that Lucas could see it. While Lucas was looking, Tomassi steered the *Eel* to a more southerly course. Lucas got back to his station, and Tomassi told him, "I've put us on course one-eight-zero. Keep her steady there."

"Aye, aye, sir."

"This'll look good in the log, won't it, Van?"

"Yes, sir," Van Wert replied. "We'll have to look through the book to see what freighter we can claim."

CHAPTER FIVE
9 SEPTEMBER 1942

After two days of lying low, the *Eel* now stood off of Singapore harbor. In the meantime, Tomassi and Van Wert looked through the Merchant Ship Recognition Manual to find one of the victims of the mines they'd laid in the Strait of Johore. It was a 6,000 ton freighter. Tomassi made note of it in the log, as if it were a torpedo sinking, and hoped to get credit for it.

It was just about 09:00 on the morning of the 9th. Mr. Odom, the OOD, had just been relieved on periscope watch by Van Wert. Van Wert looked toward the harbor, which the Japanese had made bustling with traffic. In addition to the various patrols, merchant vessels of all kinds, large and small, were moving in and out of the harbor. Among them was a leviathan the *Eel* had seen before.

Van Wert looked off to the starboard side when he saw her. His jaw just about hit the deck. "Mr. Odom, sound general quarters."

"Aye, aye, sir," Odom replied and pushed the button for the general alarm, also known as "The Bells of St. Mary's," since it's steady *bong-bong-bong* sound was rather like church bells. Odom also called over the squawk box, "Captain to the conning tower. Captain to the conning tower."

Tomassi tumbled out of his sack and slipped on his sandals. He rushed back to the control room and clambered up the ladder. The talker was just telling Van Wert, "Forward torpedo room, manned and ready."

The alarm was just stopping when Tomassi asked, "What have you got, Van?"

"Skipper, just look." Van Wert stepped aside and Tomassi stepped up to the periscope.

Tomassi didn't need any manual to tell him the ship that was steaming along a few thousand yards away. Her image had been burned into his brain over a month ago. She was over five hundred feet long, with a superstructure near the bow, cranes amidships and two smokestacks, side-by-side, near the stern.

It was her. *Luzon Maru #4.*

"Oh, my Lord," Tomassi exclaimed. He looked to Van Wert. "It's really her!"

Van Wert nodded, "I know, skipper."

Tomassi pointed to the far side of the periscope, indicating Van Wert should call the bearing and range to the fire control party. Van Wert stepped over.

Tomassi made the call, "Bearing, mark."

"Zero-eight-zero."

"Range, mark."

"Five-five-double-oh."

"Angle on the bow, one-hundred-twenty port. Estimate target speed, ten knots. Set torpedoes to five feet. Gyro angle fifteen right."

Lt. Odom was putting all the data into the Torpedo Data Computer (TDC), trying to come up with the solution that would ensure a hit. For his part,

Tomassi was hoping no errant patrol vessel would come along and ruin things for him, as had happened at Truk. He'd had to fire in a hurry then, and even though the fish were duds then, he felt if he'd had an extra moment then, he'd have gotten this big beast.

"Course and speed check, sir," Lt. Odom reported.

"Very well," Tomassi replied. "Stand by bow tubes."

"Stand by bow tubes," repeated Benton, as he reached for the firing button.

"Sound," Van Wert asked, "any other contacts?"

"Nothing else around, sir," came the answer from Marcus.

"Final check, Van." Van Wert stepped up. "Bearing, mark."

"Zero-seven-zero."

"Range, mark."

"Four-oh-double-oh."

"Check," said Van Wert.

"Set," said Odom.

Tomassi folded up the periscope handles. "Down scope," he ordered. As the scope lowered, he said to Benton, "Fire one."

"Fire one," Benton said as he pressed the button. "One's away, sir."

"Fire two."

"Fire two. Two's away, sir."

"Fire three."

"Fire three. Three's away, sir."

"Fire four."

"Fire four. Four's away, sir."

Tomassi turned to the soundman. "All torpedoes running hot, straight, and normal, sir."

Now came the most nervous part. Van Wert had his stopwatch running. "We should have a hit from number one in thirty seconds, skipper."

The seconds moved like hours. All hands knew the torpedo problems that had bedeviled them before could come on again. The deep running problem was solved for now with the settings. Five plus eleven meant a sixteen feet running depth, which would be good enough to take out this big tanker. But what of the warheads? Do they work? Only time would tell.

"Ten seconds, skipper."

"Up scope," Tomassi said. He was looking now right at *Luzon Maru #4.*

"Five seconds. Four, three, two, one."

No explosion. Tomassi could only see what would be the torpedo break against the hull of the target, with the telltale burst of air that meant the fish had broken in half.

"Number two," Tomassi asked.

"Five seconds, skipper. Four, three, two, one."

Again, no explosion.

"Sound," Tomassi asked, "what do you hear?"

"Bumping noise against the target, followed by a burst of air," Marcus answered.

"What about torpedo three?"

"Three seconds, two, one, zero."

Nothing!

"God damn it," Tomassi yelled.

Van Wert said, "Number four should hit in four, three, two, one, now."

Nothing again!

"Son of a bitch," yelled Tomassi. He slammed the handles against the periscope. "Down scope."

As the scope lowered, Van Wert said, "Can't we try again, skipper?"

"No," Tomassi thundered, "They've radioed in by now. Jap tin cans will be along quick enough." He looked down to the control room and said, "Mr. Beck, make you depth two hundred feet."

"Two hundred feet, aye, sir," came the reply.

The *Eel* would sit it out until nightfall, then come up to charge batteries. Tomassi finally said, "Secure from general quarters."

Van Wert went to the squawk box and said, "Secure from general quarters. First section, take the watch."

CHAPTER SIX
12 SEPTEMBER 1942

After the *Eel* had her brush with *Luzon Maru #4,* she spent two days trying to find something else to sink. Mostly it meant destroyers or sub chasers. Usually, a submarine would try to dodge anti-submarine warships, but Tomassi fired at them anyway. Either the torpedoes would run deep, or they would malfunction some other way, either not exploding at all, or going off prematurely. His luck finally changed on the early morning of the 11th, when the *Eel* used her deck gun to sink a Thai freighter. Since Thailand, or Siam, was Japan's ally, it was a good kill. The freighter looked to be about 1,000 tons, so at least there was something for them to make a pennant for when they would finally head home.

Before that would happen, though, Tomassi had his orders to look to the west side of Singapore Island, to see if any shipping was coming from the western entrance of the Strait of Johore. It was possible, with the Japanese advance into Burma, that some kind of shipping, either troop transports or supply ships, might try to come out of there. The *Eel* would try to intercept this.

The time was about 07:00. Tomassi had eaten his breakfast and came up to the bridge, to find Van Wert trying to cope with the fog.

"You ever been to London, Van?"

"Actually skipper, I have a couple of times. One time it was foggy as this." Van Wert laughed at little. "You know, I was –"

"Objects in the water," reported the starboard lookout.

Tomassi looked up to him and asked, "Where away?"

After a moment came the answer, "Two degrees off the starboard bow."

Both officers looked over and saw something was there, then two things, then three. It looked like people in a raft. Then a voice came up from the water, with a British accent, "My God, the bloody Nip bastards are back again."

Tomassi and Van Wert looked at each other wide eyed. After a second, Tomassi rasped, "Megaphone, now!" He then said into the squawk box, "Rescue party on deck, on the double."

Van Wert grabbed Tomassi by the arm and said, "Skipper. They could be Japs; it could be a trap."

Tomassi nodded, said, "Yeah. If a Yank could go to Oxford, I guess a Jap could, too," and turned to look down the hatch. He saw Chief Barker in the conning tower and said, "Chief, get a Tommy Gun from the magazine and join the rescue party."

"Aye, aye, sir." The Chief had been walking up to give Tomassi the megaphone. Tomassi took it and turned to the floating figures.

"Ahoy there in the water."

There was a commotion as the men in the water and raft looked at each other, no doubt startled to hear an American. "Ahoy there," one of them answered, "Who are you?"

"This is the United States submarine *Eel*. Who are you?"

"We're officers of His Majesty's submarine *Excellent*."

"How many of you are there?"

"There's seven of us, Yank."

"Say 'Lillian Russell.'"

"What?"

"Say 'Lillian Russell.'"

"Lillian Russell."

Well, Tomassi thought, no Jap could have said that name, since the letter "L" is impossible for them. But what of the rest of those figures in the water?

"How many did you say you were?"

"Seven."

"Let's have all of you say 'Lillian Russell.' I mean *all of you*." Five more English voices and one Scottish voice answered back with the actress' name. "OK, mate, I'm satisfied. Stand by to come aboard."

By this time, the rescue party and Chief Barker were on deck to fish out the British officers. Tomassi called on his men to send their guests down to the wardroom, and to sink the raft. Van Wert called for Pharmacist's Mate Matos to report to the wardroom to check them.

Tomassi told Van Wert he had the con, and then went below to check on the British. As he got to the wardroom, Matos started to look at each of them.

"How long have you been in the water," Tomassi asked the senior man he saw, a lieutenant commander.

"Oh, I think two days. I think it is, isn't it, chaps?"

The other men looked at each other and, after a couple of nods, the Scotsman said, "Aye, sir. We think two days."

Matos said to Tomassi, "I can tell you more in a minute, sir."

"OK, Doc." Tomassi stepped around the table and held his hand out to the lieutenant commander. "Commander Dominic Tomassi. You can call me Dom."

"Lieutenant Commander David Reynolds, commander, H.M.S. *Excellent*. Thanks for saving us, Dom." The men shook hands, and Tomassi introduced himself to the other men in turn.

The Scotsman identified himself, "Lieutenant Angus MacPherson, diving officer."

"Hi, lieutenant." For the life of him, Tomassi couldn't figure out where Brits got the idea that "lieutenant" contained the letter "F." After Tomassi talked to the last man, he went to the squawk box and called to the galley. "Cookie?"

"Aye, sir?"

"Bring some coffee and some milk to the wardroom for our guests."

"Aye, sir. Right away."

"Couldn't you give us something stronger, Dom," Reynolds asked.

"Sorry. Our navy has been 'dry' since 1914. I know if you had picked us up, we could have had a party." Laughter all around on that remark. "But the best we can give you is coffee nerves, and if you'd caught us just out of port, we'd have had ice cream. But that's gone now."

"The commander seems all right," Matos said. "Just a little dehydrated and malnourished. It's the same for the others."

"OK, Doc. Thanks."

"Aye, sir." Matos picked up his bag and left the compartment.

Tomassi sat down by Reynolds. "Where did you guys shove off from?"

"Trincomalee."

"Ceylon?"

"Yes. You wouldn't happen to be going that way, would you, Dom?"

"We're based in Western Australia. I'm afraid you'll have to come back with us, and our navies can arrange for your passage home."

"All right."

"So, what happened to you guys?"

Reynolds took a breath and said, "Well, we were sent here with a party of commandos. They were supposed to knock out a radio station about five miles inland that the Japs were using to pass messages forward. We had to wait for them for three days, or assume they were dead and leave without them. Well, it was four days and I waited for them anyway. We surfaced at the rendezvous and only one of the chaps showed up, and the Nips got him before he could get in the water. It's a sight I don't want to see again, what they did to that poor bloke.

"Anyway, the Japs on shore saw us, and radioed for a destroyer to come after us. We couldn't get away from him, and … well, it didn't end so well for us, either. About ten of us managed to escape, but three were badly wounded, including my Number One. Executive officer to you. They died during the night last night, and we let them go so the sharks wouldn't come after us. We figured the fog would cover us and maybe we would find a way onshore, or someone friendly would come. We'd barely had time to send a distress call. And, that's when you showed up. We'd had to play dead to keep a Nip sub from seeing us before. That's why I yelled what I did when we saw you."

At this point, Cookie showed up with a pot of coffee, and Van Wert followed him with the last big gallon can of whole milk. "Wow," Tomassi exclaimed, "I thought we'd drank that already."

"I was saving it for you, sir," Cookie said, "I know you love it, and Mr. Odom had managed to scrounge some dry ice for me to keep it cool."

"Well, God bless that Odom, and you too! OK, drinks are on me," Tomassi said with a laugh. Matos was behind Van Wert with the cups.

"Skipper, we need to dive. The fog is lifting," Van Wert said.

Tomassi got up and headed for the hatch. "I'll be seeing to that." He turned back to Reynolds.

"Lunch will be served soon. When we come up after dark, you'll all be able to stretch your legs some more. In the meantime, Mr. Van Wert will keep you company. He's been to your island, and he was going to tell me about his travels in London when we spotted you." The Brits laughed as Van Wert nodded and Cookie started to pour the coffee.

The *Eel* had settled down to periscope depth nearly an hour ago, and was on a southeasterly course, heading towards Singapore. Tomassi had just entered the conning tower with Lt. Commander Reynolds. "And now, we're back where we started," Tomassi said.

"Well, thank you, Dom," Reynolds said. "Most impressive. Compares well with my boat. Maybe a little nicer, living quarters wise."

"Maybe when you get your new boat, I could come and look."

Reynolds smiled. "That would be jolly good."

Soundman Marcus spoke up, "Sir, high speed screws bearing two-five-zero relative. It sounds like a destroyer."

"Up scope," said Tomassi. "General quarters."

"Aye, sir," said Benton, the talker. He sounded the Bells of St. Mary's and passed the word, "General quarters, general quarters, all hands man your battle stations."

"Rig for silent running."

"Rig for silent running," repeated Benton, who discontinued the alarm, and moved to turn off the fan.

The part of silent running no one liked was that the fans had to be shut off, making the submarine into a sauna.

Van Wert showed up as Tomassi looked through the scope at the Japanese tin can. "Got the book, skipper," Van Wert whispered. The book he meant in this case was the Japanese Naval Vessels Manual.

"OK, Van. This'll take a moment. The angle on the bow is ten degrees port. OK, um … two stacks."

"Two stacks."

"Three - inch guns fore and aft. Torpedo launchers forward of bridge. Um, also amidships."

"Three-inch guns fore and aft. Torpedo launchers fore of bridge and amidships," Van Wert repeated. He leafed through the book in the destroyer section and tapped Tomassi on the shoulder when he got what he thought Tomassi saw. Tomassi looked back and forth between the scope and the book. "Got it. Jap destroyer, *Mutsuki* class."

Reynolds chimed in, "That's what got us!"

Tomassi looked at Reynolds and put his finger to his lips. Reynolds nodded and grinned in embarrassment. "Sound," Tomassi asked, "any other contacts?"

Marcus did a sweep of the area before turning to Tomassi and shaking his head and whispering, "Negative, sir."

"Down scope," Tomassi ordered. The periscope was lowered, and Tomassi huddled with Van Wert. "We've only got the two fish aft, right?"

"Right, skipper."

"So if we miss, then we get pasted."

"Right, skipper."

Tomassi thought it over, and then turned to Benton. "After torpedo room, make ready tubes nine and ten."

Benton repeated, "After torpedo room, make ready tubes nine and ten."

"Helm, come left to course one-three-zero."

"Helm, coming left to course one-three-zero, sir."

"Very well. Up scope."

Van Wert raised the periscope. Soundman Marcus spoke up. "Sir, target changing course. He's coming in on us."

"Well," Tomassi said, "I thought their sound watch was asleep. Guess not. Van, get over here."

Van Wert stepped around the scope. Tomassi said, "Bearing, mark."

"One-three-five."

"Range, mark."

"Four-four-double-oh."

"Angle on the bow zero, gyro zero. Set depth to zero feet. Stand by to fire."

"Stand by to fire," Benton repeated as he put his hand on the firing button. After a few moments, Benton reported, "Both tubes ready for firing."

After a second, Tomassi ordered, "Fire nine."

"Fire nine. Nine's away, sir."

"Fire ten."

"Fire ten. Ten's away, sir."

Tomassi stared into the scope at the charging Japanese destroyer. "Come on, bitch," he hissed, "come on." A lookout on the destroyer spotted the torpedoes and the ship started to turn to starboard. But, the greatest advantage of the bow shot was that if the target saw the fish too late, and started to turn, he made a better target. That's what happened here.

"Target turning," Marcus said, "and he's speeding up."

The tin can now presented a nice port twenty degree angle. Torpedo nine slammed home and exploded, followed a couple of seconds later by torpedo ten. The rumble could be heard clearly.

"Two hits," Tomassi exclaimed. A cheer went throughout the con. "Reynolds, come look."

Reynolds rushed over to the scope like a kid at Christmas. He beamed with delight at the sight of the destroyer who'd sunk his boat, now herself mortally wounded and soon to head for the bottom. "Bloody marvelous," he beamed. Turning to Tomassi, he said, "Thanks awfully, Dom."

"Don't mention it, David. Van, come look."

Van Wert now looked through the scope and smiled as the Japanese destroyer started on her one-way trip to the bottom.

Tomassi turned to Benton and ordered, "Secure from silent running and general quarters."

"Secure from silent running and general quarters," Benton repeated. Benton smiled as he reached up to turn on the fan.

CHAPTER SEVEN
13 SEPTEMBER 1942

The *Eel* was running on the surface during the night, around 21:30 hours. Chief Grace had just called up to the bridge that the batteries were fully charged. Tomassi ordered four engine speed, all ahead standard. He liked to take in some air before he would turn in, which was usually around 22:00.

A distinctly Scottish voice came up through the hatch. "Permission to come up?"

Tomassi replied, "Permission granted, Angus."

MacPherson came up through the hatch. "I wanted to get some air, sir. It's a wee bit gamey done there."

"I understand." Tomassi pointed to the aft 20mm position. "We'll get better air back here."

Both men walked to the back of the conning tower. MacPherson started to take out a pipe and tobacco pouch, then hesitated. "Aye, did you light to smoking lamp, sir?"

Tomassi looked for a moment, then shook his head. "Actually, no, I didn't. Sorry. I hope you understand. We have no torpedoes left, and we've used up one-third of our deck gun ammo. I don't feel like diving now, since that's all I'd have left to do if we see a Jap tin can."

"Aye, sir. I'm sorry."

"Don't be sorry," Tomassi said. "If anything, I'm sorry. That's a sweet smelling blend you've got in that pouch."

MacPherson smiled, "Thank you, sir." After putting his pipe away, MacPherson asked, "If you don't mind my asking, sir, do you have magnetic exploders on your torpedoes?"

"Yes."

"We got rid of ours, and so did the Jerries. They don't work."

Tomassi nodded, "Maybe. But first of all, we need to get them to run at the depth we set them on. Then we can worry if they're causing all the duds and prematures."

"They are, sir," MacPherson said, "Trust me. Ours didn't work, and the Germans didn't either."

"Permission to come up," questioned a British voice. It was Reynolds.

"Permission granted."

Reynolds came up through the hatch and joined the two officers. "Hello, Mac," Reynolds said.

"Hello, sir."

"You wanted to smoke that pipe, did you?"

"Aye, sir. But the commander wouldn't allow it."

"I told you he wouldn't."

"You two want to be alone," Tomassi asked with a smile.

Both of the British laughed. "No, sir," Reynolds replied.

"Permission to come up," asked an American voice.

Tomassi shrugged, "What the hell. Permission granted."

It was Van Wert. "Skipper, could I see you for a minute?" He motioned for Tomassi to come below with him.

"OK. I'll just be a minute, gentlemen."

"No worries, Dom," Reynolds replied.

After Tomassi and Van Wert got to the control room, they went to the chart table. "Skipper, I'm not sure we'll have enough fuel to get home at the rate we're going. We should throttle back a little."

"Do you think we can make 'Potshot' and top off?"

"Well, skipper, wouldn't they give us a full load? And that would be no good without torpedoes to go back out on the hunt. Last I heard they didn't have a tender there."

Tomassi thought for a moment. "Well, I'd like to get back home and tell about our torpedo problems, plus –" he motioned up to the con "– I'd like to get our friends back on dry land."

"Understood, skipper, but to make sure we make Fremantle again, I recommend we slow to one-third. It will take longer, but not by much."

"All right, Van." As the two men headed back into the conning tower, Tomassi turned to the helm and ordered one-third speed.

Tomassi got back on the bridge and headed aft, where Reynolds and MacPherson stood. "Permission to go below, sir," asked MacPherson.

"Granted."

"Good night, sir."

"Good night, Mac," Reynolds replied.

"Good night, Angus," Tomassi said.

Reynolds leaned on the rail. "Nice night."

"Yeah."

"Isn't it odd there are no Japs about? I mean, no patrols."

"Well," Tomassi said, "I'm not looking a gift horse in the mouth."

"Is this your first command, Dom?"

"Actually, yes she is. Was the boat you lost your first?"

"The *Excellent*? No, she was my second. My first command was at Gibraltar when the war broke out. We sank some Eye-Ties making the run from Taranto to Tripoli. That lasted for about a year. Then, they gave me the *Excellent* and sent me to Ceylon when Hong Kong fell." Reynolds stopped to notice the glare Tomassi was giving him. Reynolds straightened up.

Tomassi broke the silence. "You think I'm angry 'cause you might have sunk one of my cousins?"

"Well, I –"

Tomassi smiled. "No, I'm not mad." Both men laughed. "No, don't worry. I'm American. Don't make fun of the U.S. and you're OK."

Reynolds leaned forward again. "Thanks, Dom. How long before we make Australia?"

"Give it a week, David."

CHAPTER EIGHT
21 SEPTEMBER 1942

Dominic Tomassi had come, since last December, to give one command with great relish. As the *Eel* was coming into port at Fremantle, he gave that command from the bridge once again. "Special sea section to your stations."

The experienced men of the special sea section were the ones who got a ship out of, and into, harbor. The rules were to have the section at their stations when coming into port as soon as possible.

"Sparks?"

The Cajun radioman, Boudreaux, answered over the squawk box, "Aye, sir?"

"Are you sure there's no tender for us this time?"

"Aye, sir. That's what they told me, for true. They done sent the *Pisces* down to Albany. We dock at a pier."

"All right. Thanks, Sparks."

"Aye, sir."

Tomassi turned to Van Wert and Reynolds. "How do you like that, Van?"

"I don't, sir."

"I guess they have enough torpedoes now, and whatever else, but somehow a tender is better for me. How 'bout you, Reynolds? Do you like being with a tender?"

"Why, yes, Dom. We rather do feel better snug up against a tender," Reynolds replied.

Tomassi shook his head again. "I was talking to one of the officers on the *Pisces*. You know, they came all the way down from Manila, through Surabaya, then Darwin, then here. Now Albany. What's next, a base in Antarctica?" Van Wert and Reynolds laughed at that.

"I say, Dom," Reynolds asked, "Did you tell your people about us?"

"Yes. They're coordinating things with your navy to get you to Ceylon. Should be tomorrow when they're ready to take you."

"Bloody good, Dom, thanks."

The base at Fremantle finally came into view about an hour after Tomassi put the special sea section on station. Van Wert knew where they were to dock and would guide the helmsman to the place.

Tomassi, Van Wert, and Reynolds were on the bridge. Reynolds looked off to port as the *Eel* began to make her way in. He noticed the submarines docked there, and they didn't look American or British. "Dom, what are those subs over there?"

Tomassi looked at them, and then told Reynolds, "They're Dutch. They came here after the Japs drove them out of Surabaya."

"Oh. They look a frightful lot."

"So did the other American boats when we got here. The *Pisces* was the only tender to make the trip all the way down, and her cupboards were bare. It was quite a feat we pulled off to get into shape here, or so I heard."

Van Wert chimed in, "Now, the *Pisces* is away, and we only have the base to feed and clothe us. I'm hoping they get us another tender, and soon."

Tomassi said, "I guess we shouldn't be greedy. The Aussies are bending over backwards for us. We didn't have to bring in Seabees for this base, like I heard we had to do at Brisbane."

"Seabees," asked Reynolds.

"Construction Battalion," Van Wert answered, "They're the master builders of the Navy. But, yeah, I heard from the tender boys that the locals were able to get everything in shape for us."

The pier where the boat would dock came into view. There was a U.S. Navy band playing "Anchors Aweigh." "Nice," smiled Tomassi.

Van Wert called down to the helmsman, "Helm, stop port. Starboard ahead slow."

"Helm, stop port. Starboard ahead slow, aye."

"Right full rudder."

"Right full rudder, aye."

The stern of the *Eel* swung left as she came close to the dock. "Stand by the lines," called Van Wert. The men with the docking lines got ready. "Get over number one," Van Wert yelled. The man at the bow threw the line to the men at the dock. Van Wert then said, "Helm, rudder amidships, stop starboard."

"Helm, rudder amidships, stop starboard, aye."

"Very well," replied Van Wert. Then ordered, "Get over two and three." The men amidships cast their lines to the dock. Van Wert turned and yelled, "Get over four." The man at the stern now sent his line to the dock. "Secure all lines," Van Wert yelled. Into the squawk box, he said, "Helm, finished with engines."

"Helm, finished with engines, aye." That signal on the telegraph told the engine room they were done for this patrol and could secure their equipment.

"OK, Van. Good job, as always," Tomassi said. He looked over to the dock and saw both American and British officers waiting for them. "Well, David, that looks like your reception committee."

Reynolds looked over. "Yes. I'll get the lads." He went below. A gangway was passed over to the sub. Tomassi and Van Wert went aft and climbed down to receive anyone who might come aboard.

As they reached the deck, Reynolds brought his men out through the side hatch.

Tomassi walked up to him with a slip of paper, with a certain address on it. He handed it to Reynolds and said, "Ask for Fiona."

Reynolds smiled. "Thanks awfully, Dom." He put the paper into one of his chest pockets, then saluted and offered his hand. "Cheers, Dom."

"So long, David," Tomassi replied as he shook hands with Reynolds. MacPherson was next. "So long, Angus."

MacPherson smiled, and shook Tomassi's hand. "Aye, look after yourself, sir."

Reynolds now offered his hand to Van Wert. "Cheers, Davis."

Van Wert shook his hand, and replied, "Look after yourself." MacPherson stepped up as Reynolds left the boat. "Look after yourself, Angus," Van Wert said.

"And you." MacPherson took his leave, as well as the other five British after him.

CHAPTER NINE
22 SEPTEMBER 1942

"So," Tomassi asked Fiona, "how was he?"

Fiona laughed, "Oh, he was bloody awful! So many of those bloody English are just awful. And he wouldn't shut up about being an officer. His family is one of those 'ten generations in the navy' types. I tell you, those are the worst. It's a wonder his family lasted that long!" They both laughed.

The best thing for Tomassi, when he was with Fiona, wasn't so much the sex. She was terrific, but that wasn't the main thing for him. It was being able to have a woman to talk to, and have one be tender with him. It was a thing he missed from back home.

Fiona asked him, "Are you married, Dom?"

"She's dead."

"Oh, I'm sorry, love." She paused, and then asked, "Do I remind you of her?"

"No," Tomassi replied, "Italian women aren't noted for green eyes and red hair."

He slowly stroked her smooth white flank as he looked into those Irish eyes. "Sophia had brown eyes, and shiny black hair. Her skin was darker, kind of like mine."

"I knew you were Italian right off," Fiona said, "I've seen enough of them, although not for, I guess, three years."

"That sounds about right," Tomassi said. Now, since Fiona asked him, he had to know about her marital status. "Are you married, Fiona?"

"He's dead."

"Oh. Now I'll say sorry. Killed in the war?"

"Yes, in North Africa."

"How long ago?"

"About a year."

"That's about how long it's been for me." They lay there for a minute. Each of them touched the other person's hair. Tomassi wanted to open up, but he felt wrong about it, since he couldn't spend forever here. Plus, her being a prostitute kept him from thinking of love, since this was just a job for her. He had to come up with something to say, though. So the first thing he came up with was Lily. "What happened to Silly Lily?"

"She left. No use staying if everyone thought she was a Jap spy. That's what you told your men, right?"

"Yeah. That's what I told them. I guess they told other guys, too. So, no one wanted her?"

"No. So she left. Ruthie told me where, but I forgot. Do you want a wife again?"

Tomassi shook his head. "Not now. When the war is over, I guess. Then it would be worth looking. Why?"

"Just asking."

"You want me to take you to America? You know our navy imposed a cooling off period for marriage to local women."

Fiona laughed. "No. I don't need that. The world literally comes to me here. I could tell you a bunch of stories. One bloke who was a regular of mine was a South African. His ship would come every couple of months from Durban." She thought for a moment. "I think it's been a year since he showed up. Maybe he joined up."

"Or maybe he got torpedoed."

Fiona frowned. "Well, aren't you a bloody optimist, Dom?"

CHAPTER TEN
7 OCTOBER 1942

"Ship's company, U.S.S. *Eel*, all present and accounted for, sir."

Tomassi returned Van Wert's salute and said, "Very well. At ease, men." The men stood at ease as Tomassi pointed out the two new men in the ship's company. "The observant ones among you will have noted that two of our happy crew have been sent for duty elsewhere and replaced by these new men with the funny badges above their stripes." Tomassi was referring to the circle with an arrow through it, which contained a line with two peaks in it. "These men are Radarman Ames and Radarman Kaplan." Ames had sandy blond hair, blue eyes and freckles. Kaplan had black hair and brown eyes. "They are here, to run for us, that new miracle of science you see up on the conning tower."

Tomassi pointed to the new appendage on the periscope shears, between the number two periscope and the radio antenna. It had a bar with lengths of wire that ran back for about two feet from either end of the bar. "That, my boys, is an air search radar. It has a range of six to ten miles, so that one of our little slant eyed friends in a patrol plane can't get the jump on us." A round of laughter came up from the crew at that remark.

Van Wert interjected, "That doesn't mean you lookouts can just stand up there and work on your tans, though. A plane going 200 miles an hour can cover six miles in about two minutes. So when the radar picks up something, you're liable to be told to look out for the plane, then when you see him, you'll be ordered below so we can pull the plug. Remember it!"

"That's right, men," Tomassi said, "You will be counting on that gadget to keep you alive, and the men who run it will count on you to keep them alive. That's all. Mr. Van Wert, when the men are dismissed, have the special sea section at their stations and prepare the ship to get underway."

"Aye, aye, sir." Van Wert saluted and Tomassi returned it. Van Wert did an about face and said, "Attention." The men came to attention, and Van Wert ordered, "Leave your quarters. Special sea section to your stations on the double. All hands prepare to get underway."

As the men went to their stations, Tomassi asked Van Wert, "Van, is our cargo stowed below?"

"Aye, skipper. It's in the magazine, all squared away."

"All right, Van. Let's take the boat out."

"I'm glad they got us a radar set, skipper. I was feeling kind of naked out there without it."

After the *Eel* was underway, Tomassi and Van Wert huddled over the chart table. "Do you have our orders, skipper?"

"Yes," Tomassi replied. "After we top off at 'Potshot,' we're to proceed to the Philippines. Specifically, we're going to Panay Island with our cargo. The guerillas will need this. You checked it before we shoved off?"

"Yes, skipper," Van replied, "It's 20,000 rounds of ammo. Ten thousand each of .45 caliber and .30 caliber ammo. The .30 caliber stuff is in stripper clips for Springfields, and the .45 ammo in boxes for loading into clips for either the pistol or the Tommy Gun."

"All right."

"Now," Van Wert asked, "did you get to talk to the admiral about the magnetic exploders, like Angus had said?"

"I didn't get a chance to talk to him, but it sounds like a good idea to disconnect them." At this moment, Chief Barker walked by. "Hey, Chief," Tomassi called.

Barker walked back to Tomassi. "Yes, sir?"

"Chief, can you disconnect the magnetic exploders on the torpedoes so they'll only explode on contact?"

"Aye, sir," Barker nodded. "Do you think that's the reason they're not going off?"

"From talking to our British friends on the last patrol, I think so. I'd like you to disconnect all the exploders. We'll see if that produces some hits."

"Aye, aye, sir. I'll get right on it." Barker walked away.

Van Wert then asked, "Did we get credit for the ships we sank with the mines?"

"I'm hoping we will. I think Lockhart is a fair man. From what that cute blonde yeoman said when I turned in my reports, I think he'll give it to us. I know he's glad we're an aggressive boat."

"You mean that you're an aggressive commander?"

Tomassi smiled, "I guess you could put it that way."

CHAPTER ELEVEN
12 OCTOBER 1942

"Happy Columbus Day, skipper," Van Wert said.

"Thanks, Van, and same to you." Tomassi woke up at 06:00 as usual, and when he'd gotten dressed, he headed to the wardroom, where the stewards had his breakfast waiting. Columbus Day had always been a special occasion at the Tomassi household growing up. Aside from being home from school, there was a parade, and his father would hoist little Dominic on his shoulders to give him a great view of everything. Then, Mama would get together with the other women of the family to make a big dinner. The only bad part, unless it was a Friday, was that Dominic would have to go to bed at the usual school night hour.

Now, of course, there was no Dad, and no parade, and no big dinner. The last Tomassi remembered there being a wartime Columbus Day was 1918. Dad was on liberty, so they could see the parade in Philly, where they lived at the time. By that year, little Dominic was eleven, so no ride on Dad's shoulders, but they still enjoyed the parade, and the dinner. Plus, that year, Columbus Day was a Saturday, so no school, so Dominic could stay up with the men as they smoked cigars and drank wine. That was his first taste of table wine.

For this Columbus Day, no parade. Just the terror of trying to get through Japanese waters, and trying to deliver supplies to a band of desperate men crouching in a jungle, on some island Tomassi hadn't heard of when he was eleven.

"Did you dive the boat yet, Van," Tomassi asked as he started in on his plate of eggs and bacon.

"Not yet, skipper. I figured if we could get a little more time on the surface –"

The Bells of St. Mary's went off, and Lt. Odom's voice could be heard over the squawk box yelling, "Dive, dive!" Tomassi dropped his fork and ran out of the wardroom to get to the conning tower. The diving alarm could be heard as Tomassi worked his way past his men going past him to their stations.

"What happened," Tomassi asked Odom as he climbed up the ladder to the con.

"Radar spotted a plane, sir," Odom replied. "I hurried up and dived, just in case."

"Up scope," Tomassi ordered. The periscope raised, and Tomassi slowly looked around. They were heading into the Flores Sea, just past Java. No doubt the sky would contain bad guys. As he strained his eye, Tomassi looked and looked. He couldn't see anything out there. It was clear and peaceful. No little black dot for a plane.

"Anything, sir," Odom asked.

"Nope. Down scope."

Odom lowered the periscope. Tomassi went down to the control room. "Make your depth 100 feet, Mr. Beck."

"Aye, aye, sir."

Tomassi went back to the wardroom. As he sat down to his plate of eggs, he told Van Wert, "Van, you need to dive at daybreak. Your intentions were good, but we need to get to the Philippines in one piece."

"Aye, aye, skipper."

"Finished with your breakfast?"

"Yes, sir."

"Then get up to the con and relieve Odom."

"Aye, aye, skipper." Van Wert got up and left the compartment. One of the stewards picked up his plate. After a minute, Odom came into the compartment and sat down. Tomassi had finished with his food, and was sipping his coffee.

The steward brought Odom his plate of eggs. He nodded, "Thanks."

"Good catch on that radar sighting," Tomassi said.

"Thank you, sir," Odom replied as he dug into his food.

"You couldn't tell your diving alarm from your general quarters alarm?"

Odom put down his fork and looked down. "Sorry, sir."

"Forget it. But you did get my blood moving."

CHAPTER TWELVE
17 OCTOBER 1942

Tomassi and Van Wert huddled once again over the chart table, with a chart of Panay Island spread before them. They were currently southwest of the island, and had to find their rendezvous point with the guerillas.

Van Wert spoke first. "I've been looking at the northwest part of the island. This little town called Union is the nearest built up area. But where we're going is over here –" he indicated a river near the town, "– on the east side of this river. Now, the mouth of river should be our best guide. The town is on the west side of the river, and also there's a reef that would block us."

"But we're not sailing into the town," Tomassi said. "We need to be away from it, so we should be over here." He pointed to a long beach that curved for about four miles from the mouth of the river.

"That's right, skipper." Van Wert pointed to a cove that was east of the beach Tomassi pointed to.

"Why not further over, further east?"

"Because there's another reef there. This point is the only good place we have to come in and deliver the goods."

Tomassi looked at the chart again. There was a reef indicated, starting there and stretching for several miles east from where he had his finger, and Van Wert was pointing to the cove just west of it. "You're right, Van." Tomassi let out a sigh. "I really need to pay attention with charts. I used to be better at it."

The lights in the boat changed from white to red. Tomassi looked at his watch. It was just turning 17:00. In half an hour, the sun should be setting, and the red lights would help the men get their eyes acclimated to the darkness when they surfaced.

"OK, Van. Let's get that chow."

After they had eaten, the captain and executive officer of the *Eel* came back to the conning tower. It was now 17:30. The boat was skirting the edge of Pandan Bay, as they came in from the Sulu Sea.

"Sound, I need a fathometer reading," Tomassi said.

The soundman on this watch, Featherstone, gave him the reading, "Thirty fathoms, sir."

"Periscope depth, Mr. Beck," he ordered.

"Periscope depth, aye."

The boat began its ascent to fifty feet. Tomassi was happy for the gray paint job at this point. If they still had their black coat, the clear waters would have given them away, as they'd done to other boats early on in the war.

"Mark fifty, leveled off," called Beck.

"Sound, do a sweep of the area."

"Aye, aye, sir," Featherstone replied. After a minute, he said, "All clear, sir."

"Up scope," Tomassi ordered. Van Wert raised the periscope, and Tomassi started to sweep the area.

A couple of miles separated the sub from the island. Tomassi kept looking around. No one up there for now. That would change when they least would want it. So, Tomassi thought, we need to be ready.

"Down scope. Stations for battle surface."

The talker, Benton, repeated the order for everyone to hear, "Stations for battle surface."

The men who would be above decks when they came up now got their life vests and helmets. This included Tomassi and Van Wert, who respectively got helmets marked "CAPT" and "XO," for their status. This also meant the men who would man the guns had to be ready with ammunition. The deck gun ammo was stowed below the deck around the gun, so no need to worry about it yet. The anti-aircraft gun ammo, and the .50 caliber machine guns, had to be up in the conning tower when the hatch opened. Men passed these items up from the magazine, through the control room, to the con.

"Sound, do another sweep," Tomassi ordered.

"Aye, aye, sir," said Featherstone. As before, he reported, "All clear, sir."

Tomassi motioned for the periscope to come up again. He took another look around, just to be safe. All clear. He motioned for the scope to be lowered, then said, "Surface, surface."

"Surface, surface," repeated Benton. The three blasts on the alarm sounded, and the boat began to rise. They could hear the water rushing by as the *Eel* came up. The boat leveled off.

"Open the conning tower hatch," ordered Tomassi. The quartermaster opened the hatch, and a splash of water hit him. After him, Van Wert went up, then Tomassi. As he looked over the deck, he saw his men spring out of the hatches and man their weapons. The machine guns went on the sides of the bridge, and the men loaded the belts of ammo into them. The 20mm crews loaded magazines of ammo onto their weapons and charged them. The deck gun crew got the ammo from under the plates near the gun, and got a shell loaded.

Van Wert called down the hatch, "Helm, right ten degrees rudder, steady up on zero-one-zero."

"Helm, right ten degrees rudder, steady up on zero-one-zero, sir."

"Very well. Skipper, do you think we should have come up now?"

"The quicker the better for me," Tomassi said, "I'd rather be sinking Jap ships than running a delivery truck." He leaned over to the squawk box. "Radio room."

"Radio room, aye," called back Boudreaux.

"Sparks, transmit to 'Lollipop' that 'Silly Lily' is here."

"Aye, aye, sir."

Van Wert gave Tomassi a puzzled look, "'Lollipop?' 'Silly Lily?'"

Tomassi shrugged, "If the Japs can't say it, it'll work."

After a minute, Boudreaux called up, "Bridge, radio room."

"Captain, aye," replied Tomassi.

"Captain, they say we plum awful early, and to come around at midnight. They'll be ready for us then."

"Very well, Sparks, and thanks."

"Aye, aye, sir."

"Well, skipper," asked Van Wert.

Before Tomassi could answer, one of the lookouts called out. "Ship off port quarter."

The men on the bridge looked off to the left, and saw the enemy ship approaching. Tomassi had sat up over the past couple of nights, looking at the Naval Vessels Manual. He didn't need it to tell him what this ship was.

"Coastal minelayer. He'll radio in when he attacks." He turned to the squawk box and called, "Helm, all stop. After torpedo, make ready stern tubes."

"Helm, all stop, sir."

"After torpedo room, make ready stern tubes, aye."

Tomassi and the others kept their binoculars fixed on the minelayer. She was about ten thousand yards away, and if she stayed on course, she'd pass astern of the *Eel*. The faint glimmer of dusk on the horizon silhouetted the Japanese ship very nicely, while hopefully the sub was too faint to be made out by any lookout on the minelayer. The single stacked ship moved along slowly, no doubt thinking no one unfriendly would be around, let alone an American submarine.

Five minutes past. The minelayer kept on chugging along, while Tomassi cursed his luck and hoped, at least, that the enemy would come after him so he could shoot. He wanted to sink something each time he got out of port. But with each passing moment, the Japanese warship kept going away. Finally, she was beyond range, and everyone on the bridge could breathe again.

Tomassi looked at his watch. "He turned out to sea," he said. "Part of me is glad, and part of me wanted him to come, Van. Is that wrong?"

"I'll let you know when I have my own boat, skipper."

Tomassi leaned over to the squawk box. "After torpedo, secure stern tubes."

"After torpedo room, secure stern tubes, aye."

Van Wert looked at his watch. "Well, skipper, we've got six hours to kill."

"That means we can take out time getting there." Tomassi turned to the squawk box. "Helm, ahead slow."

"Helm, ahead slow, aye."

CHAPTER THIRTEEN
18 OCTOBER 1942

The *Eel* had been slowly closing in on their rendezvous with the guerillas since they dodged the minelayer. Slowly, they had crept up to the point a mile east of the mouth of the river. Now, at midnight, they were getting there.

"Sound, I need a fathometer reading," ordered Tomassi.

"Ten fathoms, sir."

A light glowed ahead of them on the land. Tomassi and Van Wert looked through their binoculars. The light flashed two short and two long flashes. Tomassi looked to the signalman with the blinker light. "Give the response," he said.

The signalman flashed three long and three short flashes. After a moment, the light from shore showed two long flashes. The signalman said to Tomassi, "That's the right response, sir."

"Very well," Tomassi said. He said into the squawk box, "Bring up the merchandise, Chief."

"Aye, aye, sir," came the answer from Chief Barker. The ammunition would now come up to the deck.

"Sound here, sir, five fathoms."

"Very well. Helm, ahead dead slow."

"Helm, ahead dead slow, aye."

As the boxes of ammunition started to appear on deck, the soundman called again, "Sound here, sir, three fathoms."

"Very well. All hands, brace yourselves, we're going aground."

The sub now began to run up on the sand just out from shore. "Bridge, forward torpedo room," came over the squawk box.

"Bridge, captain, aye."

"Captain, forward torpedo room. Bottom scraping forward, sir."

"Very well. Helm, all stop."

"Helm, all stop, aye."

The sub was now well grounded in the sand. Two men emerged from the jungle. One had a Springfield rifle, the other only a pistol. Tomassi turned to Van Wert. "Van, you have the con."

"Aye, aye, sir."

Tomassi went into the conning tower, then out the starboard side hatch to head up the deck to meet the two men. He called up to the forward 20mm position. "Keep your gun leveled on them," he ordered.

"Aye, aye, sir."

As he got past the deck gun, Tomassi stopped, and then turned back to the bridge. "Mr. Van Wert," he yelled.

"Aye, sir?"

"Get Doc up here."

"Aye, aye, sir." Van Wert turned to the squawk box, and said, "Pharmacist's Mate, on deck, on the double."

Tomassi now went down to the bow of the boat, and jumped off into the water. He approached the two men on the beach. Both were definitely Filipino.

The man with the pistol spoke. "Are you afraid you'll drown?"

Tomassi looked down at the life vest he still had on and laughed. "You never know when a big wave will come."

The man laughed. "True. I am Colonel Ramirez, Philippine Scouts."

"Commander Dominic Tomassi, U.S. Navy." He saluted the colonel. "How are you, sir?"

Ramirez returned the salute, "I am fine, Commander. You have it all?"

"Everything, with compliments of General MacArthur."

"Good." Ramirez turned to the other man, and spoke to him in Tagalog. The only word Tomassi could make out was "Sergeant." The man ran back into the jungle and brought back five other men.

Tomassi turned to the sub and motioned for the men on deck to start bringing the ammunition to the bow and passing it over the side to the Filipinos. At this point, Matos came out on deck, with his helmet with a red cross on it, and his first aid bag. "Matos," called Tomassi.

"Aye, aye, sir."

"Come over here."

"Coming, sir." Matos made his way to the bow and climbed down, then ran up and stood next to Tomassi. "This is my medic, Felipe Matos," Tomassi said.

Matos saluted the colonel and spoke to him in Tagalog. Ramirez smiled and answered him.

"Colonel," Tomassi asked, "I wonder if my men couldn't help your men by unloading this stuff into a spot in the jungle, not far from here."

Ramirez nodded. "Yes, I will show you." Ramirez took Tomassi into the trees about twenty yards from the beach, and pointed to a large tree. "Your men can leave it here, and we'll come back for it."

"Very well, sir." Tomassi turned to find Matos was with him. "Oh, Doc, you startled me."

"Sorry, sir."

"Well, tell five of our guys to help bring the ammo here. Tell them to look for me, and I'll be along to help."

"Aye, aye, sir." Matos ran back along the trail. Soon, some of the men from the *Eel* were along, carrying boxes with them and setting them by the tree. Tomassi headed back with one of them to help offload the ammo. In ten minutes, the last of the ammo was by the large tree.

"I cannot thank you enough, Commander," Ramirez said. At this point, a woman came running up, talking excitedly to the colonel and pointing back into the jungle.

"Matos, what's she saying," Tomassi asked.

"She says there's a Jap patrol coming," Matos answered. It was at this point that Tomassi realized he didn't have a pistol on him. Dummy, he thought.

"OK, let's get back to the sub, on the double," he yelled. Tomassi's men started back for the boat, double time. Tomassi quickly turned to the colonel. "Hate to leave in a hurry, Colonel."

"Understood, Commander. Thank you again."

"Come on, Doc." The two of them ran like mad to get back to the sub. As they reached the beach, they could hear shooting. "Prepare to get underway," Tomassi yelled as he and Matos climbed up on deck.

"Prepare to get underway," Van Wert yelled. As Tomassi approached the forward 20mm position, he yelled, "Our little friends should be along in a moment. When they're on the beach, open up on them."

"Aye, aye, sir."

"Deck gun, open up on them when you see them, then put a couple of rounds into the trees behind them."

"Aye, aye, sir."

Tomassi made his way into the conning tower, then up onto the bridge. He turned to the squawk box. "Helm, all astern two-thirds."

"Helm, all astern two-thirds, aye." The water at the stern of the sub began to churn as the screws turned, backing the boat away. Tomassi looked forward at this point to see Japanese soldiers appearing on the beach. Japanese bullets began to ping off the hull. As per his orders, the deck gun fired, and a shell scattered the enemy. The 20mm fired at this time, cutting the Japanese down with their exploding shells. Screaming could be heard from the beach above the sound of the diesels as the three-inch deck gun put two rounds into the jungle. Glad I'm not them right now, Tomassi thought.

"Sound," Tomassi called, "I need a fathometer reading."

"Sound here, we've got four fathoms."

Twenty-four feet, Tomassi thought. We need more.

"Sound, let me know when we have ten fathoms."

"Aye, aye, sir."

By now, the Japanese soldiers on the beach were getting further away. Tomassi grabbed the megaphone, which Van Wert had thoughtfully ordered up, and yelled, "Cease fire."

"Sound here, we've got ten fathoms."

"Very well. Helm, left full rudder."

"Helm, left full rudder, aye." The boat swung around, and in no time, they were parallel to the beach. In another few seconds, the bow of the boat pointed out to sea.

"Helm, right full rudder, come to course one-niner-zero, all ahead full," Tomassi ordered.

"Helm, right full rudder, coming to course one-niner-zero, all ahead full, aye."

Van Wert yelled to the lookouts, "Keep your eyes peeled. The Japs on that beach probably radioed about us, and they'll have ships after us." He turned to Tomassi. "Maybe that minelayer will be back, skipper."

Tomassi nodded, "I don't doubt it."

A minute later, one of the lookouts called out, "Ship off port bow." Everyone looked as hard as they could through the pale moonlight. There was a silhouette there, and Tomassi recognized it. It *was* that minelayer.

"Gun crew," he yelled through the megaphone, "He should have a three-inch gun mount forward of the bridge. Aim for that, and when he cuts loose, you cut loose." He leaned over to the squawk box, and asked, "Sound, what's the fathometer read?"

"Sound here, fifteen fathoms, sir."

Ninety feet. Not enough to evade a depth charge attack, Tomassi thought. As he thought this, the minelayer fired at them. The shell splashed some twenty feet away. The deck gun crew took aim at the flash from the Japanese ship and fired back, landing a shell close to the enemy.

Tomassi called on the squawk box, "Forward torpedo room, make ready tubes one and two."

"Forward torpedo room, make ready tubes one and two, aye."

"Fire control, shifting to TBT, bearing coming down." Tomassi went to the TBT, or Target Bearing Transmitter. It was a big pair of binoculars on a mount on the bridge, connected to the Torpedo Data Computer, or TDC. With a push of a button, the target's bearing, course and speed were sent below so

81

the fire control party would have the data it needed to get the solution for firing.

The deck gun crew sent another round at the enemy, who had gotten closer with his second round. The sub's gun crew had the range this time. The gun mount on the minelayer went up like a bonfire.

"Good shot, men. Secure the deck gun," Tomassi ordered. The men of the deck gun hurried to secure. "Secure, secure," Tomassi then called to the 20mm crews. "Stand by to dive."

"Sound here, sir, twenty fathoms."

"Very well."

"Fire control, sir. Tubes one and two ready. TDC set."

"Fire one."

"Fire one. One's away, sir."

"Fire two.

"Fire two. Two's away, sir."

Tomassi could see the wakes of the torpedoes come from the bow and turn in the minelayer's direction.

"Lookouts below. Clear the bridge." As the men headed below, Tomassi gave two blasts on the alarm. "Dive, dive!"

After he closed the hatch above him, Tomassi called to the soundman. "How are those fish?"

"Both torpedoes running hot, straight, and normal, sir."

Everyone could hear the screws of the minelayer pressing in on the sub. No doubt the depth charge party was at their stations, ready to hit the sub.

As the *Eel* leveled off at fifty feet, they heard the torpedoes hit. Tomassi motioned for the periscope to be raised. He was greeted with the sight of the minelayer in flames, everything forward of the bridge engulfed. He smiled and motioned for Van Wert to come look. Van Wert smiled as he saw it.

"Down scope," Tomassi ordered. "Secure from battle stations."

Van Wert spoke into the squawk box. "Secure from battle stations. Third section, take the watch."

Tomassi could finally take off that damn helmet.

CHAPTER FOURTEEN
21 OCTOBER 1942

The night after their thrilling escape from Panay, the *Eel* got an urgent message from COMSUBSOWESPAC to proceed to Mindanao Island. There was someone very important for them to pick up. That was all Tomassi knew.

The orders told him to proceed to Mayo Bay, on the southeast part of the island. The Philippine guerillas would have the man, and once they got him, they would patrol off of Davao City, just a few hours sailing from there to the west.

Van Wert had charted the course. Once they had rounded the southern tip of Mindanao, they proceeded northeast, past Pujada Bay, then a northwest turn into Mayo Bay. As Tomassi and Van Wert huddled over the chart table again, Van Wert said, "Here's the tricky part, skipper. These reefs make it so that we can't just ground ourselves like before. We're going to only get within fifty yards or so of the beach, and send a raft to pick our guest up."

"Mm-hmm," Tomassi nodded. "First we're a delivery truck, then a taxi service. I sure hope we can go after some Jap ships after picking this guy up."

"Me too, skipper."

Tomassi looked at his watch. It was almost 01:00. "This middle of the night crap is messing with my beauty sleep."

An hour later, the *Eel* was off the reef near the peninsula that formed the southern side of Mayo Bay. They were stopped in the water, with the bow pointed northeast, paralleling the reef. Tomassi had the 20mm crews at their stations. If something big were to come along, the moonlight would give them the chance to get out and try to dive. The signalman, Oppenheim, stood next to Tomassi and Van Wert on the bridge. As they looked into the jungle, Tomassi spoke, "OK, Oppenheim. When they're ready, they're going to give us two long flashes, and you answer with three short and one long. They're supposed to then send three long flashes and one short. Got that?"

"Aye, sir. Two long flashes from them, I give them three short and one long, they give back three long and one short."

"Very good. Stand by." Tomassi looked down to the deck, where the men with the raft were standing by. "Ready there on deck?"

"Aye, aye, sir," was the answer. Two men would paddle out to retrieve the passenger, and three men on deck would help them back on board.

Presently, two long flashes from a signal light came from the shore. "OK, Oppenheim, give the signal." Oppenheim sent three short flashes and one long one from his signal lamp. The responding flashes came back.

"Lower away," Tomassi yelled to the deck. The raft went on its way to shore. After a couple of minutes, it came back with an extra man. The men on deck helped him out and pointed him to the conning tower, then helped the men in the raft back on deck and to retrieve the raft.

The man they had come to get climbed up the port side ladder and, with a salute, presented himself to Tomassi. "Sir, Major Oscar Fortin, U.S. Army Air Corps."

Tomassi returned the salute, "Commander Dominic Tomassi, U.S. Navy. This is my exec, Lt. Commander Davis Van Wert."

"How do you do, Major," Van Wert said as he offered his hand.

"Fine, uh …"

"'Commander' will do, Major," Van Wert said.

"Commander," Fortin said. "How do you tell who's calling who?"

"Someone just says 'sir,' and I get it," Van Wert smiled.

"And me, they call 'captain,'" Tomassi grinned.

Fortin smiled, "OK."

Tomassi pointed to the hatch next to him, "If you'll just go below, Major, we'll get going." Fortin went down the hatch, and Tomassi headed down after him.

As he got down the ladder, Tomassi ordered, "Helm, all ahead one-third. Right full rudder, come right to course zero-niner-zero."

"Helm, all ahead one-third. Right full rudder, coming right to course zero-niner-zero, sir," the helmsman repeated.

"Very well. Major, follow me to the wardroom. We'll get you some coffee."

"Thank you, sir."

Tomassi turned and yelled up to the bridge, "Mr. Van Wert, you have the con."

"Aye, aye, sir," Van Wert replied.

The two men went down to the control room, then proceeded up the passageway to the wardroom. Tomassi pointed the way, and Fortin went in and sat down. Tomassi grabbed a cup, filled it with coffee from the dispenser, and handed it to Fortin. "Thank you, sir," Fortin said. Tomassi filled his own cup and sat down opposite Fortin. The two men sipped their coffee as they talked.

Tomassi started. "I'm kind of curious. What did you do on this island, Major?"

"Well, sir, I commanded a pursuit squadron on Leyte. Clark Field, to be precise. After the Japs drove us out, we fell back here to Mindanao. We ended up at Del Monte Field. Well, what was left of us. When the Japs first hit us, I had some twenty planes. Hardly got anyone off the ground. We had three left after the first day. I was lucky enough to get up after them later on. I even got one of their bombers.

"When the order came down to pull back, the three of us escorted a C-47, with our ground crews in it, down here. We got into Del Monte just as the Japs came again." Fortin stared into his cup for a moment. "They got our guys before they could even get out of the damn plane. I couldn't do anything about it. I was

out of gas. I just ran away. Then they got my bird."
More silence.

"I'm sorry," Tomassi said.

"Thanks. So, anyway, I was in the infantry after that. We got word to melt into the hills. I lead a bunch of guerillas for these past months. I guess they decided I wasn't good enough, or something."

"I wouldn't say that," Tomassi said. "They probably have a nice, shiny new P-40 just waiting for you in Australia."

Fortin smiled, "I hope so." Fortin noticed Tomassi's academy ring. "You went to Annapolis?"

Tomassi held up his hand and smiled. "Yep. Class of '31."

Fortin held up his right hand with his ring. "West Point. Class of '32."

"How did you pick aviation," Tomassi asked.

"I've always wanted to fly. Saw it in the movies. Saw barnstormers. Couldn't resist running to the door when a plane flew by. How 'bout you, Commander? Why submarines?"

Tomassi smiled, "Well, in the last war, my dad was a destroyer sailor. He'd regale me with stories of how they sank U-boats each time they got out there on convoy duty. And, I don't know, I just wanted to try being a submariner."

Fortin smiled, "How did he react when you told him?"

"He laughed. He appreciated the irony." Tomassi yawned and looked at his watch. It was 02:30. "I'm going to hit the sack. I guess you can stay here until we come up with quarters for you. Try and get some sleep. We'll be having breakfast about 06:00."

"Thank you, Commander. Do you shave on submarines?"

"Oh, noticed the whiskers? We're supposed to. I won't tell if you won't. But there's only so much fresh water to be had, and I'd rather it be used for the batteries or for cooking. When we get close to home, you'll see us all shaving."

Fortin smiled, "OK."

"And when you need to get rid of that coffee, the head is down the passage on your right."

"Head?"

"Latrine to you."

CHAPTER FIFTEEN
22 OCTOBER 1942

The *Eel* rounded the Davao Peninsula during the night, and by daybreak were close to Davao City harbor. After breakfast, they dove and started to listen for destroyers and merchant shipping. The enemy had not gotten around to using convoys yet, so Soundman Marcus had plenty to listen for, but he could isolate it and figure on a target he could track. Tomassi, Van Wert, and Odom were in the conning tower to act when something they could shoot at was detected.

At about 08:00, Marcus reported, "Sir, screws bearing three-one-zero relative. It sounds like a freighter."

Tomassi turned to the talker, Benton. "Sound general quarters."

"Aye, aye, sir."

The Bells of St. Mary's tolled as the men got to their stations. Tomassi motioned for the periscope to come up. As it did, he got behind it to look at the target when a voice came up from the control room.

"What the hell happened?"

Tomassi looked over to see Major Fortin in the hatch. "It's general quarters, Major. We've spotted a Jap and we're going to attack him. I guess I didn't tell you about it, did I?"

"Sorry. Just that alarm scared me."

Tomassi looked into the periscope and saw the target against the mountains on the west side of the bay. He turned the handles to focus on the ship. "Van, get me the Ship Shapes Book."

"Aye, skipper." Van Wert got to the hatch, then asked Fortin, "Would you mind moving, Major? I need to get something."

"Oh, sorry," Fortin said as he climbed back down the ladder.

Van Wert climbed down and went to the captain's cabin to get the book, which Tomassi had carelessly left there while studying it. As he got back into the control room, he told Fortin, "Maybe you should stay on the other side of the ladder, so you're not in the way."

"All right, Commander."

Van Wert climbed back up into the con, and opened the book for Tomassi. Tomassi looked back and forth between the ship on the surface and the drawings Van Wert had in front of him. He could see the enemy ship had her stack toward the stern. He could also make out a catwalk running the length of the ship. The foremast looked centered on the foredeck. She rode low in the water, so she carried a good deal of something.

"OK," Tomassi said, "She looks like a freighter, type Sugar Able. Tonnage, oh, must be about eight or nine thousand tons. She's not going very fast. Sound, can you guess her speed?"

Marcus listened for a moment, then said, "I figure about four knots, sir."

Tomassi nodded, "I think so. Down scope." He pushed up the handles and Van Wert lowered it. "Helm, all ahead standard."

The helmsman, Lucas, replied, "Helm, all ahead standard, aye."

"Forward torpedo room, make all tubes ready for firing," Tomassi ordered.

"Forward torpedo room, make all tubes ready for firing," Benton repeated.

"Helm, left full rudder, come left to course two-eight-zero."

"Helm, left full rudder, coming left to course two-eight-zero, sir," Lucas replied.

"Very well." Tomassi looked straight ahead, waiting for a minute to gather himself. He thought about the torpedoes. They worked against the minelayer. Are they going to keep working? Are they going to go off at all?

"Helm, steady on course two-eight-zero, sir."

"Very well. Up scope." Van Wert raised the periscope. Tomassi looked ahead to the freighter. He motioned for Van Wert to step up. "Angle on the bow, fifty starboard. Estimate target speed, four knots. Set torpedoes to ten feet. Gyro twenty right. Bearing, mark."

"One-niner-zero."

"Range, mark."

"Three-oh-double-oh."

"Sound, any other contacts close by?"

Marcus listened, then replied, "Negative, sir."

Van Wert turned to Odom. "Check."

"Set," replied Odom.

"Fire one," said Tomassi.

"Fire one." Benton pushed the firing button, and the torpedo could be heard going on its way. "One's away, sir."

"Fire two."

"Fire two. Two's away, sir."

"Down scope." The periscope was lowered. "Time, Van."

"Torpedo number one to hit in twenty-five seconds, sir."

"Both torpedoes running hot, straight, and normal, sir," Marcus said.

The ticking of the stopwatch seemed louder than a bomb. Van Wert counted, "Fifteen … Ten, nine, eight, seven, six, five, four –"

BOOM.

Van Wert shook his head. Marcus reported, "Number one premature."

"Time on torpedo number two, Van," Tomassi said.

"Torpedo number two to hit in five, four, three, two, one, now."

BOOM.

"Torpedo number two hit, sir," Marcus said.

"Up scope," Tomassi ordered. Van Wert raised the periscope. Tomassi was greeted with the sight of the freighter hit. A geyser of water had gone up just aft of the bridge. She slowed down visibly, but was still moving, though just barely.

Tomassi sighed, then said, "Stand by tubes three and four."

"Stand by tubes three and four," Benton repeated. His hand went to the button again.

"Fire three."

"Fire three. Three's away, sir."

"Fire four."

"Fire four. Four's away, sir."

"Both torpedoes running hot, straight, and normal, sir," said Marcus.

"Helm, all ahead one-third."

"Helm, all ahead one-third, aye."

"Very well. Time on those fish, Van."

Van Wert looked at the stopwatch. "Torpedo number three to hit in five, four, three, two, one, now."

BOOM.

"Torpedo number three hit, sir," Marcus said.

Tomassi could see the geyser of water coming up from near the stack.

Van Wert spoke again, "Torpedo number four to hit in five, four, three, two, one, now."

Silence. Then, Tomassi could see a small burst of water aft of the stack of the stricken freighter.

"Bumping noise against the target, followed by a burst of air," Marcus said.

The enemy was dead in the water. Tomassi meant for her to go down. "Stand by tubes five and six."

"Stand by tubes five and six," repeated Benton.

"Fire five."

"Fire five. Five's away, sir."

"Fire six."

"Fire six. Six away, sir."

"Don't bother with the stopwatch, Van."

"Aye, aye, skipper."

Tomassi watched as the tracks of the torpedoes headed for the enemy. They made their way to the enemy's stern, and hit her. He smiled as they both went off.

"Both hits, sir," Marcus said.

"Thank you, sound. Van, come look."

Van Wert now looked through the periscope to see the freighter listing to port and blowing up, which could be heard throughout the boat. "I wonder if our guest might like a look, skipper."

Tomassi smiled, "Why not? Major, come up here."

Fortin climbed up the ladder and walked up to Tomassi. "Have a look."

"Thank you, sir."

Van Wert moved over as Fortin looked through the periscope at the stricken enemy ship, lying on her side and going down by the bow. Fortin smiled. "Wow."

"Captain, screws bearing zero-niner-zero relative, sounds like a destroyer," Marcus reported.

Tomassi nudged Fortin aside and turned the periscope to the right. A Japanese destroyer was charging like a maddened bull. Tomassi slammed the handles and yelled, "Down scope. Take her down to one hundred feet."

"One hundred feet, aye, sir," Lt. Beck replied.

"Rig for depth charge. Rig for silent running."

"Rig for depth charge. Rig for silent running," repeated Benton. Benton then moved to turn off the fan.

The *Eel* began to make her descent to escape the coming depth charges. Marcus reported, "Destroyer passing overhead. Picking up splashes. Depth charges coming down, sir."

Tomassi turned to Fortin. "Major, better hang onto something."

BOOM!

A depth charge went off after having passed the boat as she descended. Everyone was rattled, and a couple chips of paint came down from the overhead.

BOOM!

Another charge went off close at hand. The lights flickered.

BOOM!!

This time, two charges went off simultaneously. The sub rocked back and forth. Glass could be heard breaking somewhere. A light went out in the control room.

"Was that a bulb," Fortin asked.

"We call them 'globes.' And yes, that's what broke," Van Wert answered.

BOOM!

Another charge went off, and the sub rocked again. This time, the lights in the conning tower went out.

"Turn on emergency lights," ordered Tomassi. A moment later, all was lighted in the con.

BOOM! BOOM!

Two more charges went off, and a pipe burst in the control room, prompting Beck to yell, "Damage control to the control room, on the double."

Marcus now reported, "Destroyer coming back around."

"Mr. Beck," Tomassi yelled, "What's our depth?"

"Ninety feet, and we're leveling off, sir."

"Very well. Sound, what's the fathometer reading?"

"Ten fathoms below us, sir," replied Marcus.

"Mr. Beck, make our depth one hundred twenty feet."

"One hundred twenty feet, aye, sir."

Fortin tapped Tomassi on the shoulder and asked, "What can we do, Commander?"

"Well, I hope, he'll think he's sunk us and go away."

"Passing one hundred feet, sir," Beck reported.

Marcus listened. "I think he's going away, sir. His screws are getting fainter."

"Leveling off at one hundred twenty feet, sir," Beck reported.

Another minute passed. "He's gone sir," Marcus said. "I've lost him."

Everyone in the conning tower blew out a breath. The humid air hung heavy around everyone. "Secure from silent running," Tomassi said.

"Secure from silent running," replied Benton. With a smile on his face, Benton reached for the fan.

CHAPTER SIXTEEN
23 OCTOBER 1942

The *Eel* spent the rest of the previous day on the bottom, effecting repairs. She came up for air and battery recharge about 20:00. She dived again at 07:30 when radar had picked up a plane contact. It was now about 09:00. Sound had picked up propeller noises, and Van Wert put the boat on general quarters.

Tomassi came up to the con. "Sound, what have we got?"

Marcus replied, "Screws bearing two-zero-zero relative. Sounds like a destroyer."

"Let me listen."

Marcus took off his headset and Tomassi put it on. It was the fast beat of a destroyer's screws. He gave the headset back to Marcus. He then turned to Van Wert. "Van, have you ever sunk a destroyer before?"

"No, skipper."

"Would you like to start?"

Van Wert nodded and smiled, "Aye, skipper!"

"Well, I'll give you this one. You've seen me do this before."

"Aye, skipper."

"Go to it."

Van Wert ordered, "Up scope." Tomassi raised the scope. "Sound, what bearing did you give?"

Marcus answered, "I gave two-zero-zero relative, sir."

"Helm," Van Wert asked, "what's our course?"

Lucas replied, "Our course is three-one-zero, sir."

Van Wert turned the periscope to the left until he saw the enemy. By this time, Tomassi had pulled out the Japanese Naval Vessels Manual. "You need the book, Van?"

"He's still a little far away, sir."

"Have you turned the handles to zoom in?"

Van Wert smiled. "Thanks, skipper." He turned the handles to zoom in on the Japanese destroyer. "OK. Um, single gun mount forward. One stack, two masts, one fore, one aft. Looks like … um, torpedo tubes fore of the bridge, and also amidships. That's all I can tell."

Tomassi opened the book and looked at what Van Wert described. He walked up to Van Wert and showed him what he thought it was. Van Wert looked back and forth for a moment, then nodded. "Jap destroyer, *Minekaze* class. Make ready stern tubes."

"Make ready stern tubes," repeated Benton.

Tomassi turned to Lt. Odom. "Ready, Mr. Odom."

"Ready, sir."

Tomassi turned back to Van Wert, "OK."

Van Wert smiled, "OK, I'm ready. Bearing, mark."

"Zero-zero-five."

"Range, mark."

"Five-five-double-oh."

Van Wert stood there for a moment. He then put up the handles and said, "Down scope."

"Well," Tomassi asked.

"I think it's too soon to shoot, sir."

"You're right. What else do we need?"

Van Wert turned to Lucas and said, "Helm, right full rudder. Come right to course zero-zero-five."

"Helm right full rudder, coming right to course zero-zero-five, sir."

"Very well."

"That's good," Tomassi said. "What else?"

Van Wert had to think for a moment. "Sound, he's going to be behind us in a moment. When he's in our baffles, keep listening around for someone else."

"Aye, aye, sir."

Tomassi nodded, "Very good, Van. What else?"

Van Wert stood there. He thought for a moment, then shook his head.

"Our speed, Van."

Van Wert nodded. "Helm, all ahead slow."

"All ahead slow, aye."

Marcus spoke up, "Sir, target passing into our baffles, I can't hear him."

"Very well," Van Wert said. "Skipper, do you think he hears us?"

"I don't doubt it, Van. He should be close enough for a shot pretty soon."

Van Wert nodded. "Up scope." Tomassi raised the periscope, and Van Wert found the enemy again. He had turned slightly. "All right. Bearing, mark."

"Zero-zero-zero."

"Range, mark."

"Four-oh-double-oh."

"Angle on the bow, five port. Gyro five left. Estimate target speed, ten knots. Set torpedoes for eight feet. Bearing, mark."

"Zero-zero-one."

"Range, mark."

"Three-five-double-oh."

Tomassi called, "Check."

"Set," replied Odom."

Van Wert ordered, "Fire seven."

"Fire seven." Benton pressed the firing button. "Seven's away, sir."

"Fire eight."

"Fire eight. Eight's away, sir."

Van Wert watched as the torpedoes went downrange. The destroyer saw them and started to turn to his right. As always, the advantage of the bow shot came to the fore. As the enemy turned, he made a bigger target. Fifteen seconds after firing, the torpedoes hit. One loud boom could be heard distinctly above the sub's own prop noises. "One hit and exploded, and one bumped against the target, followed by a burst of air," Marcus yelled.

"Damn. Fire nine."

"Fire nine," Benton said. "Nine's away, sir."

"Fire ten."

"Fire ten. Ten's away, sir."

"Get ready to take her deep," Tomassi yelled down to the control room.

"Standing by, sir," Beck replied.

Van Wert looked again at the destroyer. She was wounded, but not slain. The torpedoes that had just been fired were on their way. A few seconds later, both of them hit and exploded, sending the destroyer reeling. "Two hits," Marcus yelled.

A cheer rang through the conning tower. Van Wert grinned from ear to ear. He motioned for Tomassi to come look. Tomassi saw the stricken Japanese destroyer, dead in the water and listing to port.

"Very good, Van. Another one like that, and you'll get called up to the big leagues."

"Thanks, skipper." Van Wert pushed up the handles on the periscope and said, "Down scope." Tomassi lowered the periscope. "Secure from general quarters."

CHAPTER SEVENTEEN
24 OCTOBER 1942

The Bells of St. Mary's tolled at 02:35. Tomassi headed out of his cabin, to be met by Major Fortin in the passageway. "Commander, don't you guys ever stop? You're fighting at night, too," Fortin asked.

"Tell me when the Japs punch a clock, Major, and I will too," Tomassi replied.

The two of them headed to the conning tower to find Van Wert heading up the ladder, already wearing his helmet and life vest. One of the men handed Tomassi his helmet and vest. As he struggled to put them on, he said, "Do we have some gear for the major?"

"I'll find something, sir," the man replied.

Tomassi looked up to the bridge. "Coming up," he yelled as he climbed the ladder. He found Van Wert already there, suited up and with binoculars trained on a target. "What have you got, Van?"

"It looks like a freighter off to starboard, skipper."

Fortin came up the ladder and asked, "Permission to come up?"

"Granted," Tomassi said. He then looked over to the gun crew. They were all ready to fight. The gun was being trained out to shoot at the target ship.

"All stations manned, sir. We're ready," Van Wert said.

"Very well." Tomassi looked through his binoculars. The Japanese freighter was off to starboard, some ten thousand yards away. The moon was at her back, so she was well silhouetted. She had three masts, one forward and two aft of the superstructure, and she only had one stack. "Looks like type Fox Able. She's – wait!" He looked aft and saw a gun mount. "Looks like a 4-inch gun back on the stern. Do you see it, Van?"

Van Wert looked, and said, "Yes, skipper, I see it."

"I'll call this one yours, Van. You give the orders."

Van Wert lowered his binoculars and looked at Tomassi, who was smiling at him. "Aye, aye, sir! Gun crew," he yelled, "Target their stern first. There's a gun mount there, then go for her waterline."

"Aye, aye, sir," came the reply.

Fortin smiled, "This should be fun."

"What about torpedoes? This cat may have more than one gun mount. She could even be a Q-ship."

Van Wert nodded. She could well be a freighter with many guns, waiting to pick off an unsuspecting sub. He got on the squawk box and called the talker. "Make ready all tubes."

"Make ready all tubes, aye," came the answer.

"Helm, right ten degrees rudder, come right to course one-niner-five."

"Helm, right ten degrees rudder, coming right to course one-niner-five, sir," came the answer.

"Very well."

"I'll get on the TBT," Tomassi said. He went to the big binoculars on the rail mount, opened the lens caps, and swung them out to starboard. He then lined up on the freighter and pressed the button on top. The enemy's bearing was sent down to the conning tower, where the fire control party could feed it into the TDC. "I figure she's making about six knots, wouldn't you, Van?"

"Aye, skipper. Six knots." Van Wert leaned over to the squawk box and said, "Mr. Odom, target speed six knots."

"Six knots, aye," Odom replied.

"Open outer doors on tubes one and two," Van Wert said.

"Open outer doors on tubes one and two, aye," came the talker's answer.

Van Wert turned to the gun crew and yelled, "Commence firing."

The 3 inch deck gun went off. The shell landed in the water just short of the enemy's stern gun mount. Instead of that mount firing, three guns in the freighter's superstructure fired back. Two of the shells went over the sub and hit a few yards away. The third came down just in front of the men on the bridge of the sub. Fortin was closest to the blast and feel backwards. Tomassi and Van Wert ducked down below the rim of the bulkhead. The starboard lookout grabbed his stomach and yelled, "I'm hit!"

Tomassi yelled at the gun crew, "Fire at those guns!"

"Aye, sir," the gun crew captain yelled back, and the single gun fired at one of the flashes. The American shell hit the Japanese ship and blew up a gun mount with one shot.

Van Wert got on the squawk box. "Pharmacist's Mate to the conning tower. Mr. Odom, set gyro angle fifty right. Commence firing when set."

"Aye, aye sir," Odom replied.

Another salvo from the enemy came over. These shells came down close again, wounding two of the gun crew. But they stayed on their posts, passing shells and pointing the gun to fire back.

Tomassi looked through the hatch and saw Pharmacist's Mate Matos standing in the compartment. "Get up here," he yelled.

"Aye, aye, sir," Matos replied as he climbed up.

"Check on the major," Tomassi yelled, pointing at Fortin. He hadn't moved since the first Japanese shell had hit close by. Matos looked at him, then prodded Tomassi and pointed to Fortin's head. A piece of shrapnel had gotten in through Fortin's left eye. The cye was gone, and the metal stuck out. "See to Tarpley," Tomassi said, pointing to the injured lookout still in his position.

"Torpedoes three and four fired, sir," Odom said through the squawk box.

"Very well," Van Wert said. By this time, the deck gunners had knocked out another mount in the superstructure of the enemy, as well as a near hit on the stern gun, sending its crew flying into the water.

A few seconds later, a torpedo hit the Japanese ship, sending a big geyser up and rocking the freighter. A couple of seconds later, the second torpedo hit right under the stack, sending up a fireball. The enemy was now stopped dead and listing to port. The deck gunners sent more shells into the enemy' s waterline to aid her on her way to the bottom.

"Doc, help me get the major below," Tomassi said, "then go check on the gun crew."

"Aye, sir," Matos replied. The two men got the dead flier down the hatch and then on to Tomassi's cabin, where they covered him with a blanket. Tomassi then headed back to the bridge, and Matos got onto the deck to check on the wounded gunners. By this time, they had ceased firing and were securing the weapon. Tomassi looked over to the freighter as she headed for the bottom, bow first. He turned to Van Wert.

"Good job, Van."

"Thank you, skipper."

A couple of hours after the battle, Tomassi checked with Matos on the wounded men.

"Who got hit, Doc?"

"Solo and Blanco. They'll both be all right. Just got nicked."

"And what about Tarpley?"

"His wound is more serious. I would put him on light duty until we get home and someone can dig out the shrapnel."

"OK, Doc. Thanks. I need you to help me get Fortin ready for burial."

"Aye, sir."

Towards sunrise, the men who were not on duty were assembled on deck, with a burial detail, and Tomassi, to send Major Fortin to his resting place.

Tomassi read from the book: "Unto Almighty God we commend the soul of our shipmate departed, and we commit his body to the deep, in the sure and certain hope of the resurrection unto eternal life, when the sea shall give up her dead. And the life of the world to come. Amen."

"Amen," responded the men on deck. Tomassi blessed himself. Then he nodded to the burial detail, who picked up the litter which had Fortin's body on it, covered with a white sheet.

As they prepared to send him over the side, Tomassi commanded, "Hand, *salute*." He and the men saluted. Fortin's body went over the side with a splash. "*Two*," Tomassi ordered. The men lowered their hands to their sides. "Dismissed," Tomassi said.

As the men broke it up to go below, Tomassi reflected on how many times he'd thought about doing a burial at sea. He thought that maybe after doing more of them, he might get used to it.

He hoped not.

CHAPTER EIGHTEEN
10 NOVEMBER 1942

Tomassi slammed his fist on the table of the wardroom, then looked up at Chief Grace. He shook his head at the gray-haired man standing before him, with his cap under his arm, and an embarrassed look on his face.

"Gracie, I am ashamed of you," he said through gritted teeth. "You've been in the Navy for how long?"

"Twenty-five years, sir."

"Twenty-five years. And in that twenty-five years, you should have learned to control your temper, and learned how to brush off insults, right?"

"Yes, sir."

Tomassi held up some papers and said, "Yet, here you are, with charges against you from the Fremantle police for starting a brawl with some Dutch sailors, and practically wrecking a pub!" He slammed the papers down on the table again. He looked up again at his chief engineman. After a moment, he rasped, "Well, I'm waiting."

Grace took a breath and said, "Well, sir, it's like this. I was with some of our guys, as head of the liberty party. We were toasting each others good health, and these Dutchmen, well, they started singing really loud. I try to tell them to keep it down, and one of them starts with that, 'The trouble with you Americans is that your overpaid, oversexed, and over here' crap. Well, I just said to him, 'The trouble with you Dutch is that your underpaid, undersexed, and under MacArthur.' Well, then this Dutchman asks my name, and I told him. And he says, 'I didn't' know the Americans were desperate enough to put women in their submarines.' That did it. I just let him have it right on the kisser. And the boys came up to help, and the Dutchman's boys joined in. Well, next thing you know, the whole damn place chooses sides and jumps in. Some of the locals were with us, and some with the Dutch. Next thing I know, the cops come in, and the Shore Patrol, and break us up. Mr. Van Wert was there."

Tomassi turned to Van Wert, "Is that true?"

"Yes, sir," Van Wert replied, "As you know, sir, it was my turn the other evening to head the Shore Patrol detail. When we were told there was trouble at the Anchor and Chain Pub, I shook my head. I thought, 'No way it's any men from the *Eel*. Gracie wouldn't let me down like that.' Sadly, I was wrong."

"Unfortunately, you were, Mr. Van Wert," Tomassi said. He looked back at Chief Grace. "Chief, do have anything else to say for yourself?"

Grace looked at the deck for a moment, then looked Tomassi in the eye and said, "No, sir. I know I let the boat down, and I let you down. I'll take my punishment."

Tomassi nodded, "Yes, you will. Fortunately for you, Admiral Lockhart has dissuaded the local police from tossing you in jail. You're going to make full restitution to the owners of the pub."

"Restitution, sir?"

"Yes. That means your paychecks are going to the pub owners until you've paid for the damage. Furthermore, I'm taking away your liberty for the next two times we are in port. You know that liberty is a privilege, not a right. So, while others will get off the boat and take in the local sights, you will be stuck here. You will maintain watches here. And, you can forget about any Good Conduct Medal this time. That means your stripes go from gold to red. You understand, Chief?"

"Yes, sir."

"Now, Mr. Van Wert and I have to go see the admiral. I'm hoping it's not about you. If it is, woe be to you."

"Yes, sir."

"OK. Dismissed, Chief."

"Yes, sir." Grace put his cap back on, did an about face, and left the compartment.

"Admiral, Commander Dominic Tomassi and Lieutenant Commander Davis Van Wert, of the U.S.S. *Eel*, reporting."

Admiral Lockhart returned Tomassi's salute and said, "At ease, gentlemen."

"Thank you, sir," Tomassi replied as both he and Van Wert stood at ease.

Lockhart put on his glasses and looked at the papers in front of him. "You're both here for two reasons, gentlemen. First of all, there's the matter of your Chief Petty Officer, Marvin Grace. I see by the police report that he started the fight with some sailors of the Royal Netherlands East Indies Navy."

"Yes, sir," Van Wert replied. "I had been hoping it wasn't him, Admiral. I was on Shore Patrol the other night, and was hoping Grace wasn't the instigator. He was."

"I've given him his punishment, Admiral. He's not getting liberty the next time the *Eel* makes port, and the following time, either. Plus, he's making restitution," Tomassi added. "I'd like to thank the Admiral once again for intervening with the local police on his behalf."

Lockhart nodded. "I'm glad to do it, for one of my better commanders."

"This is even after the loss of Major Fortin, Admiral? I know I was supposed to bring him home alive, but –"

"Save it, Commander," Lockhart said as he set down the papers in his hand. "I should have ordered you to come home immediately after picking him up, but this command is short on subs. I've had to send boats to Brisbane since the Guadalcanal invasion, and it's kept me from having the strength to be able to have boats come back from special assignments right away." The admiral took off his glasses. "All the same, I'm glad, first of all, that you showed some fighting spirit in sinking several enemy ships, including that destroyer off Mindanao."

Tomassi grinned, "Actually, that was Van Wert. I let him have the honor of setting that tin can up."

"Also, Commander, it seems you disconnected the magnetic exploders on your torpedoes?"

"Yes, Admiral. It was a thought I had after talking to one of the British officers we had rescued off Singapore."

"I heard from him before they went back to Ceylon. It's something for us to think about." Admiral Lockhart opened a drawer on his right and produced two envelopes, then set them on the desk in front of the two officers. One envelope was marked for Tomassi, the other for Van Wert. They looked at each other with trepidation, hoping it wasn't something terrible. "Open them gentlemen. You first, Mr. Van Wert."

The two men picked up the envelopes. As Van Wert opened his, two small objects fell out and onto the desk. As he picked them up, Van Wert saw they were silver oak leaf clusters. His eyes grew wide, and he turned to Tomassi. Both men started to grin. Lockhart smiled. "Yes, *Commander* Van Wert. You'll get your own command."

Tomassi smiled and held out his hand. "Aces, Van! Put 'er there!"

Van Wert took his hand. "Thanks, skipper. Uh, I mean Dom."

Lockhart spoke up. "There's one other player in our little drama, but I couldn't wait for him. I think

–" the buzzer sounded on his phone, and he pushed the switch, "– Yes?"

"Admiral, Lieutenant Commander Bergman is here," the yeoman said.

"Send him in, Yeoman."

"Aye, aye, sir." A moment later, there was a knock at the door.

"Enter," Lockhart said.

Lieutenant Commander Bergman entered the room, closed the door behind him, then stepped up to the desk to the left of Van Wert and saluted, saying, "Admiral, Lieutenant Commander Myron Bergman, U.S.S. *Sea Otter*, reporting."

Lockhart returned the salute. "At ease, Commander." He turned to Tomassi. "Now it's your turn to open, Tomassi."

Tomassi tore into his envelope. No captain's eagles fell out, a bit to his disappointment. Instead, he read about his transfer to the *Sea Otter*. He looked to Van Wert, and said, "Well, they gave me the *Sea Otter*." He looked over to Bergman and said, "Looks like I'm your new boss."

Bergman gave a puzzled look to Tomassi, then to the admiral. "Admiral, I… uh, thought Commander Riley –"

"Commander Riley didn't feel you were ready to command a fleet boat, Mr. Bergman," Lockhart said. He then turned to Tomassi. "Riley was wounded on the *Sea Otter's* last patrol. I'm giving you his boat, and Van Wert will take over the *Eel*."

Tomassi motioned for Van Wert to step aside, then held out his hand to Bergman. "Well, anyway, I'm Dom Tomassi. Whaddaya say, Myron?"

Bergman grinned as he took Tomassi's hand. "Well, sir, I really don't like my name very much. So if it's all the same to you, let's just go by 'Bergman' or 'Commander', please?"

"OK, Bergman. Then I'm 'Commander,' or 'Captain.'"

CHAPTER NINETEEN
11 NOVEMBER 1942

The crew of the *Eel* stood at their quarters on deck while Tomassi read out his orders. "From, Commander, Submarines, Southwest Pacific, to, Commander Dominic Tomassi, USN. Subject –" Tomassi paused, then went on, "– Relief of command. You are ordered as of 11 November, 1942, to relinquish command of the U.S.S. *Eel* to Commander Davis Van Wert, USN, and report for other duties. Signed, C.A. Lockhart, Rear Admiral, USN."

Tomassi folded up his orders and looked at Van Wert. Van Wert saluted and said, "I relieve you, Commander."

"I stand relieved," Tomassi said as he returned the salute. He turned to the crew he would leave. He had worked with these men for barely a year. In that time, through drill and practice and actual combat, he'd gotten to know and trust them. Now, he was being torn away from them. He supposed he'd get used to a new set of faces, a different boat, a strange circumstance. But, he'd lost his virginity of command, as it were, here. That never could be repeated, even if he got a Medal of Honor with his new boat.

He stepped over to Lieutenant Odom. "Looks like you're the exec now, Odom."

"Yes, sir." Odom saluted and extended his hand. "May I say what a great honor it has been to serve with you?"

Tomassi smiled, and shook Odom's hand. "Yes, you may. And sell me a bridge while you're at it." Both men laughed. "Odom, thank you for the kind words."

"You're welcome, sir."

Tomassi next turned to the other officers and shook hands with them, wishing them luck and having them wish him the same. He then came to the men, starting with Chief Barker. "Well, Chief, this is it."

"Aye, sir," Barker said. "You're about the best skipper I've had in the service."

"That bad, huh?" Laughter from both of them. "Thanks, Chief. All the best."

"And to you, sir."

He then turned to Chief Grace. "Well, Gracie, I hope you don't give Mr. Van Wert the same headaches I got from you," Tomassi said with a smile.

"No, sir."

"And the punishment I gave you still stands with him."

"I know sir."

Tomassi extended his hand. "Take care, Gracie."

Grace shook Tomassi's hand. "You too, sir. And the next time you're in the Anchor and Chain, I'll buy you a pint."

"If they let you in."

Grace laughed. "If they let me in!"

Tomassi went up and down the lines of men, shaking hands and wishing them the best. A jeep pulled up with a runner from the *Sea Otter*. Tomassi had his gear on deck by the gangplank, waiting for him. Tomassi just pointed to it, and the man loaded the jeep with it. He then turned to the ensign and saluted. He looked at the men once more and said, "*Arrivederci.*"

As he left the boat for the last time, he heard Van Wert say, "Mr. Odom, dismiss the men."

"Aye, sir," Odom replied, and after a moment, "Crew, leave your quarters."

A two minute jeep ride took Tomassi to his new command, the *Sea Otter*. Like the *Eel*, she was of the *Gato* class. Her paint job was a lighter gray than the *Eel*. Her deck gun was a 4 inch gun, rather than 3 inch. She also had two 20mm guns on the conning tower. Tomassi dismounted from the jeep and went to the gangplank. Lieutenant Commander Bergman happened to be on the bridge, talking on the squawk box, when Tomassi pulled up.

"Permission to come aboard," Tomassi asked.

"Permission granted, sir. Welcome to the *Sea Otter*."

Tomassi stepped on board, and saluted the ensign. The runner came up behind him with his gear. "Just put it in my cabin, sailor."

"Aye, aye, sir," the man replied, and headed through the hatch on the port side of the con.

"Call your crew to quarters, Mr. Bergman."

"Aye, aye, sir." Bergman turned to the squawk box and said, "Crew, to your quarters, on the double."

Tomassi watched as the men poured out from the conning tower, and up through hatches on the deck, and headed forward. For his part, he moved up, under the forward 20mm mount, and watched them assemble. These men are smart and well drilled, he thought. I don't think I'll have to shake the tree.

After a minute, the men were assembled, and Bergman reported, "Sir, ship's company, U.S.S. *Sea Otter*, all present and accounted for."

Tomassi returned Bergman's salute and said, "Have the men stand at ease."

"Aye, sir. Company, stand at, *ease*." The men complied.

Tomassi unfolded his orders for command and read them. "From, Commander, Submarines, Southwest Pacific, to, Commander Dominic Tomassi, USN. Subject, new command. You are ordered as of 11 November, 1942, to report aboard the U.S.S. *Sea Otter* and immediately assume command. Signed, C.A. Lockhart, Rear Admiral, USN." He turned to Bergman, saluted and said, "I relieve you, Commander."

"I stand relieved, sir," Bergman said as he returned the salute.

Tomassi now turned back to the men and said, "Well, I'm not one for speeches. I'll just say that I look forward to getting to know you over the next couple of days, before we all get our liberty. You timed your return to port well, since it means you'll be spending Thanksgiving ashore, albeit in a country that doesn't celebrate it." He smiled and the men chuckled. "At least we'll get turkey with all the trimmings –" he pointed to the sub tender berthed next to them "– as I see the *Pisces* is back with us. Unfortunately, it does mean that we'll be spending Christmas on patrol. Unless the Japs start taking Christmas off." Another chuckle from the men. He turned to Bergman and said, "Mr. Bergman, dismiss the men."

"Aye, aye, sir." Bergman turned to the men and said. "Company, *attention*. Leave you quarters."

CHAPTER TWENTY
12 NOVEMBER 1942

"So, love," Fiona said, "Today would have been your anniversary?"

"Yesterday," Tomassi replied. "It would have been five years."

"I'm sorry, love. Today would have been my anniversary. Trevor and I would have been married seven years today."

Tomassi scratched his chin. "Did you want children?"

Fiona nodded, "Yes. I'd have loved having at least one. Trevor would have, too."

"What happened?"

Fiona turned and looked Tomassi in the eye. "He couldn't."

"Damn," he replied. "But how about you?"

"Yes, I can. Although I'm getting up there, I mean with how much longer I can have a baby. I'm thirty-six. My looks won't hold forever. I don't know if I want to be a madam. I guess, I guess I'd like to get married again someday. But, that will have to wait for this war to end. I've got my boys, like you, to keep happy."

Tomassi touched Fiona's red hair. She put her hand on his hairy chest. It always seemed awkward after they had intercourse. Mostly, he needed someone to talk to, but his job required silence. It was "The Silent Service" after all. It wouldn't do for Fiona to repeat something Tomassi told her, and have someone pass the word along. Either he could get relieved, and sent home, to spend the war at some desk. Or worse, to the enemy. He could blab about when they would sail, and where they were going, and then a Japanese task force would be waiting to kill him and his boat. One could hope that she would just forget everything he would say. She could just put it out of her mind.

"Do you call everybody 'love,' Fiona?"

Fiona nodded, "Yes."

Tomassi looked away for a moment, then back into her eyes. She could see that look in his eyes. She'd seen it from many men and boys. It would be danger. The smile went off of her face, and she turned her head slightly, then said, "No. Don't say it."

"Please, Fiona. I want to say it."

"You don't mean it. Even if you think you do, it's just loneliness."

"I love you, Fiona."

She looked away. "No, you don't mean it. None of them ever do. You'll see."

"I just wanted to tell a woman that. I don't want to get married until the war is over. But, I just wanted to tell a woman I love her."

Fiona turned away. "No, Dom. You don't mean it."

"OK. I guess I don't, but my job doesn't let me uncork the bottle. You help me with that. Maybe it's not love I'm thinking of, but, I guess, what you do for me … that's a kind of love."

"It's companionship, Dom. That's what you get with me." Fiona turned back around and looked at him. "I will say at least that you're nice to me. Many men do it with me and just walk away. Maybe they'll say, 'thanks' or 'goodbye.' But you're nice to me, and we talk. That's all you need. I give you that, and it's my job, nothing more." She took a breath, and then said, "Please remember that."

Tomassi lay there for a moment and took in what Fiona said. He nodded, and said, "OK. You're right. And thank you." He got up, then turned back to her and said, "I've got some new mates I'll send your way."

Fiona sat up and nodded. "See. That's what I mean, just business. Thanks."

CHAPTER TWENTY-ONE
13 NOVEMBER 1942

Admiral Lockhart couldn't persuade the owner of the Anchor and Chain to let U.S. sailors back in after CPO Grace's fight. So, Tomassi and Bergman had to find somewhere else to get a drink and get acquainted. They settled on another pub close to the base called The Old Lady. They found a booth and ordered two pints of beer. As they waited, Bergman began.

"So, Commander, where you from?"

"Well," Tomassi answered, "I was born in Chicago, but I grew up in Philly, because my dad was stationed at the Navy Yard there."

"OK," Bergman answered as the beers arrived. "Well, for me, it was Barcelona, Spain. My father was a merchant captain. He met my mother there, and after I was born, he got us to America. I grew up in New York."

"Did you ever go back?"

"That's part of why I joined the Navy. I wanted to go there again. And, before the civil war there, I did get to go."

"What did you think?"

"Beautiful. I wonder if it still is, though."

"From what I understand, Barcelona was the last big city to fall to Franco. Maybe there is something left."

Bergman shook his head. "I'd like to think so. But I doubt it." After a pause, Bergman asked, "How about you? You ever been to Italy?"

Tomassi nodded. "Yeah. After I got engaged, I was posted there for a year as an assistant naval attaché. I got to see Rome, where my grandfather came from, and also Naples."

"'See Naples and die,'" Bergman said.

"I hope to put off the dying part for a while, but yeah," Tomassi said. "I got to see it. I'm happy. I got to go on a patrol in one of their subs."

"Anything as good as ours?"

"Not really. But then, they don't have to cruise as far."

Bergman took a sip of his beer, and then said, "You said you got engaged before you went to Italy."

"Yeah," Tomassi replied. "First thing after I got back, we set a date. Turned out to be Armistice Day."

"How many years," Bergman asked.

Tomassi looked away for a moment. "It would have been five years, just the other day."

"Would have been? She left you?"

"She's dead."

"Oh, I'm sorry." After a moment, Bergman said, "That makes two of us."

Tomassi looked up, shook his head, and said, "Small world." He raised his glass and said, "To absent friends."

"*L'Chiam*," Bergman answered as their glasses clinked.

After drinking the toast, Tomassi asked, "So you are Jewish?"

Bergman nodded, "Yeah."

"How did your mother's family react when she said she was marrying a Jew?"

"Delighted. She's Jewish, too."

Tomassi gulped his drink. "There are Jews in Spain?"

"We're everywhere," Bergman smiled. "It's funny how 'God's chosen people' have to keep hiding in order not to get picked on. It never works. We get picked on for trying to hide."

"Is there anywhere that you're not?"

"I wouldn't be surprised if we sailed into Tokyo and found a synagogue," Bergman laughed.

Tomassi laughed, and then looked at his watch. It was nearly 21:30. "Let's get the check. I want to go turn in."

CHAPTER TWENTY-TWO
26 NOVEMBER 1942

The crew of the *Sea Otter* went aboard the sub tender *Pisces* to have Thanksgiving dinner. As it turned out, the crew of the Eel went on at the same time. The *Eel* crew was ahead of Tomassi's new crew in line. Tomassi had his place at the head of his men, and recognized Van Wert. When Van Wert turned around, Tomassi waved, prompting Van Wert to smile and wave back.

"Are you going to eat with your old crew," Bergman asked. "I'd understand if you did."

"Well, Bergman," Tomassi answered, "you might, but the men might not. I really haven't gotten to bond with these guys since I came on board. What I do know is that I have to put my old command behind me, even if they're right here. I think if the situation were turned around, you'd understand, right?"

Bergman nodded, "Yes, sir, I understand."

The line slowly moved forward. Eventually, Tomassi got his tray and loaded up with turkey, sweet potatoes, mashed potatoes, cranberry sauce, stuffing, and a big slice of pumpkin pie. He made his way to a seat and, before starting to eat, blessed himself and said *Grace*. When he finished, he looked to see Bergman. He was slowly rocking and silently saying something. When Bergman finished, he removed his cap, and looked up at Tomassi.

"Good to know we were both brought up right," Tomassi smiled.

Bergman smiled back, "You know, sir, I don't think I've given thanks to the Lord in some time."

"What you were just doing?"

"Yes."

"I hate to admit it, but me too. Guess it takes risking your life to make you thankful."

Bergman nodded, "Yes, sir."

As they started eating, Tomassi asked, "Was Thanksgiving a big deal at your house when you were a kid?"

"Oh, yes. It was the only time I can think of when my mother wouldn't go to the kosher butcher. She'd go to the regular butcher and find a nice big turkey. Then, she'd get it home and slave over it all day, on the day. She'd get my sister to help. At about 4:30, we'd sit down and give thanks to the Lord, and then we'd go at it. There'd be nothing left inside of half an hour."

"Me, too. Mama would get a nice big turkey, and then she and my aunts and my cousins would kick the men out of the kitchen, and they'd work all day on it. We'd eat about three in the afternoon. We had to tell what we were thankful for before we could eat." Tomassi looked away for a moment, and sighed. "The last time we did that was 1918. We were thankful Dad was home. He was a destroyer sailor, and we were happy to have him back safe from the war. Then, I guess a week later, is when Mama came down with the Spanish Flu." More silence. "We ended up burying her before Christmas."

"I'm sorry, sir."

"Best of times, and worst of times, I guess," Tomassi softly said. He finished his food, and looked around. Van Wert and his officers were laughing and eating. Tomassi looked away. He had made his mind up to make a clean break of it when he left the *Eel*. He would say 'hi' to Van Wert, or Odom, when he saw them, but he didn't think it was right to be buddy-buddy with them until he'd gotten to know the *Sea Otter* crew better. He'd hardly gotten to do that before everyone went on their leave. "Bergman, have you seen the chaplain," he asked.

Bergman looked around, and then pointed toward the far hatch. "I think I see him over there."

"Thanks, Bergman, I'll see you back at the boat."

"OK, sir."

Tomassi picked up his tray and headed for the hatch, hoping to catch up with the chaplain. He did it.

"Father?"

The gray-haired priest turned and said, "Hello, son. Good dinner?"

"Yes, Father. Uh, Father, I'd… I'd like to confess."

"Certainly, my son. Come with me." They proceeded down the passageway to the chaplain's cabin. As they went in, the priest pointed to a chair in one corner, with a curtain drawn up next to it. "You prefer a screen, don't you?"

"Yes, Father."

Tomassi sat down, and the priest kissed his stole and put it on. He pulled up a chair on the other side of the curtain, blessing himself, saying, "In the name of the Father, and of the Son, and of the Holy Spirit. Amen."

"Bless me, Father, for I have sinned. It's been four years since my last confession."

CHAPTER TWENTY-THREE
27 NOVEMBER 1942

Tomassi hadn't gotten the chance to meet his division chiefs. His tradition of coming to look at each compartment when it was time to shove off would give him that chance.

He started with the after torpedo room as usual. Tomassi had briefly gotten to meet the Chief Torpedoman's Mate, Chief Petty Officer Watkins, who was there to inspect the compartment.

"Hello, Chief," Tomassi said.

"Hello, sir," Watkins replied. "Just seeing to the men, sir. The Japs gave us a good going over last time."

"Heavy depth charging?"

"Aye, sir."

"Lots of damage?"

"Well, sir, enough that the seals on all these tubes had to be replaced by the repair crew. They've certified with a test dive that they'll hold."

"How about the forward room?"

"It's all squared away, sir. Nothing like the same damage, but the parts they needed to replace are taken care of."

"Full allowance of torpedoes?"

"Aye, sir."

"Very well. Carry on, Chief."

"Aye, aye, sir."

Tomassi moved through the motor room into the after engine room. He passed from there into the forward engine room, where he saw Chief Engineman's Mate Rampone.

"Hi, Chief."

"Hello, Captain."

"Everything ready here for sea?"

"Aye, sir. Full allowance of fuel on board. We're ready for sea, sir."

"Did you have a lot of damage from your last enemy action?"

"Well, number four diesel was put out of commission, but the yard commander managed to find one from one of the Dutch subs, and we got it to work. It's not too different from ours, but we're going to get it changed out as soon as one becomes available."

"Very well, Chief. Carry on."

"Aye, sir."

Tomassi proceeded into the crew quarters. He looked for the Pharmacist's Mate. A sailor was lying in his bunk, and Tomassi shook him to wake him. "Hey, sailor."

"Bug off, I'm trying to sleep." The man turned and opened his eyes, then realized who he was talking to, and stood up very quickly. "Sorry, sir!"

"Forget it. Where's 'Doc'?"

"He should be coming back any minute, sir. He said something about getting more stimulant."

Pharmacist's Mate Avery showed up at this point. He was a redheaded young man, carrying a liquor bottle. He looked up and said, "Oh, hello, captain." He held up the bottle and said, "This is strictly for medicinal purposes, sir. You know, in case someone is hurt and I need to work on them."

"Will that be available in case I need it?"

"Aye, sir." Avery smiled.

"That's all. Carry on, Doc." He turned to the other man. "What's your name?"

"Fuller, sir. Fireman Second Class."

"You carry on too, Fuller, but not for long. You'll be called to quarters soon."

"Thank you, sir," Fuller replied. No way was he finishing his nap.

Next, there was the galley. "Cookie?"

The cook, Hawkins, answered, "Yes, sir?" Tomassi had worked with blacks in the service before, and didn't have a problem with them.

"All ready for sea?"

"Aye, sir. We got the turkey for Christmas, sir. Also, we got plenty of powdered milk, so the men can have it with their turkey."

"Too bad the whole milk will be gone by then."

"I'm sorry, sir. The tender didn't have any cans of whole milk left. The *Eel* done got 'em."

Oh, that Daniels, Tomassi thought. If I could have brought anyone over, it would have been him. He shook his head, then said, "OK, Cookie, carry on."

"Aye, sir."

Next on Tomassi's shopping list was the radio room. "Sparks?"

The radio man answered, "Aye, sir?"

Tomassi stepped into the compartment. "What's your name, sailor?"

"Troilo, sir."

"Where you from?"

"Philadelphia, sir."

"Really. I spent part of my childhood there. Was your dad in the Navy?"

"No, sir. He worked for the telephone company, and I did, too."

"Oh."

"But my uncle worked for Cramp Shipbuilding."

"He did? Well, maybe he helped build the destroyer my dad was on."

"Could be, sir."

"All ready for sea, Troilo?"

"Aye, sir. We were shaken up by the depth charges, but the radio is working perfectly now, sir."

"OK, Sparks. Carry on."

"Aye, sir."

Tomassi now went into the control room, and found the diving officer, Lieutenant (j.g.) Lloyd. "Mister Lloyd?"

"Aye, sir."

"Are you ready for sea?"

"Yes, sir. The repair crew fixed all our plane controls, and freed up the rudder. You wouldn't know we got worked over."

"Great. Carry on."

"Aye, sir."

Tomassi now passed through "officer's country" to get to the forward torpedo room. He entered the compartment as the torpedo tubes were being loaded. Torpedoman's Mate Box saw him.

"Box."

"Aye, sir."

"Loading up?"

"Aye, sir."

"Got the full allowance?"

"Aye, sir. Full allowance."

"OK, carry on."

"Aye, sir."

Tomassi turned back into the officer's quarters section of the boat when he came across Bergman. "Mr. Bergman?"

"Aye, sir."

"Do we have full allowance for the deck gun and the small arms?"

"Aye, sir. Full allowance for the 4 inch gun and the 20mm guns. Plus full allowance of .50-caliber and .45-caliber ammo. Plus, ammo for the carbine."

"Very well. Let's call the crew to quarters."

"Aye, sir." Both men went up to the conning tower. Bergman got on the squawk box. "Crew, to your quarters. On the double."

Tomassi and Bergman went out the hatch on the starboard side and went to the foredeck. After a minute and a half, the fifty-eight men and officers were on deck, and at attention.

Bergman turned to Tomassi and saluted. "Ship's company, U.S.S. *Sea Otter*, all present and accounted for, sir."

Tomassi returned the salute. "Very well. When the men are dismissed, have the special sea section at their stations and prepare the ship to get underway."

"Sir?"

"Yes, Mr. Bergman?"

"Uh, don't you have something to say to the men?"

Tomassi shrugged. "What do I have to say to them?"

"Well, sir, Commander Riley would usually give a speech to the men before we got underway."

"Well, I'm not Commander Riley, Mr. Bergman. I don't like to waste time with speeches. I'm not here for a popularity contest." Tomassi looked over to his right, past the conning tower, to the *Eel*. He could see her since the tender had been moved away during the night. Van Wert had the crew on deck, no doubt about to send the men to their special sea stations. Tomassi felt, as near as one could describe it, like a man who'd left his bride at the altar, then found himself a guest at her next wedding. He turned back to Bergman and the men. "I'm sure Commander Riley was much loved by you, and I'm sure you'd love to have him here, just as –" he looked back to the *Eel* "– just as I wouldn't mind being on my old boat there." He turned back to the men. "But, this is the Navy, not some yacht club. We go where we're told, when we're told, and we say 'Aye, sir'

137

when we get an order, then we damn well do it. So…
I'm sorry. But, we will get to know each other and get
our job done so we can all go home." He turned once
more to Bergman. "You have your orders, mister."

"Aye, aye, sir." Bergman saluted and Tomassi
returned it. Bergman did an about face and said,
"Leave your quarters. Special sea section to your
stations on the double. All hands prepare to get
underway."

The men started going to their stations. Those
who were to take in the lines went to their stations,
and Tomassi and Bergman went to the bridge.

CHAPTER TWENTY-FOUR
7 DECEMBER 1942

The Sea Otter had been ordered to patrol the port of Balikpapan on the southeast coast of Borneo. They had topped off fuel at "Potshot," which was where Tomassi found out that the tender *Pisces* had gone. Now, there was a fully stocked tender, with fuel, food and ammo, there to service any sub based at Fremantle. This meant that a sub could restock her torpedoes and fuel, take on food, and go back on patrol in less time than if she had to go to the main base.

That thought would have to wait. First, there was the passage the boat had taken through the Lombok Strait, and then passage through the Makassar Strait, between Borneo and Celebes, to the target area. They made it there on the first anniversary of the Day of Infamy. The *Sea Otter* had just made her morning dive at about 06:30. Tomassi had just finished with his breakfast when the OOD, Lieutenant Morrow, came in.

"Hello, sir," Morrow said as he sat down and the steward brought him his portion of ham and eggs.

"Hello, Lieutenant," Tomassi replied after a sip of coffee. "How's it look up there?"

"Pretty quiet, sir. Maybe the Japs don't go to work 'til 09:00."

"Who's got the con?"

"Mr. Bergman, sir. He told me he'd relieve me so I could eat."

"All right."

Tomassi didn't say anything more while Morrow ate. He had his log to update, and sometimes it just didn't do to sit in his cabin, and that cramped little desk, when he could be in the relative comfort of the wardroom, with the coffee machine right there to help him wake up.

While he had another cup of Joe, Tomassi filled in how, over the past week, they'd made their passage through the Lombok Strait, dodged a patrol craft, dove to avoid planes, and tried to go undetected through the enemy's waters. Overall, not very exciting stuff.

Morrow finished his toast and slammed down the last of his coffee. "OK, sir. I'm going back up to the con."

Tomassi looked at his watch. "You only took four minutes to finish all that food? I hope we don't have to come back up in a hurry and hit any waves."

Morrow smiled, "Me too, sir." He put on his cap and left the compartment.

Tomassi looked over the log once more. It seemed GI enough, he thought. He closed it and went back to his cabin to put it away. When he came back to the wardroom, he found Bergman was already sitting down to his breakfast. "Hello, Bergman."

"Hello, sir. You going to join me?"

"I ate before. I'm just having some coffee now." Tomassi felt an urge, then set to cup down on the table. "First, I've got to make room for it. Be right back."

Bergman smiled. "OK, sir." He started in on his food, and after a couple of minutes, Tomassi returned.

"Now I'll have the coffee," Tomassi said. After pouring it, he sat across from Bergman. "It's been a year already. Can you believe it?"

Bergman shook his head. "No. A year. Do you remember where you were, sir?"

Tomassi nodded. "I was underway in the *Eel*. We were on our way past Jacksonville when the radioman came up with the news. I guess it was about 13:00. He told me, and then after I picked my jaw up off the deck, I told the crew. Then I just went to my cabin and sat there for a while. How about you, Bergman?"

"I was at Coco Solo."

"Oh, you were stationed at the Canal?"

"At the sub base."

"What was your boat?"

"*S-52*."

"Last of the old 'Sugar' boats, huh?"

Bergman nodded as he swallowed a mouthful of eggs.

"Wow," Tomassi said. "My first boat out of sub school was the *R-12*. Then after about a year, I got onto an S-boat. The, uh … S-29. That lasted a year and a half. Then I went to the *Jawfish*. In '37, I was sent to Italy as assistant naval attaché, and that lasted about a year. Then they put me on the *Walrus*. That was until late '39. Then I got to be exec of the *Goldring*. Finally in late November of '41, I got command of the *Eel*. "How about you?"

Bergman had finished with his food at this point, and a steward came to take the plate. After he left, Bergman started in. "Well, I graduated the academy in '33, then sub school, then … well, it had been S-boats for me until now. I was on the *S-40*, then the *S-52*, based at New London, then down to Panama. I think we heard about Pearl Harbor about Noon. We had to get back to our boats right away. We started to patrol right away, in case the Japs tried to attack us."

Tomassi looked puzzled, and asked, "Isn't Coco Solo on the Caribbean side of the Canal?"

"Yeah."

"Then how did you patrol? Did they think the Japs would come around South America?"

Bergman laughed and shook his head. "No. We had to transit the canal going on patrol and coming back! We spent half a day in each direction, going to patrol and coming back from it."

"Nuts."

"It got better for us. When Germany got into the war, and we didn't know how Vichy France would go, whether they'd stay neutral or go with Germany, we had to patrol their islands."

"How did that work?"

"We got to go to Martinique. There was a French carrier there. We had to keep an eye on her. It was late April, and our skipper, Lieutenant Kelly, had us a little too close to the defenses. I went to his cabin and found him passed out."

"What happened?"

"Well, there was a gin bottle on the deck. He'd snuck it onboard and got hammered. Then the sound man reported screws underwater near us. Then he reported pinging from sonar."

Tomassi sat up in his seat. "Oh. A U-boat!"

"Yep. We played cat and mouse for about an hour, with me in command, trying to maneuver for a shot underwater. We finally got a torpedo loose on him, and he ran away. We radioed home when we came up at night, and I had to rat out Kelly. We came home, he got court-martialed, and I got promoted to Lieutenant, and got command of the boat."

"Rotten way to have to get it."

"Yeah. Well, then we were ordered to Australia. We sailed from Panama to Brisbane, with a stop in Samoa to refuel. Next thing I know, they had orders for me to come to Fremantle, and I got posted on the *Sea Otter*. I got promoted again, and here I am."

"Looking forward to getting command again?"

Bergman grinned a little. "Did it show that day? Well, I guess once you get a taste, you want more."

Tomassi nodded, "I know. You'll get it again."

CHAPTER TWENTY-FIVE
8 DECEMBER 1942

The previous day had yielded little in the way of contacts. Tomassi had wanted to go after a small lighter, which could have been a patrol craft of some kind. The enemy, however, was in shallow water and close to a Japanese gun position across the harbor from Balikpapan. This day, however, brought an old friend back into Tomassi's life.

Bergman was on periscope watch. It was about 07:50. Tomassi had just entered the conning tower when Bergman saw the ship. He probably couldn't believe his eyes, since Tomassi saw him back away for a moment and look again.

"Captain," Bergman said, "I can't believe what I'm seeing. She's huge. He turned to Tomassi and said, "She looks like –"

"Let me guess," Tomassi injected. "She's about five hundred feet long, with a forward superstructure, cranes amidships, two stacks painted black, with a white dot on either side of them. Am I close?"

"You're right. How –"

"And if you look at her bow, under the Jap characters, it says *Luzon Maru #4*. Does it?"

Bergman looked again. "Yes, it does! How did you know?"

"Because, my dear Mr. Bergman, that ship is my great white whale."

Bergman looked sideways at Tomassi. "I don't want to end up like Ahab, sir."

"I don't plan to, either. It's not going to take a harpoon for this bitch, just torpedoes that work. I was denied off Truk, and off Singapore, by torpedoes that didn't work. I'm hoping that disconnecting the magnetic exploders will help." Tomassi turned to the talker, and couldn't think of his name. He turned back to Bergman and said, "Sound general quarters."

"Aye, sir." Bergman turned to the talker. "Osborne, sound general quarters."

"Aye, sir," Osborne replied, and hit the alarm. The Bells of St. Mary's sounded, and the fire control party scrambled to their places in the con.

"Sound, do you hear her," Tomassi asked.

The soundman, Barnhart, replied, "Picking up heavy screws bearing three-five-zero relative. She sounds huge."

Tomassi nodded, "That she is. I'll take over the scope, Bergman."

"Aye, sir," Bergman replied as he moved aside.

"All stations manned and ready," Osborne reported.

"Very well. Make ready all bow tubes."

"Make ready all bow tubes," Osborne repeated.

Tomassi looked through the periscope at the target ship. It was her, all right! Her superstructure was painted white, and her stacks black with the white dots. She seemed to be running light, since some of the red antifouling paint used below the waterline on ships was showing. "She's riding light. Guess she'll take on a load of oil, if I don't do something about it. All right, angle on the bow, ten port. Gyro fifteen left. Estimate speed, six knots. Set torpedoes for … she's running kind of light, so, set torpedoes for nine feet."

Osborne relayed all of this to the forward torpedo room. Meanwhile, Lt. Morrow was working on the TDC. Bergman stood by the periscope to give the bearing.

Tomassi spoke. "Bearing, mark."

"Two-zero-five."

"Range, mark."

"Four-eight-double-oh."

"Helm, left ten degrees rudder, come left to course three-zero-zero."

The helmsman, Chastain, repeated, "Left ten degrees rudder, coming left to course three-zero-zero, sir."

"Very well. Bearing, mark."

"Two-zero-five."

"Range, mark."

"Four-four-double-oh."

"Steady on new course, sir," Chastain reported.

"Very well. Mr. Bergman, check the plot."

"Mr. Morrow," Bergman said, "I need to know about the plot."

"Course and speed check, sir," Morrow answered.

"Range, mark," Tomassi said.

"Three-niner-double-oh," replied Bergman.

"Check the plot," Tomassi said.

"Check."

"Set," Morrow replied.

Tomassi licked his lips, and then said, "Fire one, fire two, fire three, fire four."

Osborne pushed the firing button with each command and said, "All torpedoes fired, sir."

After a moment, Barnhart said, "All torpedoes running hot, straight and normal, sir."

"Down scope," Tomassi said. He put up the handles and the periscope was lowered. Bergman started his stopwatch. "Running time?"

"Number one should hit in thirty seconds, sir," Bergman said. The ticking of the stopwatch sounded clearly through the compartment. "Twenty seconds, sir … fifteen seconds … ten seconds…five, four, three, two, one, zero."

An explosion could be heard, and Barnhart reported, "Torpedo number one hit, sir."

Bergman now said, "Torpedo number two to hit in five, four, three, two, one, now."

Nothing could be heard until Barnhart said, "Bumping noise against the target, followed by a burst of air."

Tomassi grimaced, and then asked, "Torpedo three?"

Bergman answered, "Torpedo number three to hit in five, four, three, two, one, now."

"Bumping noise against the target, followed by a burst of air," Barnhart said.

Tomassi put his hand on top of his head and ran it down his face, then with his hand out, he asked Bergman, "Number four?"

"Torpedo number four to hit in four, three, two, one, now." Bergman clicked off the stopwatch.

"Bumping noise against the target, followed by a burst of air," Barnhart said.

"Son of a bitch," Tomassi muttered. "Stand by tubes five and six."

"Stand by tubes five and six," Osborne repeated.

"Up scope," Tomassi ordered. Bergman raised the periscope. Tomassi got a look at *Luzon Maru #4*. She was slower, but still going. The torpedo that did go off caught her just aft of the bridge, and a fire was started on deck, but not a very big one. "Estimate target speed, five knots. Gyro five left. Angle on the bow, fifteen port. Bearing, mark."

"Two-one-zero," Bergman reported.

"Range, mark."

"Three-three-double-oh."

"Check," asked Tomassi.

"Set," replied Morrow.

"Fire five," Tomassi ordered.

"Fire five," Osborne said as he pushed the button. "Five's away, sir."

"Fire six."

"Fire six. Six away, sir."

"Down scope." The periscope was lowered. "Helm, right full rudder, come right to course one-zero-zero. All ahead flank."

Chastain repeated, "Helm, right full rudder, coming right to one-zero-zero, all ahead flank, sir."

"Very well."

"Both torpedoes running hot, straight, and normal, sir," reported Barnhart.

"Make ready stern tubes," ordered Tomassi.

"Make ready stern tubes," repeated Osborne.

After a minute, Chastain reported, "Steady on new course, sir."

"Very well, up scope." Bergman raised the periscope, and Tomassi turned it around to see *Luzon Maru #4* still going along moving along. On the horizon, Tomassi could see smoke from the direction of the harbor. Japanese destroyers or sub chasers, he thought, maybe a tug to help bring her in. "Time check on those torpedoes."

"Torpedoes five and six both should have hit by now," Bergman said.

"Sound, did you hear anything?"

Barnhart answered, "Negative on torpedoes, sir. They might have hit and not gone off, but I didn't hear anything."

"Damn," Tomassi said. He looked at *Luzon Maru #4*. She looked like she was stopped now. "Target speed, one knot. Angle on the bow, twenty left. Gyro zero. Make torpedo depth seven feet. Bearing, mark."

"Two-two-zero," Bergman said.

"Range, mark."

"Four-three-double-oh."

"Check."

"Set," replied Morrow.

"Fire seven, fire eight, fire nine, fire ten."

Osborne pushed the firing button four times, and then said, "All torpedoes fired, sir."

"All ahead one-third," Tomassi ordered.

"All ahead one-third," Chastain replied.

"Sound, can you hear anything?"

Barnhart answered, "Torpedoes coming out of our wake. They all are running hot, straight and normal, sir."

Tomassi kept the periscope up. He watched the tracks of the fish as they ran toward *Luzon Maru #4*. Bergman reported, "Torpedo seven to hit in ten seconds... five, four, three, two, one, now."

Tomassi could see a burst of water on the side of the target. Barnhart reported, "Bumping noise against the target, followed by a burst of air, sir."

"Torpedo eight to hit in five, four, three, two, one, now."

Another burst of water, and another report from Barnhart, "Bumping noise against the target, followed by a burst of air."

"Torpedo nine to hit in five, four, three, two, one, now."

Again, just a burst of water, followed by Barnhart's weary report.

"Torpedo ten to hit in five, four, three, two, one, now."

Once more, just a burst of water and Barnhart's lamentable report. Tomassi slammed the handles of the periscope and growled, "Down scope."

As the scope went down, Tomassi turned to Chastain. "Helm, all ahead two-thirds."

"Helm, all ahead two-thirds, sir."

"Very well."

Bergman stepped up to Tomassi and asked, "Are we going to try again?"

Tomassi shook his head. "Not unless I can find the sons-of-bitches from the Bureau of Ordnance who came up with these crappy torpedoes, so I can fire *them* through the tubes." He looked Bergman in the eye. "No, I saw the smoke from Jap tin cans coming. We couldn't get around for a shot without them hitting us hard." He tilted his head back and blew out a breath. He then turned to Osborne and said, "Secure from general quarters."

CHAPTER TWENTY-SIX
10 DECEMBER 1942

The neighborhood had gotten a little too hot after *Sea Otter's* brush with *Luzon Maru #4*. Tomassi had to take his boat out into the Makassar Strait, owing to the sharp increase in patrol activity at Balikpapan. They were on the surface in the early morning, at about 07:25. They had to stay deep the night before because of a group of Japanese patrol craft. So, they had to spend an extra hour up top to recharge batteries.

Radarman Adams had the watch on the air search set. He and Radarman Zarate had the job of watching the radar when the boat was surfaced, in case a Japanese plane should show up. Zarate had just finished his watch, but couldn't sleep so he and Adams were talking.

"No, back in Arizona we don't go around flipping cows," he said.

"I was just making a joke, all right," Adams shot back. "No need for all the fireworks."

"I just think you city boys need to get off my back. It's not – Adams, look at the scope."

Adams looked at his radar set and saw the indication of an aircraft contact. He looked at the lines on the set to determine where the enemy was coming from, and then got on the squawk box. "Bridge, radar. We've got a plane contact bearing three-five-zero, relative."

Tomassi had come up to the bridge to get some air. "Radar, this is the captain. Can you tell his distance?"

"Radar here, sir. It looks like eight miles distance. He appears to be closing, but not too fast. He may not know we're here."

"All right." Tomassi turned the switch to call the engine room, "Engine room."

"Engine room, aye," Chief Rampone answered.

"Chief, how's the battery charge?"

"We could dive now, but it's not a full charge. We might have to come up before sundown."

"Thanks, Chief." Tomassi flicked the switch over to talk to the whole boat. "Battle stations, surface." The Bells of St. Mary's sounded, and men started to run out to their gun positions. Tomassi and Bergman got their helmets and life vests. "Chief," Tomassi called down the hatch, "bring up the Tommy Gun."

"Aye, aye, sir," Chief Watkins replied.

As this was going on, other men brought up the .50 caliber machine guns and fixed them to the rails of the conning tower, on either side of the bridge. They hurriedly loaded the weapons as Chief Watkins came up through the hatch with the Thompson submachine gun.

Everyone not busy with loading a weapon was scanning the sky for the plane. One of the lookouts, Barnsley, finally saw it. "Aircraft off the port bow." Everyone looked at saw the Japanese floatplane. It was a monoplane, with one large float under its fuselage and one smaller float under each wing.

"It's a 'Rufe,'" Bergman said, calling it by its Allied reporting name. "Floatplane fighter."

"Yeah," Tomassi said. "Two machine guns in the nose, a 20mm cannon in each wing, and two fifty pound bombs. And that's the good news."

"What's the bad news?"

"They have a radio, too. He'll likely call home before attacking us."

The fighter circled for a moment before swooping in from the starboard quarter of the sub. "Commence firing," Tomassi yelled. The machine gun on the starboard side, along with the 20mm guns, and Watkins with the Tommy Gun, cut loose on the "Rufe." For his part, the Japanese plane's wings and cowl lit up as he strafed the sub. No one got hit on his first pass.

The enemy plane came around to try and hit the *Sea Otter* from the port side this time. "Helm, left full rudder," Tomassi called.

"Helm, left full rudder, aye," Chastain replied.

The well timed turn kept the "Rufe" from landing his bombs on the sub. They went off in the water off either side of the boat, spraying everyone on the conning tower with water and shrapnel. The plane came around for a third pass. Tomassi suddenly realized that Watkins was right next to him with the Tommy Gun. Tomassi tried to scoot over, but there was no room, so he just covered his ear as Watkins cut loose again.

As the 'Rufe' passed over, Tomassi saw black smoke coming from his engine. Everyone let out a cheer as the enemy plane hit the water a hundred yards from the sub. Tomassi saw that the plane had come down to the left of the boat, and that the boat was still turning in a great circle. "Helm, rudder amidships."

"Helm, rudder amidships, aye," Chastain answered.

Tomassi thought for a moment, and then said, "Helm, all stop."

"Helm, all stop, aye," Chastain answered.

"Secure from battle stations," Tomassi said into the squawk box. He turned to Watkins. "Good shooting, Chief."

"Thank you, sir," Watkins replied.

"Four more like that and you'll be an ace."

Watkins smiled, "Yes, sir."

Tomassi then held out his hand. "May I borrow that for a moment?"

A puzzled Watkins handed over the Tommy Gun. "Thanks, Chief." Tomassi went down the conning tower hatch and then out the side. He went forward past the deck gun, and saw the Japanese pilot swimming towards the sub.

Watkins had come down after Tomassi. "Do you want to fish him out, sir?"

Tomassi shook his head. The pilot swam up to Tomassi, expecting him to lend a hand. Instead, Tomassi put the Tommy Gun to his shoulder and fired. The pilot let out a cry, and his arms flailed before he went silent and floated in the crimson tinted sea.

"Why'd you do that, sir," Watkins asked.

Tomassi handed back the Tommy Gun and said, "I didn't want the sharks to kill him."

CHAPTER TWENTY-SEVEN
25 DECEMBER 1942

The *Sea Otter* had stayed on station through two weeks of few sightings. Tomassi guessed that the *Luzon Maru #4* attack must have made the other Japanese tankers stay clear of him. He did manage to fire torpedoes at other ships, producing two sinkings of medium sized freighters, and they sank a sampan with their deck gun. But the thought of *Luzon Maru #4* still obsessed him.

But, that was not on his mind this evening. It was Christmas. Just about everyone on the boat looked forward to this day. Bergman, of course, simply thought of it as just another day. He'd had his holiday. Tomassi asked him about it.

"What do you do for your holiday?"

"For Hanukah? Well, I have a menorah in my cabin, and when I get a chance at night, after taking the stars for navigating, I go in there, and close the curtain behind me, and light up the candles for whatever night it is. I guess when I was growing up, I took if for granted. Now, with me being the only Jew on the boat, well, I treasure it like nothing else. I have family to write to, but that's not the same. When this is over, I'll find myself a wife and have a family to pass this along to."

Tomassi nodded, "Good for you."

The stewards came along with the turkey dinners. The officers not on watch were all there, and after saying *Grace*, they started in on their meals. Each of them had their own conversations. Tomassi and Bergman kept theirs going.

"So, Captain, you told me once you're a widower. May I ask about it again?"

Tomassi thought for a moment, and then said, "Well, Sophia meant everything to me. We met on Armistice Day of '35, when there was a dance in town in New London. Her brother was a worker in the machine shop, and she came to a mixer, and we hit it off right then. I proposed to her one year later, before I went to Italy, and when I came back, it happened to be Armistice Day that we got married."

"That made it easy to remember, didn't it?"

Tomassi laughed, "Yeah, that it did. Whenever I came back from patrol, we'd have a picnic. She'd meet me at the gate, and we'd drive outside of town, and find this old shade tree. We eat under that tree, and we'd drink some table wine. We could lose ourselves in each other's eyes." He went silent for a moment. "Then, on Armistice Day of '41, just when I'd learned I was going to get the *Eel*, I came home from my last patrol with the *Goldring*, and I busted down to that gate, expecting my Sophia to be there, with that picnic basket. Instead, it was a local cop. He asked my name, and then he told me … he told me my Sophia was dead. He took me to the hospital, we went to the basement, and they showed me the body." Tomassi had to stop to keep himself from crying. "It was some drunk driver."

Bergman looked at his plate for a moment. "I'm sorry, sir."

"It's OK." After a moment, Tomassi looked at Bergman and asked, "OK, what about you?"

"Nothing quite so joyful as your story. I was at the Academy, and I was just about to graduate. I met this girl at a dance, and we … well, we were like animals. Next thing I know, she tells me she's pregnant. She was the daughter of a Maryland state senator."

"I'm sure he was thrilled."

"Yes, especially when he found out I was a Northern Jew." Bergman chuckled, "I'm sure they'd have been less angry if our colored cook had gotten her pregnant." Both men laughed at that.

"I'm not so sure," Tomassi said.

"You don't know these people. Anyway, I agreed to do the right thing and marry her. My mother was upset I was marrying a Gentile, but I explained what happened. She still didn't like it. Luckily, the girl's mother persuaded her father not to make a big open deal about it, or I'd have been expelled."

"So, anyway, right after graduation, we got married. Four months later, she went into labor." It was Bergman's turned to pause. "She wasn't too strong, you see. Well, she died giving birth to a stillborn child."

"I'm sorry," Tomassi said.

"Thank you," Bergman replied. "Her father wouldn't even talk to me at the funeral. He just looked at me as if I'd killed her with my own hands. I left for sub school after that. I've never been back."

"Funny, I've never been back to The Yard since graduating," Tomassi mused, referring to the academy grounds.

CHAPTER TWENTY-EIGHT
21 JANUARY 1943

The U.S.S. *Sea Otter* finally pulled into Fremantle after her long patrol. She had chased after contacts, and expended all of her torpedoes. After the turn of the year, she had sunk three more ships, making this her most successful patrol, with seven sinkings, counting the sampans, one before Christmas, and one on New Year's Day. But, for Tomassi, the one that got away was the one he kept thinking over. If the damn torpedoes worked, he thought, *Luzon Maru #4* would be on the bottom.

Before they went to special sea section stations, Radioman Troilo passed Tomassi two messages. First, there was a new tender in port. Her name was U.S.S. *Capricorn*, and they were to pull up alongside her for their replenishment.

The second message was that COMSUBPAC, Admiral Irish, had been reported killed in a plane crash the previous day. The most important part of that was that Admiral Lockhart had been ordered to replace him. No more "Uncle Charlie."

There were only rumors as to who would take his place here at Fremantle. No one knew. Tomassi would find out when he delivered his reports. Someone on the tender must know. Or, he thought, maybe if I have to go into Perth to report to him, I'll find out who it is.

The *Sea Otter* proudly had pennants flying from her periscope and her radio mast. There were two small swallowtail pennants to signify the sampans, and five larger ones for the freighters. Bergman looked up at them with pride as they entered the harbor, and then turned to Tomassi. "Well, sir, I have to admit, this is the best we've done since the war started."

"Really?"

"Yes, sir. Under Riley, we wouldn't have pressed home so many attacks. Plus, even with the tin fish being so iffy, we still did better."

"Riley wasn't very aggressive?"

"No, sir. Also, sir, the crew seems to like you for it. I wasn't sure they would."

"That makes me think of General McClellan of the Union Army," Tomassi said. "He didn't win any big battles, but his men still cheered him when they saw him. Of course, they might have been sarcastic when they did it." Tomassi looked at the pennants. "Too bad we couldn't have come up with a pennant for that Jap plane."

"Maybe next time, sir. I can tell you this. I hope our new commander isn't Captain Christian."

"Why's that, Bergman?"

"Oh, something about the man just never sat well with me."

"They wouldn't put a mere captain in charge of us."

"Really, sir? When I left Brisbane, we had ten boats there, and there were only six here. We've added two more, and I heard Brisbane added two more."

"I kind of hope it's not Christian, either. You know, the magnetic exploder was his baby."

"Really, sir?"

"Yes, and they never tested the thing properly before the war."

"Lovely."

"OK, Bergman, time to dock her next to the tender."

"Admiral Christian will see you now, sir."

"Thank you, Yeoman." Tomassi stood up and went to the door. He knocked, and a voice told him to enter.

He went in, stood before the admiral and saluted, saying, "Admiral, Commander Dominic Tomassi, commanding officer, U.S.S. *Sea Otter*, reporting."

The dark haired rear admiral returned the salute and said, "At ease, Commander."

"Thank you, sir."

Christian looked at a folder on his desk. "You are to be congratulated for this patrol, I see."

"Thank you, sir. But, I regret one that got away on me."

"What's that, Commander?"

"*Luzon Maru #4*, sir."

"Oh, yes. I saw by your report that only one torpedo out of ten detonated against the target."

Christian looked up and asked, "Are you faulting the magnetic exploder?"

"No, Admiral, I had my Chief Torpedoman's Mate disconnect the magnetic exploders."

Christian stood up. "What?"

"I had spoken to some British officers about this subject. They told me they, and the Germans, had magnetic exploders, and they wouldn't function, so they disconnected them. I thought it might be worth a try, so I did that before my last patrol with the *Eel*, and we got better results."

Christian sat back down. "The British and Germans are not us. Their experiences should not be a guide for you."

"It's not just me, Admiral. If you ask other commanders –"

"I'm not asking other commanders, mister! Everyone seems to think they know the answer. How do you know this isn't the fault of your torpedomen not having the experience to handle these devices?"

"With all due respect, Admiral, you haven't been on a war patrol with these torpedoes. This is the same … discussion I had with Admiral Irish when I was at Pearl."

"How did Admiral Lockhart feel about this?"

"He seemed to be willing to try it."

"Well, I'm not. If, by the Lord's will, you make it to Pearl again, you can do what you like with your torpedoes. But while you're under my command, you will not, repeat, *not*, disconnect the magnetic exploders on your torpedoes. That will be writing very soon. Other commanders have had success with the magnetic exploder, and you'll see I'm right."

Tomassi nodded, and after a moment, said, "Yes, Admiral."

"That's all, Commander. Dismissed."

"Aye, aye, sir." Tomassi saluted and turned for the door, then turned back around. "Oh, by the way, congratulations on your promotion."

"Thank you, Commander." Christian then looked up from his paperwork. "How did you know?"

"My exec, Lieutenant Commander Bergman, served with you at Brisbane."

"Bergman," Christian muttered, "Bergman." After a long pause, he shook his head. "Don't remember him."

CHAPTER TWENTY-NINE
22 JANUARY 1943

Davis Van Wert had pulled into port with the *Eel* earlier that day, and when he saw Tomassi in the Officers' Club, the two sat down to talk while they had their drinks.

"Great to see you, Dom. How was your last patrol?"

"Pretty good, Van. We got five freighters, two sampans, and a patrol plane, a 'Rufe.'"

"All right! We got three ships ourselves. We'd have gotten two more if it weren't for our fish not going off."

"Well, you know we won't get any sympathy about that from Admiral Christian. He's issuing an order not to disconnect the magnetic exploders."

"What? Oh, bullshit. Everyone knows we've been having better results without that damn thing connected. We've both proved it."

"It won't happen, Van. You know the magnetic exploder is Christian's baby. So –" Tomassi leaned in and lowered his voice, "– we'll just have to wait until we leave port to disconnect it again. What Christian doesn't know won't hurt him."

Van Wert slammed down his bourbon. "It pisses me off, Dom. This is like Admiral Irish all over again. Did Christian blame our men for not knowing how to handle the torpedoes?"

Tomassi nodded, "Yeah, that's just what he said. By the way, you know that Irish getting killed is why we lost Lockhart?"

"I think I heard that. Irish got killed when his plane went down?"

"Yeah. He was going to Frisco for a conference, and they got lost in a fog. Ran right into a mountain. Took a bunch of his staff with him, too."

"Damn him," Van Wert said.

"I guess there's no mourning at this table," Tomassi said.

Van Wert smiled, "Nope. None here."

Tomassi looked at his watch. "I'm gonna go. I've got a certain redhead expecting me." He got up to leave.

"Tell her I'll be along pretty soon here," Van Wert said.

Tomassi turned around and smiled. "You got it."

After the climax, Tomassi fell onto the bed next to Fiona. "Thank you, my dear," he said.

"You're welcome, love," Fiona replied. She reached up and stroked his balding pate. "You know, your little bit of hair on top reminds me of my dad."

Tomassi turned at looked at Fiona. "You really know how to hurt a guy."

Fiona laughed. "Just kidding, love. But, I really do fancy it. The baldness. Most girls won't confess to it, but I love it."

Tomassi smiled. "Thank you, dear."

Fiona turned over and Tomassi reached around her side. He started to stroke her breast with one hand and ran his other hand along the seam of her stocking as he spoke. "It's funny, having it be hot in January."

Fiona reached up and touched his hand. "Well, you didn't grow up here, then. I always loved going to the beach at Christmas. It was always strange, though, having a hot plum pudding when it had just turned to summer."

Tomassi laughed, "Well, for me, January was always a time to be indoors, away from the snow and cold. Sophia and I would curl up in front of a crackling fire. We'd have hot cider, and maybe some hot toddies. We'd cuddle up and fall asleep in each other's arms."

"Sounds dreamy. When Trevor and I got married, it was June. Here that's the beginning of winter. So, our honeymoon was spent keeping warm. Similar to what you described. We'd had a fire going; nice and crackling. We drank hot toddies, and made love by the fire. When January came, of course, we'd be all hot and sticky. No matter."

"Yeah," Tomassi replied, "no matter."

CHAPTER THIRTY
4 FEBRUARY 1943

"Sir, ship's company, U.S.S. *Sea Otter*, all present and accounted for."

Tomassi returned Bergman's salute. "Very well." He turned to the crew and ordered, "Stand at, *ease*." The men stood at ease. "Well, we have a new gadget for our radarmen to play with." Tomassi pointed to the periscope shears and the new curved dish that stood behind number two periscope. "It seems they could finally spare an SJ radar set for us. That means we now have surface search capability, especially at night. This miracle of science can also extend above the surface like a periscope, so that when visibility is zero, we can still see the Japs before they even know we're there. It can also detect aircraft at a much greater range than the SD radar set."

"It also means four more radarmen. Radarman Sheffield, Kirkland, Markel, and Conroe." Tomassi pointed to each man in turn. "These guys will help us get more kills. They'll also rely on you to keep them alive and working. That's all." Tomassi turned to Bergman. "When the men are dismissed, have the special sea section at their stations and prepare the ship to get underway."

Bergman saluted and said, "Aye, aye, sir." Tomassi returned the salute, and Bergman turned to face the men. "Attention!" The men snapped to attention. "Leave your quarters. Special sea section to your stations on the double. All hands prepare to get underway."

After the *Sea Otter* had cleared the harbor, Tomassi and Bergman huddled at the chart table. "Well, sir," Bergman asked, "where are we going?"

Tomassi pointed out on the big chart. "We've been assigned to patrol Cam Ranh Bay, in French Indochina. It's in a province called Vietnam."

"Vietnam?" Bergman shook his head. "Never heard of it."

Tomassi shrugged, "Me neither." Tomassi produced a smaller chart which detailed the bay. The west side of the harbor looked a capital 'C', with a 'V'-shape northeastern section trailing away from it. "We can enter this harbor only through this mile-wide channel, once we're past Binh Ba Island." He pointed to a bow tie shaped island southeast of the channel. "But once we're in, it's our oyster."

Bergman pointed into the 'C' shaped part of the harbor. "What's over here?"

"That's the old French naval base. The Japs use it for their patrol craft now. Most of their shipping comes from there too. But here, to the northeast, there's some good targets, I'll bet."

"Has anyone patrolled this before?"

"Yeah. I've heard there's some good game in there. But I don't think anyone's tried to penetrate before."

"How big is this harbor?"

Tomassi said, "It's twenty miles, north to south, and ten miles across, from the channel to the old French base."

"Are there some French patrols in there, too?"

"We've heard that the Vichy government is only there as a figurehead. But, hey, I don't care if they're white or yellow. If someone's dropping a depth charge on me, I'll kill 'em."

CHAPTER THIRTY-ONE
19 FEBRUARY 1943

The *Sea Otter* surfaced at midnight, just as she was passing Binh Ba Island on her way to the entrance of Cam Ranh Bay. Tomassi and Bergman came up on the bridge wearing their helmets and life vests. The gun crews silently went to their positions. They counted on surprise to help them get in.

"Has anyone done this before," Bergman asked.

Tomassi nodded, "You remember reading about the U-boat that penetrated Scapa Flow in October of '39 and sank that British battlewagon? He came in on the surface. He had no other way. Dead of night. Just like this."

"I mean one of our guys?"

"Not that I know about."

"Think we'll catch a Jap battlewagon?"

Tomassi chuckled, "One can only hope."

The sub's diesel engines throbbed at full power. Tomassi figured that speed would be the essence for them to get in and out. Usually, one would put at least one engine on battery charging after coming up. Tomassi would wait until they'd cleared the harbor before doing that.

After some ten minutes, the mouth of the channel came into view. "Helm, all ahead standard," Tomassi ordered.

"Helm, all ahead standard, aye," came the reply from Seaman Henry, the helmsman on this watch. The boat slowed down so as to minimize her wake. One less thing for prying eyes to see.

All lookouts kept their eyes peeled along their sides, and likewise the gunners at their stations. Tomassi and Bergman looked around, as if they were burglars stealing into a mansion. Slowly but surely, the land to either side of the channel mouth came up. Any sentry on that land would have to strain his eyes to see the sub. They passed into the channel. No fireworks. All hands blew out a sigh of relief.

Dead ahead of them lay the city of Cam Ranh itself. To their port, lay the French base, and the Japanese patrol craft. To their starboard, most of the shipping that came from here to go to Japan.

"Helm, right full rudder, come right to course three-five-zero," Tomassi ordered.

"Helm, right full rudder, coming right to course three-five-zero, sir," came the reply.

"Very well. Mr. Bergman?"

"Aye, sir?"

"Maybe you'd better get on the after TBT, in case we have an uninvited guest."

"Aye, sir." Bergman knelt down by the hatch and asked for a talker headset. When he got it, he took off his helmet and put it on, then headed to the TBT perched on the rail by the after 20mm position.

It seemed that someone in town didn't get the idea there was a war going on, since there were lights on. None of the ships were lit, but some lights from land helped. Tomassi see the outline of a troop transport sitting at dock. She had two stacks and a single deckhouse. "Mr. Morrow," Tomassi called through the squawk box.

"Aye, sir?"

"Target looks like a transport, division Tare Baker, two stacks. Figure a bearing of two-eight-zero, speed one-half knot for the current. Depth, ten feet. Gyro angle five left. Call when set."

"Aye, aye, sir."

Tomassi then leaned into the hatch and told the talker, Saunders, "Open outer doors on tubes one and two and stand by to fire."

"Open outer doors on tubes one and two and stand by to fire," Saunders repeated.

"Helm, all ahead slow."

"Helm, all ahead slow, aye," Henry replied.

Tomassi got back up to the rail and looked for something else to shoot at. He looked to the right and saw another transport sitting at dock some fifty yards north.

Morrow called through the squawk box. "Captain, we're set."

"Very well. I have another target, bearing three-five-seven. It's another transport, division Tare Able, two stacks. Bearing two-niner-zero, speed one-half knot. Depth, eleven feet. Gyro angle ten right. Call when set."

"Aye, aye, sir."

Tomassi leaned over again, and told Saunders, "Fire one, fire two."

Saunders called, "Fire one, fire two," pushing the firing button each time he said, "fire." After pushing the button the second time, he called, "Both torpedoes away, sir."

"Open outer doors on three and four and stand by," Tomassi said.

"Open outer doors on three and four and stand by," Saunders repeated.

Tomassi looked up again to find something else. Morrow called, "We're set, sir."

"Fire three, fire four," Tomassi called.

"Fire three, fire four," Saunders repeated. "Both torpedoes away, sir."

"Very well. Helm, right full rudder, come right to course zero-zero-one."

"Helm, right full rudder, coming right to course zero-zero-one, sir," Henry replied.

"Very well. Open outer doors on tubes five and six, and stand by."

"Open outer doors on tubes five and six, and stand by, sir."

Tomassi looked to starboard again in case something was anchored out there. A bright flash showed up to port as their first torpedoes slammed home on the transport. They hit the target in her engine room and started large fires. A few seconds later, the second target was hit. Her deck was burning in no time.

Bergman called at this point. "Sir, ship bearing one-eight-five relative. Looks like a freighter."

"She's yours, Bergman."

"Aye, aye, sir," Bergman smiled. His target had a single deckhouse and four kingpost masts. He got on his talker headset. "Morrow, new target. Large freighter aft, division Fox Tare Baker. Shifting to TBT, bearing coming down." Bergman looked through the TBT and pushed the button to transmit down into the con. Bergman continued, "Gyro angle five left. Depth, eleven feet. Open outer doors on tubes seven and eight. Commence firing when set."

Meanwhile, Tomassi found another target at anchor to starboard. She was a small freighter with and split deckhouse and two masts. "Morrow, new target. Freighter, division Fox Baker. Depth, twelve feet. Gyro angle fifteen right, speed one-half knot, bearing coming down." Tomassi got on the TBT next to him and pressed the button. "Fire from tubes five and six when set."

Morrow had just finished the solution for Bergman's target and fired. Tubes seven and eight were actually above the waterline when the sub was surfaced, so Bergman got to watch the tin fish leave their tubes, first the port tube, then the starboard. Saunders reported to him, "Torpedoes seven and eight away, sir."

Next came Tomassi's third target. A few seconds after Bergman's fish were away, tubes five and six were fired. Saunders reported to the captain, "Torpedoes five and six away, sir."

"Very well. Reload all bow tubes."

"Reload all bow tubes, aye." Tomassi could already see in his mind the men in the forward torpedo room, cursing and straining to reload the six tubes.

Meanwhile, Bergman watched as his two fish headed for the freighter aft of him. One torpedo went off, while the other didn't. The burst of water from number seven torpedo told him it didn't. A moment later torpedo eight slammed into the Japanese ship and went off. He talked into his headset, "Same target. Gyro angle now zero. Bearing coming down." He looked into the TBT and pressed the button. "Target speed, four knots. Fire tubes nine and ten when set."

As Bergman was doing this, Tomassi's target was getting hit. Both of those torpedoes went off, producing a spectacular blast. No use risking my boat any more, he thought. He heard Saunders say, "Torpedoes nine and ten away, sir."

"Very well. Helm, right full rudder, come to course one-eight-zero."

"Helm, right full rudder, coming right to course one-eight-zero, sir."

"Very well. Reload stern tubes."

"Reload stern tubes, aye."

The harbor had now become a beehive of activity. Searchlights stabbed into the darkness, searching for the *Sea Otter*. Shells were going off as Japanese gunners from all over the bay started shooting at whatever they thought was the intrusive American sub. Tomassi could see the harbor entrance off to port now. Off to starboard, he could see a Japanese minelayer coming. He grabbed the megaphone and yelled to the gun crew, "Aim for his forward mount."

"Aye, aye, sir," yelled back the gun captain.

"Morrow, new target," Tomassi said into the squawk box. "Jap minelayer. Angle on the bow, fifteen port, bearing coming down." He looked into the TBT and pressed the button. "Target speed, twelve knots. Gyro angle twenty right. Commence firing when set."

Bergman's last two fish had hit their target and went off. The freighter was now listing to starboard and burning. Saunders now called, "Torpedoes one and two away, sir."

"Very well," Tomassi called. "Helm, left full rudder, come to course one-four-zero."

"Helm, left full rudder, coming left to course one-four-zero, sir."

"Very well."

The *Sea Otter* started to make her escape. The minelayer managed to dodge Tomassi's fish. Bergman was on it. He spoke into his headset. "Morrow, same target. Gyro angle five left. Bearing one-four-zero, speed twelve knots. Commence firing when set."

The after torpedo room crew made a superhuman effort to reload their tubes, and when it was done, got two fish off from tubes seven and eight. Bergman watched them splash into the water, then heard Saunders say, "Torpedoes seven and eight away, sir."

"Very well," Bergman replied. It only took about ten seconds before they both slammed home into the minelayer and blew her bow off. A cheer from everyone topside as the enemy stopped in his tracks and started for the bottom.

Tomassi had the sub turn due south so they didn't run aground at Binh Ba Island. They went on their way, and Tomassi put number four engine to battery charging. The whole episode barely took half an hour.

CHAPTER THIRTY-TWO
20 FEBRUARY 1943

Tomassi sat in the wardroom with a cup of coffee, the Merchant Vessel Recognition Manual, his logbook, Lt. Commander Bergman, and Lt. Morrow. Tomassi asked Morrow, "The first ship I said was Tare Baker?"

Morrow strained to remember. "You said … Tare Baker, with two stacks, sir."

Tomassi opened the manual to the page with the system they were using, which had been developed for the Southwest Pacific Area. He looked at the third line on the page. "Tare Baker, two stacks," he read. "Four thousand, to six thousand, gross tonnage." He shrugged his shoulders and said, "How about five thousand tons? Sound good?"

Bergman nodded, "Sounds good to me, Captain." Morrow nodded as well as Tomassi made note in the log.

"My second one was … Fox Tare Baker," Tomassi said as he looked at the second line on the page. "Fifty-five thousand to seventy-five thousand gross tons."

"Actually, sir," Morrow interrupted, "that was your third. You second was a Tare Able, two stacks."

Tomassi looked up from the manual at Morrow. "What an astounding memory you have, Lieutenant."

Morrow smiled, "Thank you, sir."

Tomassi looked at the manual, and looked on the third line, just over from his left. "Tare Able, two stacks. That's seven thousand to ten thousand gross tonnage." He smiled. "I can't lowball this. I'm calling it … nine thousand tons." He looked at the other men. "Agreed?"

"Agreed, then," Bergman said.

Tomassi noted it. "Thank you again for correcting me, Morrow, on the Fox Tare Baker." Tomassi looked on the second line again. "Let's call that –"

"Seven thousand tons, sir," Morrow chimed in.

Tomassi and Bergman looked at each other, then at Morrow for a moment, before smiling. "Yes," Tomassi exclaimed, "seven thousand." Everyone laughed as Tomassi jotted it down in the log.

"Now, for mine," Bergman said. He looked at the manual page. His target was on the top line. "Fox Baker."

Tomassi nodded and put his hand on his chest, saying sorrowfully, "Yes, poor little pipsqueak you got. Only –" Tomassi looked at the number under the description "– thirty-five hundred to six thousand gross tons." He pretended to choke back a tear, as Bergman and Morrow laughed.

"She was loaded, Captain," Bergman protested in the some joking spirit.

"Yes, you're right, I suppose, Mr. Bergman," Tomassi said. "We'll call that seven thousand tons loaded." The laughter echoed around the compartment as Tomassi wrote it in the log. "Then, of course, there was that minelayer. She couldn't have been very big. Maybe even a coastal minelayer. So … I'll call that one three hundred tons."

"You couldn't have made her bigger, sir," Bergman asked.

"Admiral Christian would get suspicious if we told him anything too big. We have to make him think we left the magnetic exploders connected. He did give us a written order not to disconnect them. If nothing else, underreporting isn't so bad. Good for the soul. After the war, our estimates can get upgraded," Tomassi said.

"Well, I can think of one other commander who does it," Bergman smiled.

"I taught him well," Tomassi said. He turned to Morrow. "You don't hear any of this, mister."

Morrow was drinking his coffee when Tomassi said that. He swallowed the mouthful and asked, "Hear what, sir?"

Tomassi nodded. "Good man." Laughter all around.

CHAPTER THIRTY-THREE
21 FEBRUARY 1943

The greatest edge that the *Sea Otter* had was her SJ radar set. Instead of skulking around underwater during the day, hoping to find an enemy ship crossing her path, she could stay surfaced, and when a contact was made, they could determine whether it was a merchantman or a patrol, and do what they had to, either to get a kill or save themselves from getting killed.

Such was the case on this day. At 09:20, radar watch reported a contact at ten miles distance, bearing northeast. Tomassi ordered the boat turned northeast at full speed. After some fifteen minutes, a lookout called out, "Smoke, bearing three-three-zero relative." Another minute passed before they could determine, along with the radar, that the target was moving across their path.

Tomassi put the boat on battle stations. Since he did not specify, "battle stations, surface," the gun crews didn't come up, nor were helmets and life vests passed up. The Japanese in this area had apparently not yet wised up to the protection a convoy offered, or the sighting would have been just the beginning.

Soon enough, the shape of the enemy ship started to become apparent. The port lookout, Seaman Howard, called out, "One Sugar Able, bearing three-four-zero relative." That meant a collier or some other kind of ore carrier. Her stack was near the stern, and she had a forward pilot house and stern deckhouse. Tomassi saw her through his binoculars. He could dive now and still catch his prey. She'd just cross his bow in a couple of minutes.

"Lookouts below," he called. The men climbed down from the positions above him and scrambled down the hatch. "Clear the bridge," he called next, and the men with him went down. He rang the diving alarm and yelled, "Dive! Dive!"

Tomassi now went down the hatch. Bergman was there to close it and hold the lanyard, while Tomassi secured it. The boat started down to periscope depth. Tomassi turned to the soundman. "Sound, what do you hear?"

Barnhart replied, "Screws bearing three-four-five relative. Sounds like a large freighter."

Osborne, the talker, reported, "Mark fifty, leveled off."

"Up scope," Tomassi ordered. The periscope was raised and Tomassi looked to port for the target. "Got her. It's a Sugar Able, all right. Must be ten thousand tons. She looks loaded. Bergman, get over here."

Bergman stepped up to the scope, opposite the captain. Lt. Morrow and the fire control party were ready. Tomassi called, "Bearing, mark."

"Three-four-seven."

"Range, mark."

"Five-oh-double-oh."

"Down scope." Tomassi put up the handles, and the periscope was lowered. It would probably be another minute before they would have the range closed. Tomassi looked at Bergman. "I don't think we talked at breakfast. How are you?"

Bergman was taken aback by this, but answered, "Fine, sir. Yourself?"

Tomassi smiled, "Just another day in paradise." After a moment, he said, "Up scope." Bergman raised the periscope. "She didn't spot us, I guess. Same speed as before. Bearing, mark."

"Three-five-zero."

"Range, mark."

"Four-five-double-oh."

"Make ready bow tubes."

"Make ready bow tubes," repeated Osborne.

"Gyro angle, five left. Depth, fifteen feet. Target speed, eight knots."

Morrow put all of this into the TDC. After a moment, he reported, "Firing solution, sir. We're set."

Tomassi answered, "Very well. Open outer doors on tubes one, two, three, and four."

"Open outer doors on tubes one, two, three, and four," Osborne repeated into the headset. After a moment, he reported, "Outer doors open, sir."

"Stand by to fire," Tomassi ordered. Osborne put his hand on the button.

"Check," Bergman called.

"Set," Morrow replied.

"Fire one," Tomassi said.

"Fire one," said Osborne. "One's away, sir."

"Fire two."

"Fire two. Two's away, sir."

"Fire three."

"Fire three. Three's away, sir."

"Fire four."

"Fire four. Four's away, sir."

"Down scope," Tomassi said. He put up the handles, and the periscope was lowered.

"All torpedoes running hot, straight, and normal, sir," Barnhart reported.

"Time, Mr. Bergman."

Bergman had his stopwatch going, and said, "Torpedoes to hit in thirty seconds, sir." Along came the nerves as the seconds ticked by. Had they finally gotten torpedoes that worked? Would they all go off, or would this be another *Luzon Maru*? "Torpedoes to hit in ten, nine, eight, seven, six, five, four, three, two, one. Now!"

The first torpedo went off, followed in rapid succession by the other three fired. Barnhart nodded and grinned. "Four hits, sir."

Tomassi smiled and motioned for the periscope to come up as the men cheered. He looked to the stricken collier. She was stopped dead in the water; fire racked her from stern to amidships. Tomassi stepped away from the scope, and motioned for Bergman to look.

Bergman looked at the wounded enemy and smiled. "We got her," he exclaimed. "Down scope." Bergman put up the handles and lowered the periscope.

"Secure from battle stations," Tomassi ordered.

CHAPTER THIRTY-FOUR
20 MARCH 1943

The *Sea Otter* had expended all of her torpedoes by the beginning of the month. Tomassi decided to try reloading and refueling at "Potshot," then heading back out to French Indochina. He had radioed ahead to both Fremantle, to tell of his last attacks, and the tender *Pisces* to let them know his plans.

The tender herself was anchored a few miles south of North West Cape, which was the tip of the peninsula that gave Exmouth Gulf her sheltering properties. Just a few miles inland was a Royal Australian Air Force base. There were the makings of a town between them, to give support to both the airbase and the tender crew. They were nearly 800 miles from Fremantle.

The sub proceeded down the west side of the gulf, closing on the *Pisces*. Bergman was on the bridge, with Tomassi behind him, to put her next to the tender. Chastain was at the helm. "All ahead slow," Bergman ordered.

"All ahead slow, aye," Chastain repeated, as he moved the lever on the engine telegraph. The tender crew stood by to lower the gangway when the *Sea Otter* was alongside.

It looked as though they might run into the ship, so Bergman called down, "Helm, left handsomely."

"Left, handsomely, aye." Chastain nudged the rudder left by a degree or so, to bring the boat parallel to the ship.

It worked. The *Sea Otter* was alongside with just enough room. Tomassi looked back, and saw the screw guards, which were almost touching the hull of the tender. "We're good back at the stern," Tomassi said.

"Rudder amidships," Bergman ordered.

"Rudder amidships, aye," Chastain responded. He brought the rudder back from her slight left jog to keep the sub going straight ahead.

Bergman looked up to see that the gangway was going to be just forward of the conning tower. "All stop," he called.

"All stop, sir," came the reply from the helm. The engines of the sub came down to a stop, and the tender crew began to lower the gangway.

"Helm, finished with engines."

"Helm, finished with engines, aye."

"Good job, Bergman," Tomassi said.

"Thank you, sir. Sir, could I get liberty tonight?"

Tomassi shrugged. "I guess. Why?"

"Well, sir, it's my birthday. I thought I'd see if they had a pub in town."

"Your birthday? Well, many happy returns on the day."

"Thank you, sir."

"Before you go into town, we'll tell the crew of the tender. We can have extra ice cream with dinner before going into town."

Bergman smiled, "Thanks, Captain."

A good time was had by the officers of the *Sea Otter* in town that night. Along with some of the sub tender officers, a singing contest was had with the Australian fliers from the nearby base. No one could really tell who won, since everyone just got loud after a few rounds. Bergman's good health was toasted by all.

Tomassi looked at his watch for a minute, and then waved to the lady proprietor. After she came over, Tomassi said, "Ma'am, one more ... one more round for the Yanks, and then –" he hiccupped "– we're going home. We got church services in the morning."

"Oh, come on, love," she said, "Why not let your lads have a lot more? You all deserve it. Besides, what's praying gonna get you? Never done me any good."

"My dear," Tomassi said, "I've been through depthchargings, strafings, and deep dives. If there wasn't a God, I'd never have made it, and I believe it, and these other guys believe it. So, we're going back home to sleep this off, after another round, mind you, and so in the morning –" another hiccup "– we can make peace with Him before shoving off again. Thank you, kind lady."

The lady just nodded. She headed back to the bar and came back with one more dose of everyone's poison.

CHAPTER THIRTY-FIVE
6 APRIL 1943

The *Sea Otter* had pulled out after divine service, or mass, back on 21 March. Since they had pulled out after lunch that day, the boat headed into Japanese held waters and toward the port of Haiphong. Tomassi hunched over the chart table with Bergman, looking at the chart for the northern Vietnamese port.

Their objective was at the mouth of the Red River, sitting in the midst of the delta. "I wish this were a deeper harbor," Bergman said.

"Me, too." Tomassi traced his finger along a line that separated the deep, blue water from the white, shallow water. "Everything south and east of this line is deep enough for us. But in the white, there's only six fathoms of water."

Bergman shook his head. "Six. That's thirty-six feet, from the surface to the bottom. Even if we're surfaced, that's too tight. We draw fifteen feet on the surface. How do they get ships in?"

"Mostly, they anchor in the outer harbor and let smaller ships and boats load them up. And brother, there's plenty to load. Besides rice, they get coal from a big vein of the stuff near the Chinese border. In addition, they've got mines nearby that give them bauxite, iron ore, tin, antimony, zinc, phosphates, and tungsten."

"Is that all?"

Tomassi nodded, "You ain't kidding. All the big ore carriers come there, like the one we got before heading home last time and load up for the emperor. Our subs are reporting that the Japs are starting to use convoys in this area. Usually three or four escorts for five or six merchants." He pointed to an island east of the river delta. "This is called Dao Cat Ba. I hope this will be a good enough place to observe shipping from, and maybe find a convoy worth breaking up, before the Japs try to break us up."

Tomassi had maneuvered the *Sea Otter* into position on the south side of Dao Cat Ba Island. They'd had to let a patrol pass by before sundown. Now, with the last fading of twilight, they looked into the darkened harbor with the radar. The island of Cat Hai loomed only a couple of miles from their position. Beyond it, though, Radarman Conroe could count seven large ships to the southwest, with many smaller contacts milling around the harbor.

Conroe and Tomassi looked at the radar scope, with the green finger of the beam making its clockwise turn. It showed the larger ships very clearly and also the several smaller contacts moving between them and the land. "Well, sir," Conroe said, "it's pretty plain."

Tomassi nodded, "Yeah. They're probably going to shove off soon. Those contacts to the north. They could be escorts."

"Yes, sir. They're the right size."

192

"OK." Bergman walked up at this point. "Well, Bergman," Tomassi said, pointing at the scope, "this is what I've been looking for. We have a chance to break them up before they sail. What do you think?"

Bergman slowly nodded, "Yes, sir."

Tomassi turned to Seaman Henry at the helm. "Helm, all ahead two-thirds."

"Helm, all ahead two-thirds, aye." Henry signaled the engine rooms to get the boat going.

"Helm, left full rudder. Come left to course two-zero-zero."

"Helm, left full rudder, coming left to course two-zero-zero, sir."

"Very well. Sound general quarters."

"Sound general quarters, aye." Saunders hit the alarm. He then grabbed the mouthpiece of his headset and said, "Go ahead, aft engine room." He listened, and then told Tomassi, "Sir, aft engine room reports number four engine won't start."

Tomassi shook his head. "Well, that's just lovely. Tell them to get it working, on the double."

"Aye, sir." Saunders passed along the order.

Tomassi looked at the radar scope and pointed to the closest contact. "That one is our first target. Mr. Morrow?"

"Aye, sir," Morrow replied.

"Stand by to track a target. I'll give you the bearing from the TBT."

"Aye, sir."

Tomassi headed up to the bridge. The twilight helped him see the target. He wasn't going to bother with the ID system in the book now. He'd guess at the tonnage later. He opened the covers from the lenses of the TBT and swung it over to the right. He pushed the button to send the bearing down into the con. He then spoke into the squawk box. "Gyro angle, fifteen right. Set torpedoes to eleven feet. Target course two-five-zero, speed one knot." He was guessing at the current. "Open outer doors on tubes one and two."

"Open outer doors on tubes one and two, sir," Saunders repeated.

"Very well. Commence firing when set." Tomassi turned the TBT to look at the next ship. She was south of the first and was facing the same way as her neighbor. After a few seconds of looking, Tomassi heard the first two torpedoes being fired.

"Both torpedoes away, sir," Saunders reported.

"Very well. Tracking new target. Open outer doors on tubes three and four."

"Open outer doors on tubes three and four, sir."

Tomassi rubbed the stubble on his face, then reached up and pressed the button. The bearing on the next ship went down to Morrow and the fire control party. "New target," Tomassi said. "Gyro angle, ten right. Set torpedoes to ten feet. Target course, two-four-five, speed one knot. Commence firing when set."

Conroe came on the squawk box. "Radar contact bearing three-one-zero, relative."

"Sound," Tomassi said, "Any report on the torpedoes?"

Barnhart answered, "Both fish running hot, straight and normal, sir."

Just then, tubes three and four were fired. Saunders called up, "Torpedoes three and four fired, sir."

"Sound?"

Barnhart listened, and then said, "Both fish running hot, straight and normal, sir."

"Very well. Radar, how close is your new contact?"

Conroe replied, "Range, one mile and closing fast."

Tomassi yelled, "Helm, left full rudder, come left to course one-seven-zero."

"Helm, left full rudder, coming left to course one-seven-zero, sir," Henry replied.

"Very well. Open outer doors on tubes five and six."

As the sub steadied up on her new course, torpedoes one and two hit their target and went off. The flash lit up the night and showed Tomassi he was playing chicken with a destroyer. He yelled again, "Gyro angle zero, depth seven feet. Angle on the bow zero. Fire five, fire six!"

Saunders repeated the order as he pushed the button. "Fire five. Fire six. Torpedoes away sir."

"Lookouts below," Tomassi yelled. The men headed below. "Clear the bridge." He hit the alarm and yelled, "Dive! Dive!"

He held the line as the quartermaster secured the conning tower hatch. "Time on three and four," Tomassi yelled to Bergman.

"Torpedoes three and four to hit in ten, nine, eight, seven, six, five, four, three, two, one, *now*!"

The crew could hear the rumble of the hits. Barnhart nodded, "Both torpedoes hit, sir."

Tomassi yelled down to the control room, "Crash dive, two hundred feet."

"Two hundred feet, aye, sir," Lt. Lloyd repeated.

"Are you sure we won't hit bottom, sir," Bergman asked.

Tomassi just looked at him for a moment. "Bottom?"

"Yes, sir. It's not deep in the harbor."

"We'd have hit bottom by now. Barnhart, what about the last torpedoes?"

Barnhart listened, and then shook his head. "Both still running, sir." He jumped a little, then said, "Depth charges coming down."

"Rig for silent running, rig for depth charge," Tomassi said.

"Rig for silent running, rig for depth charge," Saunders repeated. Bergman reached up to turn off the fan.

"Passing one hundred feet, sir," Lloyd called up from the control room. This was followed by the rumble of depth charges going off above them. The boat shook a little, but no leaks were sprung. After another couple of charges went off, Lloyd called up softly, "Passing one-hundred-fifty feet, sir."

"Start leveling off," Tomassi said.

"Aye, sir," Lloyd replied, and whispered to the planesmen to level off. The Japanese destroyer dropped one more pattern of charges, then turned into Haiphong harbor.

After another ten minutes, Tomassi passed the order, "Secure from silent running." Everyone breathed easier with the fans back on.

CHAPTER THIRTY-SIX
8 APRIL 1943

Commander Tomassi now took the *Sea Otter* northeast, between Haiphong and Hainan Island, off the southern coast of China. A nice convoy would come their way; the odds were with them on this. Sure enough, radar picked up a convoy coming from the southwest, no doubt heading for Hong Kong. There it could refuel and head for Japan. Not if Tomassi had something to say about it.

Contact had been made about Noon, and Tomassi had the radar watch track the ships. They could pick out four large merchantmen with five escorts. After radar had been tracking their targets for two hours, the lookouts could see the smoke. They were on course for interception in another hour. At about 15:00, they could start to see the ships themselves.

Tomassi stood on the bridge with Bergman, and both officers kept straining their eyes, looking at the convoy. "I hope they're all ore carriers," Bergman said.

"Me, too, brother."

"Do the Japs have radar?"

Tomassi shook his head, "I don't think so, at least not according to the intelligence people. Even if they did, we'd probably look like a fishing smack to them."

"Good."

Another fifteen minutes passed before they could make out the ships. Being only able to use three engines added to the drama and tension, since it seemed they were almost inching along. Tomassi reeled off the list for Bergman.

"Frigate in the lead. Four merchant ships in pairs on either side, with two frigates outboard of them on either flank." He lowered his binoculars. "When we've closed a little more, we can dive and shoot at the freighters closest to us. Maybe we can shoot at all four before the escorts counterattack."

Bergman smiled, "You know, in the movies it never takes this long. It seems like they're right there when our heroes spot them, and we just shoot."

"Yeah. I'd love to drag a writer along on a patrol sometime. It would be something to see what kind of a script they'd come up with."

"Can you make out the lead merchant, sir?"

Tomassi looked again. "She's an ore carrier, and the trailing ship too. I hope the ones on the other flank are too." He went to the squawk box. "Radio room."

Troilo answered, "Radio room, aye."

"Sparks, send a contact report on this convoy. Include info on five frigates and four merchant ships, all ore carriers. Include also enemy course is zero-eight-zero. Get our position from Mr. Morrow, and transmit immediately."

"Aye, aye, sir," Troilo replied.

Tomassi now called the radarman. "Radar."

Radarman Sheffield answered, "Aye, sir."

"What's the range, Sheffield?"

"Range ten thousand yards, sir."

"Very well." Tomassi set the squawk box to address the boat. "General Quarters, all hands man your battle stations." The Bells of St. Mary's sounded.

"Are we diving now, sir," Bergman asked.

"We need to get closer." Tomassi got back on the box. "Radar, let me know when the range is six thousand yards."

"Aye, aye, sir."

The deck gun crews started to show up on deck and go to their weapons. "No, no," Tomassi waved at them, "This is going to be a submerged attack. Get back below."

"Aye, sir," called back the gun captain, who then waved his men back below. Inexorably, the *Sea Otter* drew closer and closer to the Japanese ships. Finally, Sheffield called up, "Radar here. Enemy range six thousand yards."

"Very well," Tomassi replied. He turned to the men. "Lookouts below." They went below. "Clear the bridge." He rang the diving alarm. "Dive! Dive!"

He got below and the hatch above him was secured. "Make ready all tubes," he said to talker Osborne.

"Make ready all tubes," Osborne repeated into his headset.

"All ahead full," Tomassi said to the helm.

"All ahead full, sir," Chastain replied.

Lieutenant Lloyd called up from the control room, "Leveled off at fifty feet, sir."

"Very well," Tomassi called back. "Up scope." The periscope came up. He could see the lead escort and turned the scope to the right to see the first ore carrier. He motioned for Bergman to come over to him with the manual. Tomassi looked back and forth between the book and the ship, and declared, "Ore carrier, division Sugar Able. Bearing, mark."

"Zero-two-five," Bergman answered.

"Range, mark."

"Five-oh-double-oh."

Tomassi turned to Osborne. "Set forward torpedoes to thirteen feet. Open outer doors on tubes one, two, three, and four. Gyro angle, five right. Stand by." Osborne passed the orders on. Tomassi looked again. The frigate next to the target ship was dropping back. He allowed himself a smile. "I'll bag a nice big one," Tomassi murmured. "Bearing, mark."

Bergman answered, "Zero-two-zero."

"Range, mark."

"Three-eight-double-oh."

"Fire one, fire two, fire three, fire four."

Osborne pushed the button four times, and answered, "Torpedoes away, sir."

After a moment, Soundman Barnhart said, "All torpedoes running hot, straight and normal, sir."

"Stand by tubes five and six," Tomassi ordered.

"Stand by tubes five and six," Osborne repeated.

There was a problem. The frigate that had dropped back now started to pull forward again, getting herself in line with the target. "No, no, damn it," Tomassi said. "Damn you bastard. Fall back again!"

The four ribbons that were the wakes of the torpedoes showed the thing Tomassi was dreading. The frigate was going to take the fish he'd meant for the ore carrier. Could they have seen them coming, Tomassi wondered. It wouldn't matter now.

Tomassi saw the big explosion as the first torpedo hit the frigate in her forward magazine. Fully half the vessel disappeared. The second torpedo caught the enemy escort just aft of her stack and finished the carnage. Hopefully the other two fish would pass under and go on to the target. "Sound, what do you have?"

Barnhart listened for a moment, then said, "Torpedoes one and two went off on something, and three and four are still going. I've got high speed screws coming in."

Tomassi muttered, "I hope that Jap burns in Hell for all eternity for fucking up my shot!" He then turned the scope to see the lead frigate was turning his way. He looked back to the main body of the convoy and, miracle of miracles, saw the target ship getting hit. "Sound?"

Barnhart replied, "Hits with torpedoes three and four. Target stopping."

"Bearing, mark," Tomassi called.

Bergman looked and replied, "Zero-zero-niner."

"Range, mark."

"Three-oh-double-oh."

"Fire five, fire six."

"Fire five, fire six, sir," Osborne said as he pushed the button. "Both torpedoes away, sir."

"Down scope." The periscope went down. Tomassi yelled down to the control room. "Crash dive, two hundred feet."

"Crash dive, two hundred feet, aye," Lloyd answered.

"Both torpedoes running hot, straight, and normal, sir," Barnhart reported.

"Very well. Time on the torpedoes, Bergman."

Bergman had his stopwatch running. "Torpedoes to hit in fifteen seconds, sir... Ten seconds... five, four, three, two, one, now."

Barnhart nodded, "Torpedoes five and six are hits, sir." He listened for another moment. "Target is fully stopped... breaking up noises." He paused. "Depth charges coming down, sir."

"Rig for silent running, rig for depth charge," Tomassi ordered.

"Rig for silent running, rig for depth charge," Osborne repeated.

An hour passed while the Japanese frigates dropped their charges around the *Sea Otter's* position. Tomassi kept the boat turning and did a couple of dives. Sweat was on everyone's faces, and condensation ran down the bulkheads. Finally, the Japanese got sick of playing the game and went away.

Barnhart did a sweep of the area, and said, "All clear, sir."

Tomassi gave the order, "Periscope depth."

The boat came up. Tomassi looked around and saw no ships. He did see wreckage. The scope was lowered, and Tomassi ordered, "Secure from silent running and depth charge."

Osborne passed on the order and turned on the fan in the conning tower.

CHAPTER THIRTY-SEVEN
1 MAY 1943

"Special sea section to your stations." Tomassi was glad to give that command this time. The men and officers had all shaved, and with one engine out, this patrol felt never-ending. The engineer had not been able to come up with the parts to keep the number four engine going. So, it was that Tomassi had radioed ahead to Fremantle that they would need a new engine as soon as possible.

As the *Sea Otter* pulled into the base, and Bergman maneuvered the boat up to the pier, Tomassi noticed a figure clad in white standing near the band. Tomassi saw him, along with two other men, and pulled up his binoculars to see who it was. It was Admiral Christian!

"What the hell," Tomassi exclaimed. He handed the binoculars to Bergman, who also couldn't believe his eyes. "I can't imagine why he's here."

Bergman said, "Maybe we're in trouble. Why else would he be here?"

"Maybe someone ratted us out about the exploders."

"A spy in our midst?"

"I'd hate to think one of our crew is a rat. All I know is I'm glad we've shaved."

Bergman guided the sub to her place at the dock, near the tender *Capricorn*, and gave the "finished with engines" command. The lines were secure, so Tomassi and Bergman stepped down through the conning tower, and onto the deck. They each saluted the ensign, then moved onto the dock. They walked up to the admiral and saluted him.

"Welcome home, gentlemen," Christian said as he returned the salute.

"Thank you, Admiral," Tomassi replied. "To what do we, uh … owe the pleasure, sir."

Christian pointed to a commander standing next to him, who read from the citation: "For action at Cam Ranh Bay, French Indochina on 19 February, 1943, Commander Dominic Tomassi, USN, is hereby awarded the Silver Star. With extreme daring, aggressiveness, and skill, Commander Tomassi took his submarine, *Sea Otter*, into an enemy harbor and with sagacity and great planning, launched a through and complete attack on enemy shipping at dock in the inner harbor. His brilliant torpedo and gun attacks resulted in the sinkings of one warship and four large transports. His boldness also allowed for his ship to escape from the pursuing enemy. His actions are a great credit, not only to the submarine service, but to the United States Navy in general."

Tomassi tried hard to maintain his composure while the citation was read. How could they pin a medal on me so fast, he wondered. These things take a year sometimes. He tried hard to keep himself from blushing as Admiral Christian took the medal from its case and pinned it on Tomassi's chest. "How am I getting this so fast, sir?"

"I approved the medal myself, Commander," Christian replied. "It speeds up the process. I think it's better for morale, don't you?"

"Yes, sir!" Tomassi saluted the admiral, who returned same with smile.

Van Wert couldn't believe it. The two men sat in the Officers' Club, with Tomassi sticking his chest out to show his new bauble. "You got a Silver Star? You lucky dago."

"Smile when you say 'dago,' you damn Dutchman," Tomassi smiled.

Van Wert laughed, "OK." He took a sip of his beer. "Where did you earn that?"

"French Indochina, at Cam Ranh."

Van Wert nodded, "All right."

"Where have you been lately, Van?"

"Well, my last patrol was in the Philippines. We had another delivery for Colonel Ramirez. He says 'hello,' by the way."

"'Hello, Colonel.' How's the boat running?"

"Purring like a kitten. How about you?"

"Well, we're going into drydock to replace an engine. Pisses me off."

"Oh, well. You're lucky to do it. This is the first time the Aussies have let anyone else use it. My boat should be next. It'll probably take a trip to Mare Island for that to happen. I didn't realize the *Eel* could seem so old, so soon."

"Yeah," Tomassi nodded. "I've heard Mare Island is a great facility. And right by San Francisco. That's what I want. I've never been there."

"Me neither, Dom."

CHAPTER THIRTY-EIGHT
24 MAY 1943

"At ease, Commander," Admiral Christian said. "Sit down."

"Thank you, sir," Tomassi replied as he sat down opposite the admiral.

"Been enjoying your extended leave?"

Tomassi smiled, "Oh, yes, sir. I managed to do some sightseeing around these parts. I even went to an old gold mine just northeast of here. They say it's played out, but maybe after the war, I'll come back and look for something they missed."

Admiral Christian laughed, "Good man. Well, I've struck a kind of gold of my own. Two boats are being transferred here from Brisbane. They should be here tomorrow. That, and two other new boats are coming from Pearl. They should be here be the end of the week."

"That's terrific, sir. What does that give us?"

"That will give me at least parity with the Brisbane base. Since the securing of Guadalcanal at the beginning of the year, I've begged for some of their boats to come here. It was one thing when I was commanding there, but now, I'm glad to get boats from there. Some crews I know, and that know me."

"That's swell, Admiral. We can cover more areas now, and for longer."

Christian nodded, then picked up a paper on his desk and looked at it while speaking. "I see that your boat is all better now. The drydock commander reported that he's replaced that dead engine of yours, plus he's had the generators rebuilt. The repair crew took the *Sea Otter* out and given it the green light to go."

"Great, Admiral. I can't wait to get out there again."

"That's the next thing on my mind, Tomassi." Christian withdrew an envelope from his desk and handed it to Tomassi. "With the new boats coming in, I can spare you now to go back to Pearl."

Tomassi couldn't believe it. He opened the envelope and read the orders sending the *Sea Otter* to Pearl Harbor. Christian continued, "Normally, you'd stay for a year before rotating back, but Admiral Lockhart pulled some strings, and he made a deal with me. If he gave up two boats, he'd get back two in return. He specifically asked for you and Commander Van Wert to come back with your boats."

Tomassi could only look up and stare for a moment. Then, he slowly said, "Admiral Lockhart … asked for me and Van Wert, sir?"

Christian nodded, "He was very pleased to hear about your Silver Star. He thinks very highly of you two." He paused, then said, "It's really more than I can say."

Tomassi nodded, "I know we've had our differences, Admiral. But, I can say, and speak also for Mr. Van Wert, that we're proud to have known you."

Christian smiled, "Well, all right. I will be able to say the same. I'm telling Van Wert the news after you leave. You two can figure out how to work your return trip. That is, whether you sail together as a team, or separately. Also, COMSUBPAC just issued an order for their boats to disconnect the magnetic exploders on their torpedoes. Since you'll be passing into their command when you're near Truk, you … can do that also."

Tomassi smiled at that.

"What do you mean, love?"

"Well, Fiona, all I can say is that I won't come back after tonight."

Fiona and Tomassi lay alone in the dark, touching each other for the last time. She asked, "Can you tell me where you're going, Dom?"

"No. I'm sorry. You know how it is. Submarines are called 'The Silent Service' for a good reason. I just wanted you to know that, if it's God's will, and I'm here again, I'll definitely come see you."

Fiona realized this time would come. Dom has always been a gentleman, she thought. But I could count on him coming to see me. At least he's telling me he's going. Some of these bloody Yanks don't. I know it's part of the war. But I find myself liking Dom more than the others.

For his part, Tomassi had come to like Fiona so much that, unlike other "ladies of the evening" he'd known, he just had to tell her he would be going

away. As he stroked her long red hair, he knew he'd
been a fool to tell her he loved her that time. You're
just a dollar sign, or pound sign, or whatever to her.
Also, I didn't think of her every night, like I did with
Sophia. I still think of Sophia. But she's gone. Fiona
is here. I had her to look forward to when I came back
from patrol.

"Fiona?"

"Yes, Dom"

"I…I want to thank you."

"What for, love?"

"I want to thank you for your companionship,
and for your tenderness."

A man hadn't said that to me since Trevor
died, she thought. "Oh, Dom. Thank you. That was so
sweet."

Tomassi gave Fiona a kiss on the shoulder. He
slowly got up and dressed himself. As he opened the
door to leave, he blew Fiona one last kiss. She reached
up to grab it, and then touched her heart and smiled.

CHAPTER THIRTY-NINE
7 JUNE 1943

Tomassi and Van Wert planned, before they shoved off, that they would work together on this patrol. Tomassi, as the man with more time in grade, would be in command, and would direct things from the *Sea Otter*. Whenever they made a contact, they would take turns in attacking. If it was a convoy or task force they came across, one would give the other time to reach the enemy's other flank, and both would attack as close as they could to simultaneous.

That was the plan. In reality, they hardly saw anything after they topped off at "Potshot." Nothing worth shooting at, at any rate. They passed through the Solomons without making any contacts bigger than a frigate. They didn't even bother with sampans. They would simply dive to avoid them, except for the one Tomassi just had to sink. The idea was to make their big splash at Truk.

Now, the two submarines had been at sea for nearly two weeks. They were approaching the "Gibraltar of the Pacific," Truk Atoll. They had pre-arranged that the *Sea Otter* would search the area and surface first. That would be the signal for the *Eel* to come up. Tomassi had had Bergman plot a course to take the two subs to the west side of the atoll before the two captains would confer again.

It was nearly 16:00 when the *Sea Otter* came up to periscope depth. Tomassi had the radar antenna extended. A sweep was made with no enemy detected. He then checked with the periscope, and, satisfied that all was clear, surfaced the boat. As the men made their way to the bridge, the port lookout called, "Submarine surfacing to port."

Tomassi and Bergman looked. She was the *Eel*. Van Wert had brought her up fifty yards away. Tomassi told his helmsman to bring her left, handsomely. She would just move over a bit, while Van Wert told his helmsman to bring her right, handsomely. After a couple of minutes, the boats were within ten yards of each other, and the skippers told their helmsmen to put rudder amidships. Now they could converse, using their megaphones.

"Ahoy on the *Eel*!"

"Ahoy on the *Sea Otter*!"

"Well, Van, how have you liked this trip so far?"

"I wish the Japs would have come out and played, Dom. I wish we'd have seen more than sampans."

"You could have come up and sunk one with us, like the one I got at New Ireland."

"My gun crew didn't need the practice like yours did."

"Enough chatter," Tomassi said. "I want you to take your boat around the north side of the atoll. You should have good hunting around North Pass. I'm going around the south. I expect you to rendezvous with me in four days near Northeast Pass. And make sure about any submarine contacts before you shoot at them. There could be other American boats around here."

"Aye, aye, skipper."

"Last one in at Pearl buys the drinks. Good hunting, Van."

"Good hunting to you, Dom. And get ready to buy the drinks!"

Tomassi laughed as he handed the megaphone over to Bergman. "I'm not letting that mug beat us to Pearl."

"I should say not, sir," Bergman replied as the two officers headed down the hatch.

"Helm, right ten degrees rudder. Come right to course one-two-zero," Tomassi said.

Chastain, the helmsman, replied, "Helm, right ten degrees rudder. Coming right to course one-two-zero, sir."

"Very well."

Down into the control room went the captain and exec. They both hunched over the chart table and looked at the chart of Truk Atoll spread before them. "I'm hoping we can catch any supply ships heading south to Rabaul. The best spot for that is here." Tomassi pointed to the spot marked "Otta Pass" on the chart.

"We shouldn't neglect these other exits though," Bergman replied, tracing his finger on the other passages running to the west of Otta Pass, and ending up at Piaanu Pass, the western entrance to the lagoon.

"We'll give them a look as we go by, but I don't think we find more than frigates. I want you to plot a course that lets us look at those passes, but we shouldn't go at them unless there's something worth shooting at. I just … have this feeling."

CHAPTER FORTY
9 JUNE 1943

"Captain to the conning tower! Captain to the conning tower!"

Tomassi struggled out of his bunk and hurried to put on his shoes. He glanced at the clock on the bulkhead. It was 06:30. His first thought was, why did they let me sleep this late?

He rushed up the ladder to the conning tower and said, "Report."

Radarman Markel replied, "Sir, contact bearing three-five-five relative. Distance, fifteen thousand yards." Tomassi stepped up next to the radar scope as Markel continued, "At first, I thought this was another little island in the atoll. But then it was moving." Tomassi looked at the scope and saw the big blip Markel was talking about. It seemed to be clearing Otta Pass, and Tomassi got the feeling he knew what it was.

"Helm, all ahead flank."

Chastain replied, "Helm, all ahead flank, aye." The diesels were cranked up to their highest speed. Tomassi stared at the scope, trying to guess the blips course.

"Do you think she'll go past Givry, and into the lagoon there, sir," Markel asked. He was referring to the northernmost island of the atoll called Kuop that was just south of Otta Pass.

"No. If she is who I think she is, she'll be too heavy, and the lagoon would be too shallow. Mr. Morrow?"

Lt. Morrow answered, "Aye, sir."

"You have the con. I'm going up."

"Mr. Bergman is already up there, sir."

Tomassi climbed up onto the bridge, where he found Bergman. "Did you sound the alarm, Mr. Bergman?"

"Aye, sir, as soon as the radar reported the blip."

"Thanks for letting me have the extra half-hour of sleep."

Bergman smiled, "You're welcome, sir."

"Bridge, radar here."

Tomassi leaned over to the squawk box. "Captain, aye."

"Sir, I make three contacts now. Two smaller ones fore and aft of the larger one."

"Still on the same heading?"

"Aye, sir. I estimate target's heading as two-two-five true."

"Good job, Markel. Keep it up."

"Aye, sir. Thank you, sir."

Half an hour passed before the lumbering target and the two frigates that were with her came into view. Tomassi was first to spot her. He smiled.

It was her. *Luzon Maru #4!*

"Ships bearing zero-two-zero relative," he called out. He then leaned over to the squawk box. "Radar, this is the captain."

"Radar, aye."

"What's the range you have?"

"Range ten thousand yards, sir."

"Very well."

"Don't you think we should slow down a little, sir," Bergman asked.

Tomassi looked him in the eye and coldly said, "She tasks me, and I shall have her. I'm not slowing down a knot until I'm close enough for a good shot. If it takes my last drop of fuel, I'll do it."

Bergman couldn't believe his ears. He didn't know men could behave like this outside the pages of a book. "This isn't just your show, sir. There's a whole crew –"

"Oh, I have no intention of dying, Bergman." Tomassi pointed out to the mammoth tanker. "*She's* the one that will die. We'll get in there and fire all six forward tubes, then dive under her and give her the four stern tubes. That should do it, if the damn torpedoes work, that is." He gave Bergman a pat on the shoulder and grinned. "I've waited two years for this. Let's go."

"Radar here. Range niner-oh-double-oh and closing."

"Very well. Make ready all bow tubes."

"Make ready all bow tubes," replied talker Osborne.

"Helm, right full rudder. Come right to course one-four-zero."

"Helm, right full rudder, coming right to course one-four-zero, sir."

"Very well."

"Shall we stand by to dive, sir," Bergman asked.

"Negative. Every moment I can squeeze out up here brings us closer and gives us the best shot."

Bergman shook his head. He felt the captain was risking the boat and the men, but he wouldn't say anything. Not my place, he thought.

"Radar here. Range eight-oh-double-oh and closing."

"Very well," Tomassi answered.

The radar watch called the range every thousand yards, until the gap was down to six thousand yards. At this point, Tomassi ordered the lookouts below. Also, at this point, a lookout on one of the frigates saw the American sub and the word passed between the Japanese ships.

Tomassi was unfazed at the sudden commotion. He calmly ordered the forward torpedo settings: gyro angle five right, angle on the bow one hundred starboard, depth twenty feet. Commence firing at five thousand yards.

While he did this, the trailing frigate began to turn towards the *Sea Otter*. She began to close, but when the sub reached the five-thousand-yard range to the tanker, all her bow tubes fired. Tomassi then yelled, "Clear the bridge," sounded the two blasts and ordered, "Dive! Dive!"

As he went down the conning tower hatch, a Japanese shell blew up near them, rocking the boat as she dove. "Take her to one hundred twenty feet," Tomassi yelled down to the control room.

"One hundred twenty feet, aye," replied Lt. Lloyd.

Soundman Barnhart reported, "All torpedoes running hot, straight, and normal, sir."

"Very well."

Once again, the special agony of time passing was felt. Bergman had his stopwatch counting down the seconds. "Fifteen … ten … five, four, three, two, one, *now!*"

One by one, the six torpedoes went off. Barnhart nodded, "All torpedoes hit, sir." He kept listening and reported, "The target has stopped. Jap frigates circling. Depth charges coming down."

"All ahead slow," Tomassi ordered. "Rig for silent running, rig for depth charge."

"All ahead slow, sir," Chastain replied.

"Rig for silent running, rig for depth charge," Osborne repeated, then reached up and turned off the fan.

The sub leveled off as the Japanese depth charges went off over them. She kept going, passing under the giant tanker, as the enemy escorts kept hammering away behind her. After a few minutes, Tomassi looked around at the sweat soaked men in the conning tower. "Sound, is the target still up there?"

Barnhart replied, "Aye sir. She's dead in the water."

"And the enemy escorts?"

"Still circling where we were, sir."

"All right." Tomassi looked down to the control room. "Periscope depth."

"Periscope depth, aye."

The boat slowly rose to fifty feet. Tomassi turned to Osborne and said, "Make ready stern tubes."

"Make ready stern tubes."

Shortly thereafter came the report, "Leveled off at fifty feet."

"Up scope." Tomassi turned the periscope aft and looked. He saw the *Luzon Maru #4* listing to starboard and bellowing smoke for her stern. A smile played across his lips. "Now I'll get you, bitch," he murmured. Bergman came up to the scope opposite Tomassi. "Gyro angle five left, angle on the bow eighty port, torpedo depth nineteen feet. Bearing, mark."

"Two-three-zero," Bergman said.

"Range, mark."

"Three-five-double-oh."

Tomassi took a breath, then said, "Five seven, fire eight, fire nine, fire ten."

Osborne pressed the firing button with each command, then said, "All torpedoes away, sir."

Barnhart reported, "All torpedoes running hot, straight, and normal, sir."

Tomassi watched as the torpedo tracks headed for the side of the behemoth. Presently, they all hit and exploded. Barnhart reported, "All hits, sir. She's breaking up and going down!"

Everyone in the con, indeed throughout the boat, let out a cheer. Tomassi cheered the loudest. He'd slain his white whale. Now he'd have to get home to tell about it. Meanwhile, everyone in the con got a turn at looking through the periscope as the great tanker went down. Tomassi finally ordered, "Secure from silent running," so that everyone could turn on their fans and breathe again.

The sub was secured from battle stations. Tomassi went to his cabin and made note in the log. "07:37 hours. Sunk off Otta Pass, Truk Atoll, tanker *Luzon Maru #4*. Estimate tonnage at 18,500 tons."

CHAPTER FORTY-ONE
11 JUNE 1943

Tomassi was in his cabin, taking care of the log. Since the thrill of sinking *Luzon Maru #4*, there had been, for the past day and a half, the added thrill of being hunted. As the *Sea Otter* made her way along the southeastern side of Truk Atoll, she'd had to dodge many patrols. Even when she came up at night to recharge her batteries, the radar watch was kept busy. Between picking up tankers and freighters, frigates and destroyers, and the odd patrol plane, it made for a lively cruise.

This also meant using up more fuel than anticipated, so Tomassi had to slow down the boat so there would be enough juice to get them to Pearl. He wondered if Van Wert and the *Eel* were having such a time. They'd maintained radio silence since parting ways four days ago.

The good side of all these contacts was that Tomassi had sunk another three Japanese merchantmen, and now when he made his rendezvous with Van, they could go home with empty torpedo racks, and he could set the men to work on sewing a battle flag for the boat.

There was a knock on the bulkhead. "Enter," Tomassi said as he looked up. Pharmacist's Mate Avery entered. "Hi, Doc. Did I miss my time with the sun lamp?"

"No, sir. This is more serious."

"OK, Doc."

"Torpedoman Box is suffering from a high fever. He also has pain and tenderness in his abdomen. Down here." Avery pointed to the lower right quadrant.

Tomassi leaned back in his chair. "You think it's his appendix?"

"That's what it looks like, sir."

"So, you'll have to operate?"

"Yes, sir."

"I was wondering when I'd get to see an appendectomy. Actually, I won't see it. But, all right. You can use the wardroom table for it. If anyone gives you crap about it, send them to me."

"Aye, sir." Avery stood there for a moment.

"Well, get going!" Tomassi stood up and pushed past Avery as he headed forward. As he reached the control room, he look up into the con and called, "Is Bergman there?"

"Aye, sir," Bergman answered.

"Please come here, Mr. Bergman."

"Aye, sir." Bergman climbed down the ladder and joined Tomassi at the chart table.

"One of the men needs his appendix out. We need a place to set down so we can operate."

Bergman looked at the chart in front of him, which showed the underwater features near their position. "Well, there looks like a shelf just ahead of us. Deep enough to keep us from a casual Jap patrol, but not deep enough to crush us."

"Does it say the depth?"

"It says one hundred twenty feet."

Tomassi thought for a moment, then headed back to the ladder and called up, "Sound."

Barnhart answered, "Sound, aye."

"I need a fathometer reading."

Barnhart took the reading and said, "Two hundred seventy fathoms, sir."

"So, forty-five feet below us." Tomassi nodded, "That's about right. OK." He turned to Lt. Lloyd. "Mr. Lloyd, make your depth one hundred twenty feet."

"One hundred twenty feet, aye, captain."

Tomassi and Bergman now headed up the ladder into the con. Tomassi got on the squawk box. "Attention all hands. We're going to set down on the bottom. One of the men, Box, needs to be operated on. We're going to be silent. But I'm having the fans left on. Otherwise, observe silent running rules. No unnecessary movements or talking. Secure nonessential equipment. And, while you're at it, say a prayer. We know God has gotten us through tough scrapes, and he'll get Box through this one if we pull together on it. That is all."

Two hours had passed since they set down on the bottom. The worst part was the sitting around, waiting to find if Avery could do the job. Tomassi had read about appendectomies being done on subs. He never thought his boat would be the next one. He glanced at his watch. It was nearly 16:00. Soon, they were supposed to rendezvous with Van Wert and head back to Pearl. He should be along any time.

Barnhart broke the silence. "Sound here. We've got high speeds screws bearing three-one-zero relative. Sounds like a destroyer."

Bergman turned to Tomassi. "Shall we secure the fans?"

"Negative. I hope he won't hear us, that's all. Stay with the silence we have."

"Another contact, sir," Barnhart said. "Bearing three-zero-zero relative." Long pause. "It sounds like a submarine."

Tomassi perked up. "Are you sure, Barnhart?"

Barnhart listened again. "Aye, sir." He jumped a little, then said, "New contact bearing two-eight-zero relative. Sounds like another destroyer."

Bergman chimed in, "Oh, no. I hope that's not the *Eel*."

"Bite your tongue, mister," Tomassi said. "Let's think a happy thought. Maybe it's a Jap sub."

"I've heard Jap subs before, sir," said Barnhart. "I don't think this one is." He jumped a little again. "Picking up splashes. Depth charges coming down."

Tomassi leaned down and softly said to Lloyd, "Pass the word, rig for depth charge."

"Aye, sir," Lloyd replied in a similar soft tone. He tapped the shoulders of his planesmen, whispered to them, and saw each of them on their way forward and aft.

BOOM!

A charge went off. This wasn't directed at them. The other submarine was getting it.

BOOM! BOOM!

Whoever it was, ours or theirs, it was clear the Japanese destroyers smelled blood, and would go for it.

BOOM! BOOM!

"They're really pasting him, sir," Barnhart said.

"What the hell is taking Avery so long," Bergman asked.

"Why don't you go ask him," Tomassi replied.

BOOM! BOOM! BOOM!

The other sub was clearly on the ropes. Tomassi started to say the *Lord's Prayer*. He mouthed it out, lest his talking should somehow get picked up by the enemy and they should turn on him. He looked around and saw the other men in the con had their lips moving, too. He recognized the words as the same ones he was saying. Even Bergman's lips were moving, though Tomassi couldn't tell what he was saying. No doubt he was praying in Hebrew or Yiddish.

BOOM! BOOM!

Tomassi turned to Barnhart. The soundman's eyes were getting bigger and bigger. He started to shake his head. All the while, he still prayed. Everyone swallowed hard as they heard the depth charges go off. The two destroyers were circling the mortally wounded sub not far from the *Sea Otter*.

Tomassi looked down the hatch to the control room. The planesmen were back at their stations. "Mr. Lloyd, send a runner up to the wardroom and see if they're done yet."

"Aye, sir." Lloyd tapped the bow planesman on the shoulder again and sent him on his way.

BOOM! BOOM!

Tomassi looked to Barnhart again. Barnhart shook his head. "The sub is breaking up, sir," he whispered. Everyone stopped their praying.

The silence in the con was finally broken by the talker, Saunders. "Go ahead, wardroom." After listening, he turned to the captain. "Sir, Avery is done with the operation. Box should be fine. He apologizes for taking so long."

Tomassi just nodded. "Tell him 'thank you.'" He turned to Barnhart again. "Anything else up there?"

Barnhart listened and said, "One of the destroyers has left. The other one is circling."

"Mr. Bergman, didn't we load a couple of those new acoustic torpedoes when we left Fremantle?"

"Aye, sir. The 'cuties.'"

"Well, where are they?"

"I don't know, sir. Chief Watkins supervised the loading, and he was just giving the ether to Box."

Tomassi turned to Saunders. "Call the forward torpedo room. Ask if they have the 'cuties.'"

Saunders called, "Forward torpedo room. Do you have the 'cuties' loaded?" A moment passed, then Saunders said, "They don't have them, sir."

Tomassi shook his head. "I've gotta yell at the Chief for that. Who the hell puts acoustic torpedoes in the stern of a sub? Call the after torpedo room and ask if they have them loaded."

"Aye, sir. After torpedo room, do you have the 'cuties' loaded?" A moment passed, then Saunders said, "They have them loaded in tubes eight and nine."

"Very well. Stand by tubes eight and nine."

"Stand by tubes eight and nine." Saunders put his hand on the firing button.

"I still don't know if I want to risk my life on a fool gadget like that," Bergman said.

Tomassi replied, "I just hope they work. And what better time to fire them than when the enemy is the only noise maker."

"Tubes eight and nine ready, sir," Saunders said.

"Fire eight."

"Fire eight. Eight's away, sir."

Tomassi turned to Barnhart. Barnhart listened. "Torpedo eight rising. The Jap doesn't –wait. The tin can is speeding up. He's trying to –" An explosion cut him off. "Torpedo eight hit, sir. The Jap is going in a circle."

"Fire nine."

"Fire nine. Nine's away, sir," Saunders said.

Barnhart listened. "Torpedo nine rising. It's catching up to the destroyer." Another explosion. "Torpedo nine hit. He's dead in the water."

Tomassi clapped his hands. "All right. Helm, all ahead one third. Periscope depth."

Chastain the helmsman replied, "Helm, all ahead one third, sir."

The sub started to rise. When they got to periscope depth, Tomassi asked Barnhart, "What was the last bearing you had on the tin can?"

"Two-niner-zero relative, sir."

"Up scope." The periscope came up, and Tomassi looked at the stricken Japanese destroyer. "Stand by tubes seven and ten."

Saunders repeated the order.

"Gyro angle fifteen right. Angle on the bow one thirty port. Depth six feet. Bearing, mark."

"Three-zero-zero."

"Range, mark."

"Four-one-double-oh."

"Check."

Lt. Morrow worked the TDC, then yelled, "Set."

"Fire seven."

"Fire seven," Saunders said. "Seven's away, sir."

"Fire ten."

"Fire ten. Ten's away, sir."

"Both torpedoes running hot, straight, and normal, sir," Barnhart said.

Tomassi watched as the torpedoes headed for the enemy. The tracks closed on the destroyer, and the torpedoes hit. After a moment, the smoke cleared and it became apparent that the destroyer's stern was gone.

"Secure from battle stations. Down scope," Tomassi said. The periscope came down. "Stand by to surface."

"Stand by to surface," repeated Saunders.

After a moment, Tomassi yelled, "Surface! Surface!" Three blasts on the alarm, and the boat went up. After surfacing, Tomassi ordered a detail on deck to check for survivors of the sunken sub. "Helm, ahead dead slow."

"Helm, ahead dead slow, aye," came the answer from the helm.

The lookouts spotted the wreckage from a submarine floating off to port. The boat was turned towards it. There were planks, and bits of metal, plus life vests and gear. There were also bodies clad in dungarees and khaki. She'd been an American sub.

Bergman saw a body he'd known. He grabbed Tomassi by the arm and pointed. Tomassi looked. It was Van Wert. He'd lost his right arm, and part of his right leg, but his face was intact. Tomassi covered his eyes. He'd just found a real purpose to fight the Japanese.

After a moment, he told the men on deck, "Look for her ensign. It's gotta be floating here."

The men looked in the water intently to see if Old Glory was floating there. A man forward spotted it and pointed, shouting, "There."

"Get a hook and fish it out," Tomassi said, "then bring it below so that engineering can hose it off."

"Aye, sir," the man said. He got a boat hook from another man and brought the flag up from the water.

Tomassi just stared ahead for a moment. He finally turned to Bergman and looked at him for a moment. "They killed my friend."

"Aye, sir."

"I'm going to kill their friends, Bergman. As many as I can."

"I will too, sir."

"Let's set a course for Pearl."

CHAPTER FORTY-TWO
20 JUNE 1943

Tomassi had run the *Sea Otter* as far from Truk as fast as he could. It was catching up to him now. He called from the bridge to the engine room, "Bridge to engineering."

"Rampone, aye."

"Chief, are you sure we're almost out of fuel?"

"Aye, sir. Those high speed runs we took at Truk used up a lot of our reserve fuel."

Tomassi looked up at Bergman, who looked ready to say, "I told you so." Tomassi glared at his exec and scowled. "Don't say it!"

"I don't have to, sir. You knew the risk."

Tomassi turned back to the squawk box. "Chief, how long?"

"At slow speed, sir, it'll be about an hour."

"Great! OK, Chief, thanks."

"Aye, sir."

Tomassi glared at the squawk box for a moment. He then looked down into the con. "Helm, ahead slow."

"Helm, ahead slow, aye."

"Very well." They wouldn't make much headway in an hour, but they'd be closer to Pearl.

The engines began to sputter. Tomassi could kick himself for this. He'd be a laughingstock when he got home. That's on top of whatever Admiral Lockhart might think of. As the engines died out, Tomassi took his cap and threw it onto the deck. "Damn it! Damn it!"

Bergman just shook his head.

Chastain called from below. "Sir, shall I switch to battery?"

"No," Tomassi thundered back, "Then we'll really be stuck. No juice at all!" He exhaled loudly, then looked at Bergman. "This means we'll have to call for a tow."

"Aye, sir."

"Get down and figure our position, then pass it on to the radio room."

"Aye, aye, sir."

As Bergman headed below, Tomassi could have sworn the man was grinning at him. He turned to the squawk box. "Radio room."

"Radio room, aye," Troilo answered.

"Raise Pearl Harbor, and tell them …tell them we've run out of fuel and … that we need a tow. Mr. Bergman will give you our position to relay to them."

"What, sir?" Troilo sounded as if he was going to laugh.

"You heard me, Sparks. And don't laugh, or I'll have you busted to seaman apprentice."

"Aye, sir." Troilo was probably laughing anyway. Tomassi looked at his watch. It was almost lunchtime.

Nearly four hours had passed since the call to base. They were expecting a destroyer and a tug to come and get them. Just to be safe, Tomassi had ordered the ensign to be hoisted on the conning tower. He looked back to see it flying from the standard by the after 20mm. The lookouts strained their eyes to see if anyone was coming. How much good would it do? Even if they dived, they couldn't maneuver. Plus, they couldn't stay down very long.

"Aircraft off the port bow, sir," called one of the lookouts. Tomassi looked up to see it was a PBY Catalina patrol plane. The plane made a pass and everyone waved to it. On its second pass, it wiggled its wings to signal it knew who they were down there.

"Radio to bridge," Troilo called.

"Captain, aye."

"Sir, an airplane has signaled. He says our relief is coming. It should be another hour before they get here. We have to look for a tug and a four-stack destroyer. They've given me the recognition codes to give to the signalman."

"Thanks, Sparks." Another hour, he thought. I hope we get into port before the bars close.

The sun was setting behind them. The ships coming to relieve them would be perfectly visible, but not a little submarine on the surface. Finally, the lookouts sounded, "Two ships off the starboard bow. One destroyer and one tug."

Tomassi and Bergman looked through their binoculars. A tug and an old destroyer. "Signalman to the bridge," called Tomassi.

Signalman Petersen came up. Tomassi pointed to the destroyer. "Give the challenge."

"Aye, sir." Petersen lit up the signal lamp and flashed the message to the tin can. There was no answer.

"Try again."

"Aye, sir." The challenge was flashed a second time. After a minute, the destroyer signaled back. "It's the right answer, sir."

Everyone on deck cheered. Tomassi asked, "Who did they say they were, Petersen?"

"They're the tug *Yaqui* and destroyer *Leighton*, sir."

"*Leighton. Leighton*," Bergman muttered. "I should know that name, right?"

Tomassi nodded, "If your old man was a destroyer sailor like mine, you'd never forget it. In the last war, Seaman Harold Leighton was at his battle station on a tin can in the Atlantic. He was on the depth charge party. The lookout spotted a torpedo coming. The officer in charge ordered everyone off the fantail. Leighton stayed behind on his own. He knew if the torpedo hit, it would set off the depth charges. So, he opened the racks and let all the depth charges go. When he ran out of them, he turned to run forward when the torpedo hit. A trailing ship fished his body out of the water. What was left of it, anyway. He got a posthumous Medal of Honor."

"And a tin can named after him. Do you think we'll get a tin can named after us?"

"My old man would be proud. U.S.S. *Tomassi*. Plus, the Navy could do with another boat named *Sea Otter*." Tomassi called into the squawk box. "Chief Watkins?"

Watkins showed up at the conning tower hatch. "Aye, sir."

"Get a party on deck to take the tow line."

"Aye, sir."

CHAPTER FORTY-THREE
21 JUNE 1943

The tug got the *Sea Otter* back to Pearl Harbor about midnight. After getting into the inner harbor, the tug took them on the easterly turn into the sub base. From there, Bergman supervised getting her docked under battery power. Then, Tomassi and Bergman, and the maneuvering watch, all hit the sack.

With the dawn, the crew came up on deck to be reviewed by Admiral Lockhart. Everyone had washed as best they could, and Tomassi made sure they had shaved before going on deck. Lockhart gave his commanders freedom at sea, but when they got home, it was strictly by the book.

The admiral came on board at 07:00. The men got a looking over, and Lockhart liked what he saw. He said to Tomassi, "Your crew looks very smart, mister."

"Thank you, Admiral. We keep in line."

"Um, Dom, how does a fleet boat run out of fuel before coming home? Was there damage you didn't mention in your radio messages?"

Tomassi blushed. "Well, uh, it's like this, Admiral. I, uh, wanted very badly to get a certain ex-whaling ship." He pointed up to the battle flag the men had sewn together while under tow, and had stretched across the periscope shears. It showed a gigantic sea otter, with teeth bared, biting a Japanese ship in half, and with the name "U.S.S. *Sea Otter*" under it. Below that were various marks to denote the sub's kill record, with a section for merchant ships, warships, sampans, and an airplane silhouette. Below these, however, was the silhouette for *Luzon Maru #4*, with the words "18,500 tons" emblazoned on it.

"Ah."

"So, you see, sir, I used up more oil than I'd expected in trying to catch her. And, uh, well, you know, sir."

Lockhart nodded, "I get the picture, mister. Well, you did get her. You once said you would. Good for you."

"There is something else, Admiral."

"Yes."

Tomassi turned to Troilo, who had the ensign from the *Eel* tucked under his arm. Troilo handed the folded flag to Tomassi, who turned to the admiral. "Admiral Lockhart, we were able to recover the ensign from U.S.S. *Eel*, after her loss with all hands off of Truk Atoll."

Lockhart opened his mouth in surprise. "Oh, my."

Tomassi held the flag out to Lockhart. "I wonder, sir, if you'd make sure Van Wert's father gets this flag, or if not, that any new boat with the name *Eel* should get it."

Lockhart took the flag and held it for a moment. He looked at it, speechless. He'd lost boats in his command before, but he'd never gotten even a plank, let alone an ensign from one. He looked at

Tomassi with moist eyes. "If Van Wert's father doesn't want it, may I keep it?"

Tomassi nodded, "Yes, Admiral, I'd be honored if you had it. But I'd rather –"

"Understood. I'm sure Mr. Van Wert will gladly keep it." Lockhart handed the flag to his aide next to him. "Thank you, Dom. You did a splendid thing, and all of your crew. Enjoy your liberty."

"Thank you, Admiral."

Tomassi raised his glass unsteadily and yelled, "To Felipe Matos. Pharmacist's Mate, First Class, in every sense of the term!" He swallowed his shot of whiskey and slammed the glass onto the bar. "Another one, good sir," he bellowed to the bartender.

"I don't think so, Navy," the man replied. "You've had enough."

"But I'm only halfway through the roster," Tomassi yelled. "I've got more dead shipmates to drink to."

"No," the man said as he snatched away the glass. He reached for the bottle, but Tomassi took it first. "One more, then I shall depart your establishment." He raised the bottle and said, "To Commander Davis Van Wert, USN. A fine friend. A kick ass submarine commander. A great addition to the ranks of the men still on patrol." He slammed down the last third of the bottle and threw it against the wall.

"That does it," the bartender said. He grabbed Tomassi and dragged him to the door. "I'm closing. If you don't go, I'll call the Shore Patrol."

"No need to get rude," Tomassi yelled as he stumbled into the street. He staggered a bit and looked at a woman who was staring at him as she walked by. "What do you want, toots?" She turned her nose up as she walked on. "Same to you, my tarty friend."

As he proceeded in a zigzag down the street, he came across another woman standing on a porch. "Hey, babe," he yelled.

"Hey, sailor," she yelled back, "Come here. It'll be curfew time soon. You look like you need a place to lay your head."

"A capital idea, my good lady!"

He staggered up to the porch and stumbled up the steps. The woman grabbed him as he hit the floor. "Whoa, sailor. Looks like you found us just in time," she said. The pretty blonde helped Tomassi to his feet and inside the house.

As they entered, Tomassi saw a parlor full of young women. They came in all shapes and sizes, and had brunettes and redheads, as well as blondes, among them He rubbed his eyes and exclaimed, "I'm sorry, young ladies! I didn't mean to walk into a sorority house."

The women all laughed. The blonde holding him up told Tomassi, "No, this ain't no sorority."

"Where am I?"

"You're on River Street, sailor."

It now hit Tomassi. River Street was where the "ladies of the evening" were allowed to operate while martial law prevailed in Honolulu. A smile came across his face. "Oh! Sorry, girls. It's been almost a year since I graced this fair city with my presence." That drew more laughs.

CHAPTER FORTY-FOUR
22 JUNE 1943

"Good Morning!" The blonde opened the door on Tomassi, just as he was resigned to the idea his head would hurt for the rest of his life.

He rolled away from her, pulled a pillow over his ears and said, "No need to be rude, my dear."

She walked over to his side of the bed, then stopped and recoiled. "Oh. I forgot how sick you got." Tomassi looked over the side of the bed and saw that, indeed, he'd emptied out his stomach sometime during the night.

"Oh, damn. I'm sorry, miss."

"It's OK. Not the first time I've seen it." She stepped around the mess and set a cup of coffee on the nightstand. "Thought you might need this."

Tomassi contemplated it for a moment, then put his head back down. After a moment, he was struck with the fear he might have been robbed. He reached back for his wallet and was relieved to find it. He took it out and opened it.

"It's all there, sailor," the blonde said. "If you'd gone a couple of doors down, you'd have gotten rolled for sure. But you stumbled in a good house."

Tomassi looked up at the young woman. "What's your name?"

"Betty Jane. Just call me Betty."

"Thanks, Betty." He looked more closely at her. She had brown eyes. "What's a blonde doing with brown eyes? Blondes are supposed to have blue eyes."

Betty shrugged, "I had to be different." She headed for the door. "Do you want breakfast?"

Tomassi looked at his watch. It was nearly 09:00. "Oh, damn! I should go."

"You need to be at your ship?"

After thinking a moment, he replied, "Actually, I need to be at the Royal Hawaiian."

"Oh. You a flier, or a sub sailor?"

"You couldn't get me to be a flier. Airplanes are dangerous." Tomassi sat up and looked at Betty. "How do you know about who's at the Royal Hawaiian?"

"Every working girl knows. We get invited there a lot. We're snuck in and out of there all the time."

Tomassi finally turned to the cup of coffee and started in on it.

The taxi dropped off Tomassi at the Royal Hawaiian Hotel about an hour later. It had been a year since he'd seen the place. Its art deco style and pink paint job made it unforgettable. Admiral Lockhart had been good enough to secure its use for his resting submarine crews. Various aviators also used it for their rest and relaxation.

Tomassi walked up to the front desk and asked about his crew. The man directed him to the third floor, where the sub commander found his men and officers had set up their home. Bergman happened to be at the elevator when Tomassi got upstairs.

"Hi, Commander," Bergman said, "I got your luggage put in your room. It's next to mine –" he pointed "– down near the end of the hall."

"You're a pal, Bergman. I hope no one asked where I was, 'cause frankly, I don't really remember."

"Oh, I can guess. I was down at River Street."

"Did I look OK?"

"I think you looked better than I did." They both laughed.

"Thanks again. See you at the beach?"

"No, sir. I've had enough of the ocean for a couple of weeks, thank you very much."

CHAPTER FORTY-FIVE
22 JULY 1943

It was funny how things could change in a month. When they'd shoved off from Pearl Harbor, it had been a sunny early July day. Two weeks later, they were on station, and freezing their butts off.

Since Tomassi had last been at Pearl, there had been many changes. For starters, the admiral who disliked him had been killed in a plane crash and replaced with a man he idolized. It didn't necessarily mean being sent to a tropical paradise. One of the other changes was that areas the U.S. submarines patrolled in the Pacific no longer had numbers; they had names.

The sector of the North Pacific that the *Sea Otter* had been sent to was called the "Polar Circuit." This was the Kurile Islands, the chain that ran north from Japan's northern main island, Hokkaido, to the Kamchatka Peninsula. The enemy maintained garrisons and airfields along this ugly strand of rocks to guard their northern flank from U.S. forces in Alaska. They had to be feed, clothed, fueled, and relieved. That meant Japanese shipping. It was Tomassi's job to sink it, and here he had been sent to do it.

However, the biggest change Tomassi felt was inside. Before Truk, this had been just a job. Sure, he felt it was a job worth doing, but with no special animus, other than that of defeating an enemy who'd struck at the U.S. first. But now, with having seen the body of his best friend in the water, mangled and broken, there was a special anger; more than he'd even felt when he first saw Pearl in January of '42. Not even the wreckage they had yet to clear away on that day could kindle the purpose Dominic Tomassi now felt in his heart, soul, and bones.

The cook, Hawkins, was down in the conning tower with a pot of coffee. He'd been giving it to the men on watch, with Tomassi's permission. He looked up the hatch to the bridge. "Permission to come up, sir?"

Tomassi looked down. "Permission granted, Cookie. Come up with that hot java."

Hawkins had neglected to put on a sweater, or even a sweatshirt. He shuddered when he got topside. "Never was this cold in Florida, I tell you what, sir." He handed over a mug and poured the bottom of the pot into it.

"Thanks, Cookie." Tomassi blew on it, then took a mouthful. He squinted for a moment while swallowing it.

"Sorry I took so long to get to you, sir."

"I don't mind it being the bottom of the pot, Cookie."

"Thanks, Captain. I'd better get down there and see to my stew." He went back down the hatch with his empty pot.

Tomassi looked ahead into the fog bank. Without radar, that would be the ideal place for the enemy to hide. Even a year ago, the sub wouldn't have found anything if they sailed into fog, unless they collided with it. He turned to the squawk box and called, "Bridge to radar."

Radarman Markel replied, "Radar, aye."

"Do you have anything ahead of us?"

"Aye, sir. Just picked up something and was going to call. Contact bearing zero-five-zero relative. One ship. She's medium sized."

"Very well, radar. Range?"

"Range six thousand yards, sir."

"Very well." Tomassi hit the button to talk to the whole boat. "Battle stations, surface." The alarm began to go off in the conning tower, and after a moment, the gun crews showed up to get their weapons ready. "Helm, all ahead full, right full rudder, come right to course three-four-zero."

Chastain called back from the helm, "Helm, all ahead full, sir. Right full rudder, coming right to course three-four-zero, sir."

"Very well." Bergman showed up at this point. "Good of you to join us, Mr. Bergman."

"My pleasure, sir," Bergman replied. "Just had to take care of something."

The sub began to sail into the fog bank. Tomassi got on the megaphone to the deck gunners. "We may be right on top of him before we see him, so be ready."

The deck gun captain waved and said, "Aye, sir."

The sub was now enveloped in the pea soup fog. Every eye on the deck and bridge strained to find something to reveal the enemy. Tomassi called again to Markel. "Radar, what do you have?"

Markel replied, "We'll be on him in a minute, sir. Range, two thousand. We'll be catching up to him any second."

"Very well. Gun crews, stand ready," Tomassi said.

A green running light could now be made out in the fog. Tomassi turned to Bergman. "Who the hell would have their running lights on in a war zone?"

"Maybe they're too complacent, sir."

"Range one thousand, sir," called Markel.

"Helm, right ten degrees rudder."

"Helm, right ten degrees rudder, aye."

The sub was now overhauling the target along her starboard side. Tomassi could see now her shape. A nice sized freighter. But what was that on her hull? A big red flag was painted on her side. It had a hammer and sickle in the upper left corner. It was outlined in orange, with the letters "USSR" in black on the orange outline.

Damn it!

"We can't sink her," Tomassi exclaimed.

"Damn," Bergman exclaimed. "They have no right to tease us like this!"

"Helm, rudder amidships."

"Helm, rudder amidships, aye," Chastain replied.

"Secure from battle stations. She's a damn Russian!"

The gun crews slowly secured their weapons. A lookout on the Russian ship saw them and waved, exclaiming, "*Tovarich*!"

Tomassi smiled and waved back, then curled his lip and turned his palm away and twirled his hand four times. Don't you *tovarich* me, he thought.

CHAPTER FORTY-SIX
24 JULY 1943

Tomassi sat at the wardroom table, looking glumly at the chart of the Kuriles that Bergman had brought in to look over while he had his coffee. "I wish the hell we could find something big to attack," he fumed.

Bergman looked at the chart and pointed further north up the chain of islands. "Couldn't we hunt here, at Matsuwa?"

Tomassi looked at him and said, "You know who's up there? The *Narwhal*. We picked up her report on the radio. She was there, pounding at the airfield there with her six-inch guns. That was to cover the breakout of three other subs from the Sea of Japan. I hope the attention she got is enough to get the Japs around here –" Tomassi pointed on the chart to Simushiru "– to give us a chance to hunt. Mostly it's been those fishing trawlers we've seen."

"By the way, sir, how did you rate the gun crew on that trawler we got yesterday?"

"We did a good job. Maybe just a little more practice. I'd like it to be a freighter, or maybe a transport this time."

"Too bad that other ship was Russian. Do you think the Japs are painting their ships that way to fool us?"

"Nah," Tomassi shook his head as he swallowed his coffee. "If that happened, the Russians would go to war with the Japs."

"Why haven't they yet?"

"I guess they need the right excuse. Plus, they've got the Germans still in their front parlor."

"Have the Japs ever done that?"

"No. The last skipper to think that, the skipper of the *Sea Panther*, sank two Russians in these waters on his first patrol, under the idea it was a Jap trick. When he got home, he got yelled at and threatened with court-martial if he did it again. The Russkies screamed bloody murder about it."

"Captain to the conning tower," came over the PA. Tomassi slammed down his last swallow of coffee and grabbed the chart as he headed forward, with Bergman right behind. He deposited the chart on the table in the control room before heading up the ladder. He stopped at the radar set.

"Report."

Radarman Markel said, "SJ radar contacts bearing three-two-zero relative. Range ten thousand yards. First check puts enemy on southeasterly course."

Tomassi smiled. "Coming right to us. Simushiru *is* a good hunting ground, after all. Battle stations, surface."

"Battle stations, surface," talker Osborne repeated as he hit the alarm.

Tomassi headed up to the bridge. Lt. Morrow was on the watch. Tomassi got on the squawk box.

"Mr. Bergman, come up here, please." Turning to Morrow, he said, "Get down and start working the plot."

"Aye, sir," Morrow replied, and headed down. Bergman took his place next to Tomassi.

"Helm, left ten degrees rudder. Come left to three-two-zero."

"Helm, left ten degrees rudder, coming left to three-two-zero, sir," Chastain replied.

"Very well. Mr. Bergman, how many contacts did radar have?"

"Two, sir. The lead contact looked smaller."

"Big enough to be a destroyer?"

Bergman smiled, "It wasn't another trawler."

After a moment, Markel called up again. "Contacts now dead ahead, sir. Range eight thousand yards and closing."

"Very well."

Fog was rolling up to the right of the sub. Ahead they could see the two ships. The officers looked through their binoculars at them. Bergman spoke first. "The lead ship looks like a sub chaser."

Tomassi nodded, "That's what I'm thinking. What about the trailing ship?"

"She's really big. Maybe *Luzon Maru* had a sister we didn't know about."

Tomassi laughed, "That'd be nice. But, no." He strained to look at her. "I think she's a transport."

Bergman now strained his eyes. "I think you're right, sir."

Tomassi smiled and looked at Bergman. "I think those soldiers need a refreshing cold water dip, don't you?"

Bergman smiled back, "It would be quite exhilarating."

Tomassi called down on the squawk box. "Stand by bow tubes."

Osborne repeated, "Stand by bow tubes."

Tomassi then called down, "Mr. Morrow, lead ship is a sub chaser, angle on the bow, five right. Gyro angle five right. Set torpedoes for six feet. Target bearing one-four-zero. Speed, ten knots. Range five-oh-double-oh yards. Fire torpedoes one and two. Commence firing when set."

"Aye, sir," Morrow called back after a moment. A few seconds after that, Tomassi could see the torpedoes leave the bow and head downrange. Osborne reported, "Both torpedoes away, sir. Sound reports both running hot, straight, and normal."

"Very well. Shift target to transport. Bearing coming down on the TBT." Tomassi pointed to the TBT, and Bergman got on it. He pushed the button, sending the bearing down to Morrow and the fire control party.

At about this point, the sub chaser started to speed up and fire her bow gun at the *Sea Otter*. Right after that, the torpedoes hit and blew her bow off.

Tomassi nodded, "That'll teach him." The transport started to speed up. "What's the range," Tomassi asked.

"Six thousand yards, sir," Bergman replied.

Tomassi grabbed the megaphone and called to the gun crew, "Aim for her waterline. Commence firing, fire at will."

"Aye, sir," came the answer, followed by the first round from the 4-inch gun. It came up short. The gunners adjusted and fired again. This shell came down on the transport's deck.

Tomassi called down again to Morrow, "Angle on the bow, ten right. Gyro angle, five right. Fire torpedoes three through six. Commence firing when set."

"Aye, sir," came the answer. The gunners fired twice more before Tomassi could see the four bow tubes spit out their tin fish.

Osborne reported, "Torpedoes away. Sound reports all torpedoes running hot, straight, and normal, sir."

"Very well."

The gunners were finding the range better now. They managed three hits on the waterline of the transport. She was now stopping. A couple more seconds passed before the torpedoes started to hit and go off. A cheer went up from the gun crew. Tomassi and Bergman shook hands and smiled. "They could use that cold water dip," Tomassi said.

"Yes, sir."

"Helm, left full rudder. Come left to course one-niner-zero."

"Helm, left full rudder, coming left to course one-niner-zero," Chastain replied.

"Very well. Secure from battle stations."

The fog started to cover the sub as she turned away from the sinking transport. The Japanese soldiers started to take their cold water dip.

CHAPTER FORTY-SEVEN
16 AUGUST 1943

The *Sea Otter* had been running up and down the Kurile chain for the past month. She'd sunk another transport since late July, plus another escort. She's also taken out five more trawlers since then. It could be described as a good haul. But there were torpedoes still on board, plus enough fuel to keep her on station for another two weeks.

Tomassi and the officers were having their dinner. Bergman finished his portion and waited for the steward to take his plate. When that happened, he excused himself and headed into the passageway. A moment later, he came back with Hawkins. Hawkins had a nice big chocolate cake with three candles burning.

Tomassi looked up and smiled, then turned away laughing. The men present sang "Happy Birthday" to him as Hawkins set the cake on the table. When they finished singing, they applauded. Tomassi grinned and said, "Oh, fellas. Thank you."

"How many is it, sir," Bergman asked.

"I'm thirty-six."

Morrow chimed in, "You don't look a day over thirty-five, sir."

Tomassi exclaimed, "Thank you!" Everyone laughed.

"Go on, sir. Make a wish," Hawkins said. Tomassi looked at the cake. It said, "Happy Birthday,

Commander. August 16, 1943. Seventh war patrol of the *Sea Otter*."

Tomassi closed his eyes and wished for the boat to get home safely. He clenched his fists and also wished for more chances to kill more Japanese. He opened his eyes and blew out the three candles. Everyone applauded. Then, Hawkins brought out a knife and handed it to Tomassi.

As he cut the cake, plates and forks were passed to him. Pieces of the delicious chocolate cake were then passed around. "Do we have milk for this, Cookie?"

Hawkins snapped his fingers. "Knew I forgot something. It's powdered, sir."

"Oh well. This is war, after all."

As Hawkins left, Morrow asked, "Is this as good as mother's?"

"Oh, wow," Tomassi said. "Well, nothing could be as good as mother's. The last time she made me a birthday cake was when I turned eleven."

"Why not after that, sir?"

"Well, before I turned twelve, Mama died. It was ... it was February of '19. My little brother, Mike, had just turned eight. Mama was sick, and Dad said she had the flu. We'd had the flu, and we knew it was tough. But not that tough. Mama had the Spanish Flu. She was dead by March."

Bergman spoke up, "My father died of the flu about that time."

Morrow then said, "I lost my older sister to it."

Hawkins showed up at this point with the milk. "What did he say, sir," he asked Tomassi.

"We were talking about people we lost to the Spanish Flu."

"I lost my grandmother to it," Hawkins said.

Tomassi nodded, "Well, small world, ain't it? Anyway, after Mama died, my father asked to be transferred to Great Lakes. He figured the new Navy needed men like him, with battle experience, to teach the new sailors. Besides, we still had family in Chicago. My Uncle John, and my Aunt Olive, had moved with us when Dad was transferred to Philly, but my Aunt Gina stayed in Chicago. She'd married the owner of an ice cream shop. He'd joined the Marines when we got into the last war. He was killed in France.

"So, my little brother, my Dad, and I, came back to live with Aunt Gina. While we were at school, and Dad was working with the recruits, she kept house. She cooked and cleaned. She made our birthday cakes. But, of course, it was never like Mama's." Tomassi looked around the compartment. Everyone had a pensive look. Whether it was for home, or someone they loved that was gone, everyone thought about it.

Hawkins broke the silence. "Everyone like the cake?"

Tomassi smiled, "It's wonderful, Cookie. Whose recipe?"

"My mama's, sir."

"You do her proud, Cookie."
"Aw, thank you, Captain."

CHAPTER FORTY-EIGHT
17 SEPTEMBER 1943

Tomassi wanted to shave off his whiskers. It was almost time to get back to Pearl. The *Sea Otter* had a successful patrol. Since his birthday, Tomassi and his crew sank another transport, two tankers, another sub chaser, and six more trawlers. That meant twelve trawlers altogether. Not a glamour target, to be sure, but still it meant twelve less boats to catch fish to feed hungry enemy soldiers.

As he waited by the head, Tomassi wondered who was in there, and why they were taking so long. He finally knocked on the hatch. "Hey, come on."

"Just a moment, please," came the answer. Tomassi knew the voice was that of Torpedoman Witherspoon. He was the new man in the forward torpedo room. A skinny nineteen-year-old from Kansas. He can't have much of a beard from what I've seen, Tomassi thought. Come on, kid, let me in before I actually have to go.

A moment later, the toilet flushed and the hatch came open. Tomassi looked at the kid. He held a picture of a blonde actress. She was sprawled across a diving board, with her head tilted slightly, and a sweet smile. She had on a flower pattern swimsuit and had her left leg stretched out along the length of the board. Her right foot was tucked under her left knee.

Witherspoon looked up at his commander and grinned. "I think she's beautiful, sir."

Tomassi nodded his approval. "Yeah. Virginia's quite a tomato, isn't she?"

Witherspoon nodded.

"Tell you what, Witherspoon. When we get into Pearl, and get squared away, I'm going to take you into Honolulu. I'll introduce you to girls that will make you forget all about Virginia. Sound like fun?"

Witherspoon nodded. "Yes, sir. It does!"

"Well, you let me into that head, and let me get shaved. When we get liberty, I'll introduce you to those girls. OK?"

"Oh, yes sir! Yes sir!" Witherspoon took off down the passage.

"Witherspoon!"

"Yes, sir?" The young man stopped, his body shaking with anticipation.

"Let's not tell everyone about this, all right? They might not, um, appreciate that I'm doing this for you. They might get jealous."

"Oh, I understand, sir. Not a word. Scout's honor!" Witherspoon made the Boy Scout salute, then turned and hurried down the passage.

Tomassi smiled. I shall make you a man tonight, youngster, he thought.

After the crew settled in at the Royal Hawaiian, Tomassi waited for Witherspoon in the lobby. The young man showed up after he'd told his buddies he had plans for the night. "Hello, sir," the young man said.

"All ready for it," Tomassi asked.

"I, I think so, sir."

"Are the others following you?"

"No, no sir."

"Don't be so nervous. Women smell fear like animals do. They'll pounce and they'll tear you up! Even Virginia would."

"Oh, OK sir."

As they headed out the front door to the taxi stand, Tomassi asked, "Have you always been nervous around girls?"

"I guess, sir. I have trouble sometimes talking to them."

"Well, don't you worry. These girls will be nice, and you can talk to them, and everything. I promise."

"Thank you, sir."

They approached a taxi and Tomassi told the driver, "Sugar's House on River Street."

The driver smiled and said, "OK, sailor."

The taxi pulled up to the house where Tomassi had spent his night of sickness. He paid off the driver and turned to Witherspoon. "Well, they don't have a doorman. Open up and go to the door."

"Aye, sir." Witherspoon opened the taxi door and got out. Tomassi went out after him. As the car pulled away, Tomassi saw that Witherspoon was staring at the two women, one blonde and one redhead, sitting on the porch.

"Hey sailors," called the redhead. "Come on in."

"Hi, girls," Tomassi called to her. "Is Betty here tonight? I got a friend who I'd like her to meet."

"Oh, sure. Can we meet him too?"

"OK. This is – I forgot your first name."

"Homer, sir."

"This is Homer."

The blonde spoke up. "Oh. Hi, Homer, and what's your name, Captain?"

"Dom." Witherspoon seemed riveted to the ground. "Well, go Homer." Witherspoon nodded and started up the steps to the door. He ran into the doorframe on his way in as he stared at the redhead.

Tomassi followed him in and looked for Betty. "Hey, Betty?"

"Here." The brown-eyed blonde came up front and center.

"Hey, Betty."

"How are you, Dom?"

"Better than last time."

"You know the military says we're not allowed to have steady 'boyfriends,' right?"

"I know. But, hey, I have someone else who'd love to meet you. Homer?" Witherspoon wasn't looking. "Hey, Witherspoon?" Still nothing, as Witherspoon was entranced with the redhead. "Torpedoman!"

Witherspoon snapped to attention. "Sir!"

"Come here." Tomassi wiggled his finger. The young man stepped up to him. "Meet Betty. Betty, meet Homer."

"Hi, Homer." Betty smiled sweetly at the young man.

"Hi, Betty." Witherspoon smiled back.

"Betty, I'm here – we're here, tonight, so Homer can be a man. Whaddaya say?"

"Sure. Does he have the money?"

"Well, sure he does! We just got paid."

"OK." Betty smiled again at Witherspoon and took him by the hand. "Come on, sailor." Witherspoon looked back at Tomassi and smiled nervously. Tomassi gave Witherspoon thumbs up and smiled back.

Tomassi now turned around to look at the other girls. "OK. Where's that redhead?"

CHAPTER FORTY-NINE
16 OCTOBER 1943

The orders for the *Sea Otter* on her eighth war patrol took her to "Convoy College." This was the name for the Luzon Strait, between Luzon and Formosa. This was a vital choke point for Japanese shipping coming from the empire to the home islands. Many boats were given their maiden patrols here, hence the funny name for the area. For the veteran boats, like *Sea Otter*, and skippers like Tomassi, this could be considered a chance for a master's degree.

This area also marked the northern boundary between the Pacific and Southwest Pacific Areas. So, any submarine had to be verified as friendly or enemy, not just fired at. Admiral Lockhart had offered Tomassi a chance to be in a "wolf pack" for this patrol. Tomassi declined, since he wouldn't have liked to be tethered to anyone else.

The admiral had also told Tomassi that tankers were now the new priority target in any convoy they met. Only a battleship on an aircraft carrier would take priority over a tanker.

Tomassi took his boat off of the South Cape of Formosa. This might be a good hunting spot, he thought. Convoys coming up from the Philippines and Dutch East Indies came by here routinely. They needed thinning out.

At 20:00 that evening, Radarman Conroe called to Tomassi in his cabin, "Captain, SJ radar contacts bearing two-niner-zero relative. It looks like five merchantmen and four escorts. Enemy's course estimated at zero-four-zero."

"Very well. On my way." Tomassi headed for the conning tower. He found Bergman coming out of his cabin at the same time. "Did you hear it, Bergman?"

"Yes, sir."

As they got to the control room, Tomassi yelled up, "Battle stations torpedo!" Seaman Saunders, on the talker watch, sounded the alarm and repeated the order. Tomassi got to the radar station and told Conroe, "Show me the convoy."

Conroe pointed out the blips on his radar scope. "I figure their range to be nine thousand yards. Speed, seven knots."

Tomassi turned to Seaman Henry, on the helm, and ordered, "Helm, left full rudder. Come left to course one-one-zero."

"Helm, left full rudder, coming left to course one-one-zero, sir."

"Very well. All ahead full."

"All ahead full, aye."

The diesels started to throb as the boat turned for her attack. Tomassi headed up to the bridge with Bergman behind him. Tomassi got on the squawk box. "Mr. Morrow?"

"Morrow, aye."

"Stand by. We'll have some action for you in a few minutes."

"Aye, sir."

"Mr. Bergman?"

"Aye, sir."

"I think you need some experience in attack. How about you handle this one?"

Bergman smiled, "Aye, sir."

The officers and lookouts strained to see the convoy in the darkness. Finally, a lookout said, "Convoy to starboard. Five degrees off the starboard bow."

As they looked where the lookout had said, Tomassi and Bergman saw the ships, just as the radar had described their size. There was a frigate in the lead, plus one trailing, and one on either flank. Inside their protective ring, there were four freighters, two on each flank, one leading and one trailing. Between them, there was the prize. She was a medium sized tanker.

"What do you figure for her tonnage, Bergman?"

Bergman squinted through his binoculars and guessed. "I'm thinking, oh, about nine thousand tons, sir."

Tomassi stepped back from the squawk box and pointed to it. "OK. Give the orders."

Bergman smiled as he stepped up to the box. "Helm, right five degrees, come right to course one-two-five."

"Helm, right five degrees rudder, coming right to course one-two-five, sir."

"Very well. All ahead two-thirds."

"All ahead two-thirds, sir."

"Very well. Mr. Morrow, bearing coming down on the TBT." Tomassi took his cue and pointed the large binoculars at the tanker and pressed the button, transmitting the bearing down to the fire control party. Bergman continued as the sub steadied on her new course, "Angle on the bow, fifteen port. Gyro angle zero." He stopped himself.

"Forget something," Tomassi asked.

Bergman nodded, "Yes, damn it. Open outer doors on bow tubes."

Saunders repeated, "Open outer doors on bow tubes."

"That's better," Tomassi nodded.

Bergman wiped his forehead, then continued. "Mr. Morrow, set torpedoes for eight feet. Range, six-oh-double-oh. Fire tubes one and two."

Fifteen seconds passed, then Morrow reported. "Set." Bergman looked at Tomassi.

"Well," Tomassi said. "Give the order."

Bergman gasped. He hadn't ordered Morrow to fire when set. So, Bergman gave the order, "Fire one."

"Fire one," Saunders said as he pressed the firing button. "One's away, sir."

"Fire two."

"Fire two. Two's away, sir."

"What's next, Bergman?"

Bergman looked to the freighter on the port bow of the tanker. He then said into the squawk box, "Mr. Morrow, shifting targets, bearing coming down." Tomassi swung the TBT to the freighter Bergman pointed to and pressed the button. Bergman continued, "Angle on the bow, five port. Gyro angle five right." He took a breath. "Range, five-five-double-oh. Set torpedoes for seven feet. Fire tubes three and four. Commence firing when set." He looked to Tomassi, who made the OK sign.

Some fifteen seconds later, tubes three and four sent their torpedoes downrange. Saunders reported, "Torpedoes three and four away, sir. Both running hot, straight, and normal."

About this time, the torpedoes fired at the tanker hit their target. A spectacular fireball was sent up into the night sky. Now, the Japanese escorts got a clear view of the American sub. Their retaliation would come quickly.

"Lookouts below," ordered Tomassi. The men went down the hatch fast. "Clear the bridge," he yelled.

Bergman sounded the diving alarm and yelled, "Dive, dive!"

The *Sea Otter* started down. As the conning tower hatch was secured, Tomassi yelled, "Take her down to two hundred feet! Rig for depth charge and silent running!"

Saunders repeated, "Rig for depth charge and silent running." He then reached up to turn off the fan.

Bergman asked Tomassi, "How I'd I do, sir?"

"I'll let you know after the Japs are done bombing us."

"Passing fifty feet, sir," Lt. Lloyd reported.

The soundman on this watch, Messi, reported, "High speed screws bearing zero-zero-five relative, sir. It's one of the escorts."

"Passing seventy-five feet, sir," Lloyd reported.

Tomassi looked into the control room. "Mr. Lloyd, just tell us when we're at two hundred."

"Aye, sir."

"Enemy passing overhead, sir," Messi reported. A few seconds passed, then he said, "Splashes. Depth charges coming down, sir."

"I hope those won't be my only kills, sir," Bergman said.

"Keep the happy thoughts coming," Tomassi replied.

BOOM!

A depth charge had passed them and went off under the boat. Everything shook. A few globes could be heard breaking.

BOOM! BOOM!

These two went off very close and rattled everyone. Messi blessed himself and started to pray out loud. Tomassi tapped him and said, "The Lord can hear you when you mouth it out, too."

Messi nodded, "Aye, sir."

BOOM! BOOM!

The lights in the con flickered. Lloyd could be heard in the control room ordering someone to secure a line. Some oil might have gotten out.

BOOM! BOOM!

Lloyd could be heard again. He was telling someone to look alive and fix that leak.

Tomassi yelled down the hatch, "Do you need some help down there?"

Lloyd replied, "Yes, sir."

Tomassi pointed at Bergman. "Get down there and help him."

"Yes, sir," Bergman replied as he went down the hatch.

"What's our depth, Mr. Lloyd," Tomassi asked.

"One hundred twenty feet, sir!"

Messi reported, "High speed screws diminishing, sir."

After an eternity, Tomassi could feel the boat leveling off. Bergman came back up the hatch from the control room. "We had a bit of a leak, sir. But we've got it fixed. We were taking a little water."

"Did anything short out?"

"Negative, sir."

"Sound, do a sweep."

Messi rotated the sound heads to check the area. After a moment, he said, "All clear, sir."

Tomassi scratched his whiskers, then said, "All right. Let's hope they gave up easily."

Bergman said, "Maybe we're leaking oil. That could have been enough for them."

"That would be all we need. We'll know better when we come up and see if we're trailing oil." Tomassi turned to Saunders. "Secure from depth charge and silent running."

CHAPTER FIFTY
17 OCTOBER 1943

It turned out that the *Sea Otter* hadn't sprung an oil leak. A valve had been jarred loose during the depth charging that the engineer was able to fix. Tomassi was glad to be able to keep his boat on station.

Being a submarine on war patrol was rather akin to being a sniper. After a sniper takes a couple of shots at the enemy, he needs to move so that his opponents don't get a fix on his position and move to kill him. With a submarine, it wasn't wise to stay in the same part of one's patrol area for very long. Tomassi knew this and decided to take his sub further south.

He couldn't go very far south, however, without leaving the area that COMSUBPAC held sway over. The boundary between COMSUBPAC and COMSUBSOWESPAC was at 21 degrees north latitude. That was halfway through the Luzon Strait, just north of the Bashi Islands. So, Tomassi had to stay north of those islands.

At around 13:00 that day, radar detected a convoy southwest of *Sea Otter's* position. Tomassi turned the boat towards the enemy. Within twenty minutes, the convoy was sighted by a lookout. Tomassi and Bergman were on the bridge. Radarman Sheffield was on watch.

Tomassi called down to him, "Tell me again how many contacts you have."

Sheffield replied, "I have seven contacts, sir. Three escorts, one leading and one on either flank, with four merchantmen in a line."

"Very well."

"What are you thinking, sir," Bergman asked.

"Well, I figure if we sink the lead escort, we can stampede them, then if one of the merchantmen is a tanker, we can have him. Then, we just go deep and avoid the depth charges."

Bergman nodded, "I'd love to have a crack at that, sir."

"Yeah, you do need to try a periscope attack. That'll be yours when we're close enough." Tomassi nodded, "That's what we'll do." He turned to the lookouts. "Lookouts below." The men got down the hatch. "Clear the bridge." Bergman headed down the hatch, while Tomassi sounded the alarm. "Dive, dive."

As Bergman secured the hatch, Tomassi yelled down to the control room, "Periscope depth, Mr. Lloyd!"

"Periscope depth, aye, sir."

The boat headed down, then leveled off. Seaman Osborne, on the talker watch, reported, "Leveled off at fifty feet, sir."

"Very well," Bergman said, "Up scope."

Tomassi raised the periscope and opened the handles for Bergman. Bergman looked at the lead ship while Tomassi grabbed the Japanese Naval Vessels

Manual. He flipped to the destroyer section and held the book up for Bergman. As Bergman looked back and forth between the scope view and the book, he shook his head. "Turn the page," he said. Tomassi flipped ahead, and Bergman shook his head again. After flipping through two more sections, Tomassi came to the one Bergman was looking at. "She's a *Fubuki* class, *Amagiri* sub-type," Bergman said, "Coming in, bow on."

"Even if he turns away from our fish, they can go on to hit someone, provided they don't turn quick enough."

Bergman nodded. "That's what I'm thinking, too, sir." He looked through the scope again. "The merchants are almost directly behind him."

Lt. Morrow spoke up, "Fire control party ready, sir."

"OK. Angle on the bow zero. Bearing, mark."

Tomassi read it. "Zero-two-zero."

"Range, mark."

"Four-five-double-oh."

"Gyro angle zero. Set depth to six feet. Open outer doors on tubes one and two."

Osborne repeated, "Open outer doors on tubes one and two."

Bergman let the range close. Only the most eagle-eyed lookout would have seen the tip of the periscope that they were showing. After another moment, he said, "Bearing, mark."

"Zero-two-zero," Tomassi said.

"Range, mark."

"Two-five-double-oh."

"Fire one."

Osborne said, "Fire one. One's away, sir."

"Fire two."

"Fire two. Two's away, sir."

"Down scope."

Soundman Barnhart reported, "Both torpedoes running hot, straight, and normal, sir."

"Left five degrees rudder," Bergman ordered.

Chastain repeated, "Left five degrees rudder, sir."

Barnhart reported, "The destroyer is speeding up, sir." Right after saying this, the torpedoes hit the enemy. "Both torpedoes hit, sir."

"Up scope," Bergman ordered. The periscope came up. Bergman was rewarded with the sight of the Japanese destroyer going down. "Helm, rudder amidships."

"Helm, rudder amidships, aye."

"What's next," Tomassi asked.

Bergman turned his scope to the lead freighter. "Set up on lead freighter. Gyro angle ten right. Angle on the bow, fifteen right. Set depth to ten feet. Bearing, mark."

Tomassi read it. "Zero-two-five."

"Range, mark."

"Three-five-double-oh."

"Open outer doors on tubes three and four. Commence firing when set."

"Open outer doors on tubes three and four," Osborne repeated.

After a moment, Morrow called, "Course and speed check, sir."

"Fire three," Bergman ordered.

"Fire three," Osborne said. "Three's away, sir."

"Fire four."

"Fire four. Four's away, sir."

"Down scope." As the periscope lowered, Bergman called down to the control room. "Mr. Lloyd, take us to two hundred feet."

"Two hundred feet, aye, sir."

Barnhart reported, "Both torpedoes running hot, straight, and normal, sir."

As the sub headed down, the explosions could be heard. "Both hit, sir."

The *Sea Otter* headed down through the cold water layer that saved her from a Japanese counterattack. Tomassi spoke up. "Did we forget something, Mr. Bergman?"

Bergman closed his eyes and nodded. "Rig for silent running."

Osborne repeated, "Rig for silent running."

Tomassi shook his head and said to Osborne, "Rig for depth charge."

"Rig for depth charge," Osborne said.

Bergman shook his head again. "I'm sorry, sir."

"When you have your own boat, there'll be no time for sorry," Tomassi said. After a few minutes, with the remainder of the convoy heading away,

Tomassi gave the order, "Secure from depth charge and silent running."

"Secure from depth charge and silent running," Osborne said as he turned the fan back on.

CHAPTER FIFTY-ONE
25 NOVEMBER 1943

Another Thanksgiving spent at sea. Not much to be thankful for since mid-October. Several convoys were sighted since Bergman had sunk the tanker and destroyer four and a half weeks ago. All the *Sea Otter* had gotten from them were torpedoes expended for nothing, and several loads of depth charges dropped on her.

Tomassi had to be content with sending contact reports of the enemy shipping back to Pearl, so that someone else up the patrol chain could go after them. It didn't sit well with anyone.

At least, he thought, we have plenty of turkey and dressing. Plus, Hawkins the cook had opened up his mother's recipes to bake a pecan pie, as well as several pumpkin pies. All the same, this Thanksgiving wasn't the festive occasion he'd experienced every other time before. As he looked around the wardroom at the other officers present, he saw it was in their eyes, too.

"Gentlemen, look at it this way," he said to them. "At least we –" indicating with his finger those sitting there "–get to have this meal hot and not warmed over like those on watch right now." One or two men chuckled at this, and the rest nodded.

Bergman leaned forward at his end of the table and said to Tomassi, "I'm sorry if I took all your luck, sir."

Tomassi looked at him and smiled. "What? That makes it sound like after you sank those Japs, I all of a sudden became a Jonah."

"No, I guess …I didn't mean you were all of a sudden bad luck, sir. I don't know if you think of those things or not."

"Well, Bergman, it's a stereotype of naval men that we're all superstitious. Not me. I'm not superstitious, and you know why?" Tomassi paused for effect. "Because it's bad luck!" Everyone in the compartment laughed at that.

"Thank you, sir," Bergman said.

At this point, Hawkins and the stewards showed up with the turkey, dressing, and mashed potatoes. Applause rang through the wardroom as the officers saw the bounty put before them. "Happy Thanksgiving, sir," Hawkins said.

"Happy Thanksgiving, Cookie. And thanks to you for this wonderful spread. Get ready with that pie."

Hawkins nodded, "Aye, sir," as he left the compartment.

"Should we say *Grace*," asked Lt. Morrow.

Tomassi looked around. "Well, my version may not be the same as all of yours. So, everyone say your version of *Grace* to yourselves." Tomassi blessed himself and looked up to see Lt. (j.g.) Lloyd doing the same. Bergman started to rock in his seat and murmur the Hebrew version. When everyone was done, Tomassi said, "OK. Dig in."

CHAPTER FIFTY-TWO
18 DECEMBER 1943

"Helm, finished with engines," Bergman called down to Chastain.

"Helm, finished with engines, aye," the helmsman replied.

"Mooring lines all secure," Chief Watkins called up from the deck.

"Very well," Tomassi replied. He turned to Bergman. "Good job, as always, Mr. Bergman. Also, you added to our battle flag." They looked up to see the banner stretched across the periscope shears. Despite its aggressive pose, Tomassi still thought the sea otter on their battle flag looked like a goofy animal. At least they didn't have it breaking ships on a rock perched on its belly, like a real sea otter did with shellfish.

But, aside from that, one more destroyer and four more merchantmen were added to the record of the U.S.S. *Sea Otter*. She was fast becoming an ace of the sub service.

That was something beautiful.

Tomassi told Bergman, "Call the crew to quarters. Admiral Lockhart should be pulling up any minute now."

"Aye, sir." Bergman touched the button on the squawk box. "Crew to your quarters."

After a minute, the crew formed up on the foredeck. Tomassi and Bergman went down on deck to check that each man had shaved. Admiral Lockhart may have forgiven his sub skippers for some things, in the name of getting kills. But he wouldn't forgive them for not passing inspection.

Bergman saluted Tomassi and reported, "Ship's company, U.S.S. *Sea Otter*, all present and accounted for, sir."

"Very well." Tomassi returned the salute and told the men, "Stand at ease." He looked over his shoulder to see if the admiral's car was coming. The band had stopped playing "Anchors Aweigh." They were no doubt waiting for the admiral, too.

Bergman looked at his watch. "Shouldn't the admiral have been here by now?"

Tomassi nodded. "I guess something held him up. He's usually here to greet us. Just like with every other sub."

As if on cue, the admiral's car pulled up at the end of the dock. Tomassi saw this and called to the men, "Attention!" The men came to attention as "Anchors Aweigh" was struck up by the band.

Admiral Lockhart got out of the car and walked up the dock to the sub's gangplank. He crossed it and as Tomassi and Bergman saluted him, he asked, "Permission to come aboard?"

"Permission granted, sir," Tomassi said. Lockhart returned the salute, then the two men shook hands. "Welcome home, Dom."

"Thank you, Admiral. Good to be home."

"Sorry I was late. Flat tire."

"Oh well. The men are ready for your inspection, sir."

"Thank you, Dom."

After inspection was done, the men went on liberty. All hands went to the Royal Hawaiian Hotel, as always. There would be time to write home, or maybe send a cable, wishing a Merry Christmas, or Happy Hanukkah, and Happy New Year.

CHAPTER FIFTY-THREE
31 DECEMBER 1943

Tomassi had managed to get the girls from Sugar's House into the ballroom of the Royal Hawaiian. No way was he letting his men spend the New Year with only each other for company. Besides, there was a certain brown eyed blonde he wanted to kiss at midnight.

At about 23:00 the girls arrived. Tomassi had paid off however many people it took. It was money after all. He brought them to the stage and called his men through the microphone. "Attention, officers and men of the *Sea Otter*. I've made sure we're not going to be lonely this night. I don't want to see any of you without a girl."

A cheer went up from the men as the ladies filtered into the crowd. Tomassi grabbed Betty's hand and told her, "You're with me, babe."

"OK, baby," she replied.

As the minutes to midnight ticked away, the band played and the men and officers danced with the girls. Some of them, though, didn't want to wait for the turn of the year to start kissing the women. Tomassi could see from his perch that Bergman and Lloyd, and Chief Rampone, each had a woman in his grasp and were doing the kinds of things that should have waited until they went upstairs.

"Some officers and gentlemen *they* are," he said.

Betty asked him, "How long has it been for your, skipper?"

Tomassi looked into her eyes and said, "Long enough that maybe another half hour won't matter." He took her hand and said, "For you, I'd wait a whole other year."

Betty giggled, "Oh stop it, Dom."

Tomassi looked at his watch. It was just a couple minutes to midnight. He hurried to the stage just as the band leader said, "OK everyone. It's time to count down. We've got two minutes. Everyone get with your girls."

Betty had joined Tomassi near the stage with two champagne glasses. He took his glass and held Betty's free hand. The couple next to them bumped him and nearly spilled his drink. "Hey, watch it man!"

The man of that couple was Torpedoman Witherspoon. "Oh, I'm sorry sir." He was with the redhead Tomassi had enjoyed the night Witherspoon became a man.

The band leader started the countdown. "OK everyone. Fifteen seconds." Everyone joined him. "Fourteen, thirteen, twelve, eleven, ten, nine, eight, seven, six, five, four, three, two, one. HAPPY NEW YEAR!"

"Auld Lang Syne" started playing. Everyone drank a toast with their girl. Before Betty could drink hers, Tomassi planted a kiss on her lips. "OK, Dom," she said when he finished.

"Happy New Year, sweetie."

CHAPTER FIFTY-FOUR
3 JANUARY 1944

After having the weekend to recuperate from the New Year's festivities, the crew of the *Sea Otter* got back to their boat and prepared for an inspection from Admiral Lockhart before shoving off for another war patrol.

The ship's company was lined up on the foredeck, as always. Bergman reported everyone was present and accounted for. Before Tomassi could tell the men to stand at ease, Admiral Lockhart pulled up in his staff car and made his way to the gangplank. "Permission to come aboard," he asked.

"Permission granted, sir," Tomassi answered.

Lockhart held out his hand. "Hi, Dom. All ready to go again?"

"Yes, Admiral."

"Everyone recovered from New Year's?"

"Yes, Admiral. We're done with partying until we come home again."

"Excellent, Dom. Let's get on with the inspection."

Admiral Lockhart passed in front of the first rank of men. He looked at their appearance and asked one or two of them how they were. They answered they were OK.

He asked Hawkins if he was getting everything he needed to feed the men. Hawkins answered he was getting what the men needed. Lockhart went on to the next man.

WUMP!

The sub shook from something exploding inside her. It wasn't a catastrophic blast; just enough to shake up the boat and the men on deck.

Lockhart stopped and cocked his head. Tomassi looked around, then to the men. One of them caused this. He saw Hawkins slowly close his eyes in terror. Tomassi looked at Hawkins, then at Bergman. Bergman nodded and grimaced. He knew what this was.

"What was that," Admiral Lockhart asked.

"What was what, Admiral," Tomassi answered.

"I thought I heard something, and that the boat shook." He looked at Bergman. "Did you feel it, Mr. Bergman?"

"No, Admiral," Bergman replied.

"Did you feel it, Hawkins?"

"No, Admiral."

"Hmmm." Lockhart proceeded with the inspection. He stopped after looking at the second rank, then looked at Tomassi for a moment. "I think I've seen all I need, Mr. Tomassi."

"Very well, Admiral."

Lockhart walked up to Tomassi and shook hands with him. "Good hunting, Dom."

"Thank you, sir." Tomassi and Bergman saluted Admiral Lockhart, who returned it, then headed for the gangplank.

As he stepped on the gangplank, he turned back to Tomassi. "Dom?"

"Yes, Admiral?"

Lockhart winked at him and smiled, "Hope it was good." He turned around and went up the dock, got into his staff car, and drove off.

Tomassi and Bergman glared at each other for a moment, then Tomassi's gaze shifted to Hawkins. Hawkins was making applejack. If he'd kept an eye on it, it wouldn't have blown up and nearly gotten everyone in trouble. Hawkins himself realized if he'd kept a stone face, no one would have guessed it was him making the potent potable.

Tomassi pulled himself together and told Bergman, "When the men are dismissed, have the special sea section at their stations and prepare the ship to get underway." He turned to Hawkins, pointed at him, and said, "You are coming with me."

Bergman turned to the men and said, "Leave your quarters. Special sea section to your stations on the double. All hands prepare to get underway."

As the men went to their stations for getting underway, Tomassi and Hawkins went below, down even below the control room, to a void space that was used mostly to get to the sub's batteries. Here, Tomassi found the remnants of a five-gallon glass jug. The ceramic lid, and wire hasp that had held it, were the biggest pieces left. The compartment reeked of alcohol.

Tomassi turned to Hawkins. "Do you know what kind of trouble you can be in for making booze on a ship of the Navy?"

"Yes, sir."

"Did you get this jug from Chief Rampone?"

"He didn't need it anymore, sir. Once that water is used for the batteries, it's just a glass jug. He didn't mind me taking it." Hawkins' voice sped up as he talked, since this was something that could cost him his stripes.

"I suppose Mr. Bergman didn't know why you needed raisins? That's one of the important ingredients."

"I told him I was making tapioca pudding, and would use the raisins in that, sir."

Tomassi rolled his eyes and shook his head. He then sighed, and said, "I'll figure out what to do with you another time. Right now, you clean up this mess. You've got half an hour to do it."

"Aye, sir."

Tomassi climbed out of the void space and saw one of the stewards. "What's your name, sailor?"

"Reese, sir. Steward Apprentice."

"Well, get down there and help Hawkins."

The stewards, aside from Hawkins, were the only black men on the sub. This made it more surprising to Tomassi when he heard Hawkins bellow, "Well, boy, don't just stand there! Get a mop! Help me clean this!"

CHAPTER FIFTY-FIVE
29 FEBRUARY 1944

"Hit Parade." That was the name for the patrol area off the eastern coast of Japan. For the *Sea Otter*, the hits just weren't coming. Tomassi had taken his boat up and down the eastern coast of the big island of Honshu. There were lucky to see anything bigger than a sampan. They had sunk two of those with gunfire. It had been this way for five weeks on station.

It was at 03:05 that Tomassi got called from sound sleep. "Captain to the radio room. Captain to the radio room."

Tomassi hurried to the radio room, where Troilo gave him the message. "Thanks, Sparks," Tomassi smiled. He went to the bridge to find Bergman getting his stars. He had to use the positions of the nighttime stars to get an accurate position for the boat. "Hey, Bergman."

"Sir?"

"Radio room just picked up a message from the *Needlefish*. She torpedoed a tanker just south of us and left her dead in the water. She said she's been driven off by escorts and need someone to finish the tanker." Tomassi beamed, "That's us! We can do it."

Bergman smiled, "Yes, sir!"

Tomassi ordered all ahead full, left full rudder, course one-eight-zero. The lookouts could spot a glow in the sky ahead of them, just a couple of miles away.

Kirkland was on radar watch. He reported one large contact and three smaller ones. They were escorts. Kirkland said they were making a screen around the stricken merchantman.

"All right," Tomassi said. "Battle stations, torpedo."

The Bells of St. Mary's rang through the boat. Tomassi called down to the fire control party to get ready. Kirkland called up, "Bridge, radar. The tanker is dead ahead. Range niner-oh-double-oh."

"Very well," Tomassi called back. He then called the talker, Saunders. "Make all bow tubes ready for firing."

"Make all bow tubes ready for firing," he relayed.

"Bridge, radar. Escort closing off starboard beam. Range eight-five-double-oh."

The lookout to starboard called at the same time. "Frigate closing on starboard beam." Tomassi looked to the right for a moment. The pale moonlight betrayed the Japanese frigate's presence. He hoped the same wasn't true for him and his sub.

"Helm, all ahead flank," he called down.

"Helm, all ahead flank, aye," answered Seaman Henry.

"Radar, bridge. What about the other Jap escorts?"

Kirkland answered, "They're both going in a large circle, one going southwest, the other southeast. The one off of our beam is still heading towards us, but he's not going fast. Maybe he doesn't see us."

"What about the range to the tanker?"

Kirkland answered, "I make our range to him as six-five-double-oh."

"Very well. Bergman, go aft and keep an eye on our friend. We may have to take a shot at him with the stern tubes. You deal with that."

"Aye, sir." Bergman headed aft to the after TBT.

Tomassi called down to Saunders. "Make ready stern tubes."

"Make ready stern tubes," he repeated.

"Mr. Morrow," Tomassi said into the squawk box, "Setup for target is as follows: Gyro angle zero, angle on the bow forty right, target course three-one-zero, speed one knot, set torpedoes to eleven feet. Fire tubes one and two. Commence firing when set."

"Aye, sir," Morrow replied.

Bergman called down the hatch, "Fire all stern tubes!"

"Fire all stern tubes," repeated Saunders as he pressed the button.

"The Jap's coming up our ass, sir," Bergman yelled. Tomassi looked over his shoulder to see the enemy frigate bearing down on their stern.

Saunders reported, "Tubes one and two fired, sir."

Tomassi yelled down, "Very well. Clear the bridge." Everyone topside hustled down the hatch as Tomassi rang the diving alarm, "*Dive! Dive!*"

As the boat headed down, explosions shook everyone up. "What the hell," could be heard by

Tomassi from everyone in the con and the control room, as well as a few saltier phrases.

"Sound, what have you got," Tomassi asked.

Soundman Messi replied, "I heard a big explosion aft. It sounded like a freight train, sir." After a moment, he reported, "Torpedoes one and two are running hot, straight and normal, sir."

"What about aft of us?"

Messi listened, then said, "I'm only getting our screws, sir. I think we got that Jap tin can."

Bergman nodded, "That'll teach him."

"That's *my* line," Tomassi said.

"Sorry, sir," Bergman replied with a grin.

"Keep listening, Messi," Tomassi said. "Those other Jap frigates will be on us any second."

"Aye, sir."

After another few seconds, Messi nodded, "Both torpedoes hit, sir." He listened some more, then said, "High speed screws bearing three-two-zero relative. Another set of high-speed screws bearing zero-six-zero relative, sir."

Tomassi sighed, then said, "Rig for depth charge and silent running."

"Rig for depth charge and silent running," Saunders repeated. The fan was turned off.

"What's our depth," Tomassi called down to the control room.

"One hundred feet, sir," Lt. Lloyd answered.

"Make our depth two hundred feet."

"Two hundred feet, aye, sir."

"Picking up splashes," Messi reported. "Depth charges coming down."

BOOM! BOOM! BOOM!

The sub got knocked around, and the lights went out in the con. "Emergency lights," Tomassi ordered. In a moment, the lights were back.

BOOM! BOOM! BOOM!

Everyone got shaken up, and lights could be heard breaking in the control room. Next came the sound of water rushing in.

BOOM! BOOM! BOOM!

"Hurry up and level us off," Lloyd could be heard saying.

"The bow planes aren't answering, sir," came the desperate voice of the planesman.

"You have the con, Bergman," Tomassi said as he went down the hatch.

BOOM! BOOM! BOOM!

"What's going on, Lloyd?"

Lloyd and the planesman were struggling with the control, trying to get the boat to level off. "The bow planes are jammed, sir."

BOOM! BOOM!

Tomassi tried to help. The three men struggled with all they had to try and unjam the bow diving planes. Meanwhile, the depth charges kept going off around them. Tomassi glanced at the depth gauge. The needle was past three hundred feet, the designed maximum depth for the submarine.

Finally, the three men managed to wrestle the bow plane control to level the boat off. They were past four hundred feet!

BOOM!

The enemy probably couldn't believe a submarine could go that deep and not have broken up. As Tomassi climbed back into the con, he heard Saunders saying into his headset, "Forward torpedo room, report." He shook his head.

"What," Tomassi asked.

Bergman answered, "The forward torpedo room was telling me they were taking water when the line went out."

BOOM! BOOM!

The lights were flickering. "I hope there's no gas leaking up there. The batteries can't take this without cracking, and worse, giving off chlorine gas." He paused to think, then said, "I'm going up there."

As he bounded down the hatch, another depth charge went off close by and knocked everyone to the deck. Lloyd yelled in pain.

"What happened," Tomassi asked.

"I think I broke my arm," Lloyd replied.

Tomassi got on the squawk box. "Pharmacist's Mate, to the control room on the double." He headed forward, pounding on bulkheads as he went. "Everyone aft of the control room, on the double." Men who were there headed aft as he said.

When he got to the forward torpedo room, Tomassi pounded on the closed hatch. A man opened it and he went in. Torpedo tubes five and six were already submerged. Men were struggling to get the water that was pouring in into buckets to put into the bilges. Chief Watkins was lifting one of the full buckets himself.

"Chief, report."

"We can't stop the water, sir. I've lost three men already; Box, Witherspoon and Hegarty." Watkins pointed to the bunks across from him. The three dead men were lying on them, their faces bloody. Box's eyes were nearly closed, and Witherspoon's and Hegarty's were closed.

BOOM! BOOM! BOOM!

Tomassi yelled at the top of his lungs, "Clear the compartment! Everyone aft of the control room! On the double!"

Men dropped their buckets and ran for the hatch. Tomassi followed them, and after Watkins had gotten out, Tomassi left, securing the hatch behind him.

As the men went aft, Tomassi could detect the odor of chlorine. He secured the hatch behind him when he got to the control room. He pushed his way past the men in front of him to find Lloyd sitting up, with Pharmacist's Mate Avery working on the officer's right arm.

"It's broken, sir," Avery said.

"What happened up forward, sir," Lloyd asked.

Tomassi exhaled loudly, then said, "Forward torpedo room is flooding. Three dead."

"Who, sir," Avery asked.

"Box, Witherspoon and Hegarty."

Avery's jaw dropped. "Oh, God. Box is dead?"

BOOM!

"Yeah, and we'll join him, if they –" Tomassi pointed up "– have anything to say about it. Also, the forward battery is giving off chlorine gas. Secure vents coming from forward."

"Aye, sir." Lloyd craned his neck and said, "Secure vents coming from forward."

Tomassi looked up the hatch to the con and said, "Mr. Bergman, do you have any other news?"

"Aye, sir." Bergman came to the hatch and knelt down to talk to Tomassi. "After torpedo room reports their port bulkhead is dished in four inches. The tubes are working, and I've ordered them to reload. Engineering reports they have dished in bulkheads, also we have a dished in bulkhead in the con. Many machines are broken, sir. We're leaking oil. Chief Rampone doesn't know how much we can take."

BOOM!

Tomassi stood for a moment and looked down. This is the loneliness of command, he thought. Well, these men look to me, and I look to God. I don't want to die down here. I'd rather die up there.

"Well, sir," Bergman asked.

Tomassi looked up and yelled, "Stations for battle surface!"

Saunders repeated, "Stations for battle surface."

Tomassi climbed back into the con and said, "Make ready stern tubes."

"Make ready stern tubes," Saunders said into his headset as he got his talker's helmet on.

"Secure from silent running," Tomassi said.

Saunders repeated, "Secure from silent running." The fan came back on. At least they could get a little cool before the heat was back on upstairs.

"Surface! Surface!"

"Surface, surface," Saunders repeated as the three blasts went on the alarm.

It seemed like they were coming up stern first. "Mr. Lloyd, are the bow planes working?"

"Negative, sir."

"Sound, do a sweep."

"Only one of my sound heads is still working, sir," Messi replied. He took a sweep with the port sound head and answered, "I make out high speed screws, but it sounds like they're going away. They think were dead, I guess."

"If their sound watch is still awake, they know now that we've blown our tanks."

Tomassi glanced at his watch. It was only twenty-five minutes since they had dived.

"Passing one hundred feet, sir," Lloyd reported.

The sub seemed to be coming up fast, but not on an even keel. Tomassi called down, "Try to steady us, control."

"Aye, sir, we're trying."

Finally, the *Sea Otter* came up to the surface. "Open the conning tower hatch," Tomassi ordered. Three men pushed as hard as they could and finally managed to open it.

The men got out on deck and manned their guns. They struggled to cope with the boat's ten degree list to port. Tomassi called on the squawk box, "Control room, we're listing ten degrees to port. We need to steady her."

"Aye, sir. We're trying."

"Don't try, just do it!"

"Aye, sir."

There was no glow from the burning tanker as before. She had to have gone down. The Japanese frigates were circling the area, and one of them saw the *Sea Otter* and turned towards her.

As the range closed, the sub was finally on an even keel, making seven knots. The frigate that saw her was closing fast. Tomassi called to his gunners, "Commence firing." Everything opened up on the enemy, both 20mm guns, as well as the deck gun. The twenties were raking the deck of the frigate, as well as taking shots at their bridge. The 4-inch gun was taking on the forward mount, then the waterline. Japanese machine guns were shooting at the sub, their strings of red tracer bullets licking at the hull and chewing up planks.

The enemy began to turn away as the second frigate came into range. The same procedure was performed, this time with a steady boat. Lloyd and the control room crew had gotten them on an even keel.

The second frigate also ended up pulling away, licking his wounds.

Bergman called out, "Rain squall, off the starboard bow." Tomassi looked over and saw it. He then looked at the enemy escorts. They were starting to turn towards the *Sea Otter* again.

"Helm, right full rudder, come right to course zero-eight-zero. All ahead full."

Henry replied, "Helm, right full rudder, come right to course zero-eight-zero. All ahead full, sir."

"Very well."

As the enemy saw the sub head for the rain squall, they turned away also. Tomassi got on the squawk box. "Radio room." No answer. "Radio room." Tomassi then looked down the hatch and said, "Talker, try to raise the radio room."

"Aye, sir," Saunders replied. He called into his headset, "Radio room." After a moment, Saunders reported, "He's answering, sir."

"Tell Sparks to send a call for other boats to come help us. Have him spell out our damage and send it in the clear; we've no time for other people to decode it. Any friendlies come help us and have him give our grid position."

"Aye, sir."

While Saunders told Troilo this, Bergman tapped Tomassi on the shoulder and pointed up. Tomassi saw that the radio antenna was broken. Tomassi looked down the hatch again. Saunders had just finished telling Troilo the message when Tomassi said, "Tell Sparks the antenna is broken, and he needs to fix it before transmitting."

"Aye, sir."

Troilo did come up and tie up the antenna with a coat hanger. He stopped before going down the hatch and said to Tomassi, "I just realized, sir. My birthday's tomorrow."

"Really? Well, many happy returns on the day." Tomassi then took up his megaphone and told the deck gun crew, "Battle stations, stand easy." He looked down the hatch and told Saunders to repeat that message for the boat.

The rain began to come down on the tired sub and her men.

CHAPTER FIFTY-SIX
1 MARCH 1944

Troilo's message did get heard by other subs. The *Needlefish* and the *Garlopa* rendezvoused with the *Sea Otter* just after 08:15. With their help, the chlorine gas in the forward sections was expelled from the stricken *Sea Otter*. They also helped the wounded boat by sending their Pharmacist's Mates to help treat the wounded men. They provided parts to get some engines running again, and to help with getting the pumps in working order so they could clear out the forward torpedo room.

However, the bow planes still wouldn't budge. Some of the machinery was wrecked beyond repair. Number one engine couldn't be made to run. There were still leaks in the hull, and it took keeping the pumps on all the time to keep the boat from taking a fatal dive.

Bergman also pointed out to Tomassi that the sub was leaving a trail of oil behind her. It meant that this patrol was finished. They also used up most of their deck gun ammo in the fight with the two frigates. The other subs each provided some of theirs to make sure the *Sea Otter* could defend herself.

Tomassi had a bit of a headache. He went to Doc Avery's cabin to get something for it. As he got to the hatch, he heard sobbing. He knocked on the bulkhead and was told, "Go away!"

"Doc, it's the captain. I need something." Avery just kept sobbing. Tomassi let himself in. He found Avery sitting on the edge of his bunk, with his bottle of whiskey over half empty. Tomassi knelt down and asked, "What is it?"

Avery wiped his face, and with red eyes looked into his commander's face. "Box is dead, sir."

"I know. I saw him."

"But sir, I saved that man's life once. I can't believe he's gone."

"I know, Doc. I know you two were thick as thieves after you saved him that time. You always went skirt chasing when we got home." He put his hand on Avery's shoulder. "Everyone loses a buddy in war. I lost a buddy that same patrol where you saved –"

Avery threw his bottle onto his bunk and said, "But sir, I saved him! And for what? For him to die at a later date? What the hell good am I doing?" He broke down, and Tomassi had to hug him.

"You'll put it behind you. You have to. When we bury him and the others –"

"I'm not going to watch him get buried!" Avery pushed Tomassi away. "I'm sick of this fucking war!"

"I'm not in love with it either, Doc! You didn't corner the market on bitterness and loss. You have a crew of men that need your skills. We don't have the luxury of choosing to shut out the world. This crew still needs you, Doc!" Tomassi touched his forehead. "Especially me right now. My head is killing me!"

Avery looked up and said, "I'm sorry, sir." He got up and opened his medicine cabinet. He took the aspirin bottle, opened it, and gave Tomassi two pills. Tomassi took a cup and filled it from the sink, then took the aspirin.

Bergman showed up at this point. "Sir, we're ready to bury the dead."

"Very well, Mr. Bergman. I'm coming." Bergman left. Tomassi then turned to Avery. "Doc, I'm going to have to take that bottle. You don't need anymore 'stimulant.' If someone needs it, send them to me."

"Aye, sir," Avery said. He then picked up the bottle and handed it over.

After performing the burial, Tomassi went back to his cabin. He'd set the whiskey bottle on his desk before going topside, and now it was gone. He ran back to Avery's cabin and knocked on the bulkhead. "Doc! Doc! Answer me!" He then went in.

He found the young medic lying on the deck. The empty bottle was in his right hand, and a medicine bottle was in his left. Tomassi looked at the bottle. It was for sleeping pills.

"Oh, God! No, Doc!" Tomassi tried to feel for a pulse on the man's neck. Nothing. Tomassi picked up the whiskey bottle, looked at it for a moment, then threw it against the bulkhead, shattering it.

Bergman walked in to find Tomassi sitting on the deck, holding the dead man's body. "Sir? What happened?"

Tomassi looked at him for a moment, then said, "We'll have another burial soon. I'm…I'm putting in the log that he killed himself by drug overdose. We'll add his dog tags to the others."

Bergman looked at the deck for a moment. He then looked up and said, "Sir, Cookie made a cake for Sparks' birthday. They'll be serving it in a few minutes, when Sparks gets off his watch."

Tomassi nodded, "Sounds good. We'll just shut up about this until someone asks."

CHAPTER FIFTY-SEVEN
12 MARCH 1944

The *Needlefish* and the *Garlopa* escorted the *Sea Otter* to Midway, at which they arrived on the 8th. They had radioed ahead, and got a PBY Catalina to escort them in. The other subs topped off their tanks and headed back to patrol. Tomassi had graciously let the subs have what was left of his torpedoes. This was, in part, because he knew that without Doc's "stimulant" bottle to go to anymore, the men might just break into the torpedoes and drink the "torpedo juice," the alcohol that propelled them. Tomassi wanted to be sure that didn't happen.

The *Sea Otter* herself only took on fuel to get back to Pearl. Tomassi didn't even let the men go ashore, since he figured they would take advantage of the beer ration and get smashed. He didn't want to waste a day in getting them, and the boat, back home.

As they got closer to home, the old destroyer *Leighton* came out to get them. Another PBY was also there to lead them in. They followed the four stacker into the harbor and moored at the sub yard. As always, Admiral Lockhart was there to greet them.

He was on the dock, and when the gangplank was extended, he and his aide stepped up. "Permission to come aboard," he asked Tomassi.

"Permission granted, sir," Tomassi replied. As the admiral and his aide came aboard, Tomassi and Lockhart saluted and shook hands.

"Welcome back, Dom. Congratulations on bringing her home."

"Thank you, Admiral. The high spot on this run, other than that tanker, is being able to come home on my own boat."

"I'm writing you up for a Navy Cross for this, Dom. Brilliant work getting the boat home."

"Well, sir, I think this boat deserves a decoration more than me." Tomassi held up the ID tags of the dead men. "These men more so, even than the rest. These are the men we lost."

Lockhart looked at them for a moment, and said, "Of course, Dom. They do deserve more. Tell me about them."

Tomassi held up the first tag. "Torpedoman's Mate Box." He smiled. "This was going to be his last patrol with us. He was going to be rotated out. Always held his cool under fire." He handed the tag to Admiral Lockhart.

With the second tag, Tomassi said, "Torpedoman Witherspoon." Another smile. "I took him to Sugar's House on River Street, and made him a man."

Lockhart smiled. "You told me about that one, Dom. Give me the tag." Tomassi complied.

As he held up the third tag, Tomassi said, "Seaman Hegarty." An awkward silence. "Well, Admiral, I can't really tell you much about him. He was a new man rotated in at New Year's. I only talked to him when he reported aboard. I looked at his personnel file. We talked a minute. I asked if he had questions, and he said, 'No, sir.' That' s the last time I talked to him." Lockhart nodded and took the tag from him.

With the last tag, Tomassi paused before saying, "Pharmacist's Mate First Class Avery. He's the one who saved Box's life with the appendectomy."

"I read that report. What nerves of steel that took."

"Yes, sir. He and Box were thick as thieves after that. Always chased skirts together. Now, they're at the bottom of the Pacific together. He committed suicide by drug overdose. I don't think his folks need to know that, though."

Lockhart shook his head. "No. They only need to know he's gone." After he took that tag from Tomassi, he looked at them for a moment, then handed them off to his aide. "Have you written the letters yet, Dom?"

"No, Admiral. I –"

"Don't worry," Lockhart said. "You have two weeks of leave, and you can hold off writing their folks. If you like, I can do it."

Tomassi looked at Lockhart for a moment, then said, "What kind of a commander wouldn't write? No, I'll do it. I just need a day or two to come up with the words."

"It never gets easier, Dom. Trust me."

CHAPTER FIFTY-EIGHT
27 MARCH 1944

Tomassi ran up the hallway on the second floor of the Royal Hawaiian Hotel. There was plenty of big news. He had to find Bergman.

He got to Bergman's door and knocked. After a few seconds, he knocked again, much harder, and yelled, "Bergman? You awake?"

"What," Bergman yelled back.

"We need to get the men together. Open this damn door!"

After a few more seconds, Bergman opened the door. He was only half dressed. "Did I catch you in the middle of someone," Tomassi asked. He pushed the door open enough to see the bed. Betty was in it. "Oh, Betty. Whaddaya say?" He waved to her.

Betty waved back and smiled, "Hey, Dom. How's tricks?"

"That's *my* line." Tomassi turned back to Bergman. "Is everyone on this floor?"

"Yes, sir."

"Well, we need them all in the ballroom in ten minutes. You work this side of the floor, and I'll work the other." Bergman stood for a moment. Tomassi yelled, "Well, get your shirt on, man. Chop, chop!" He turned to the bed again. "So long, Betty."

"So long, Dom."

In the requisite time, all the officers and men of the *Sea Otter*, except Tomassi and Bergman, were gathered in the ballroom. They were talking among themselves, wondering what could be so damned important that their commander and exec had to get them out of bed so early. They were looking forward to finishing their liberty quietly.

"Attention," Bergman yelled. Everyone snapped to attention as Bergman and Tomassi walked up to the stage. Tomassi looked over at one man whose cap was pushed back on his head, showing his forehead.

Tomassi let him know about it. "Square up that cap, sailor! What do you think this is, the movies?"

The two officers mounted the stage and stepped up to the microphone. Tomassi blew out a breath, then spoke to the men. "Well, fellas. I have some good news, I have some bad news, and I've got some great news. First, the good news. As you might have guessed, we're going to take our boat to Mare Island Naval Shipyard. That means liberty in San Francisco!" The men cheered at this.

Tomassi looked at the floor for a moment, then went on. "Now, the bad news. The boys here at the sub yard have...they have determined that the *Sea Otter* was too badly roughed up by our last patrol to go on. The damage done to her would take too much time and manpower, and equipment, to fix. That effort could be better put, they say, to the building of a new sub. So...when we get to Mare Island, we turn her over…to be scrapped. Whatever they can salvage, they'll cannibalize and put into either fixing a current boat, or put towards a new one being built." This time, the men stood in stunned silence. A sailor's ship is his home, and losing her was as traumatic as seeing one's own home be demolished.

"Now," Tomassi said as he stepped back, "Mr. Bergman will give you the great news."

Bergman stepped up to the microphone. "Thank you, Captain. Well, boys, they say every dark cloud has a silver lining. For us, that silver lining comes in two parts." He held up a paper in one hand and a folded pennant in the other. "The first part of it, is that our boat is getting the Navy Unit Commendation, for our effort to bring home our wounded boat." The men cheered this. "That means an extra ribbon for your goodie bars, and this nice pennant that we'll fly on the trip to Frisco. It also means that, the next boat to get the name *Sea Otter* will have this pennant, and her men will get the ribbon, but you men know you're the ones who earned it." Another cheer from the men.

"Go on and read it, Mr. Bergman," Chief Watkins yelled.

Bergman turned to Tomassi, who nodded and smiled. Bergman tucked the pennant under his arm and unfolded the citation. He cleared his throat and began reading: "The Secretary of the Navy takes pleasure in presenting the Navy Unit Commendation to the United States Ship *Sea Otter* for service as set forth in the following citation:

'For outstanding heroism in action during her Ninth War Patrol in the area east of the town of Sendai on the island of Honshu on the night of 29 February, 1944. Despite severe enemy countermeasures, including gunfire from hostile ships and severe depth charging, and grievous damage, and loss of lives among her crew, the U.S.S. *Sea Otter* not only managed to save herself from sinking, she counterattacked the enemy, striking with devastating force in a series of brilliantly executed gun attacks. She dispatched one Japanese ship totaling some 9,500 tons, and damaged two frigates, saving herself from their determined attacks. This splendid record of achievement attests the courageousness of her crew, and reflects the highest credit upon her gallant officers and men and not only upon the United States Submarine Service, but the United States Navy in general.'" Once again, the men cheered. Great to get a pat on the back like this, and as a unit, which is how they had always fought.

Tomassi held up his hands to get the men to be quiet so Bergman could finish his announcement. As the men became quiet, Bergman continued. "The better news is this. There is a new sub being built at Mare Island right now. They were going to put together a crew for her. But, it has been decided that we are going to be retained as a fighting unit, and we are going, together, to be her crew. Those of you who were going to be rotated out will instead come aboard her with the rest of us!" The men cheered even louder at this news. Instead of getting used to whole other bunches of men, they would stay together and get a new boat in the bargain.

Tomassi stepped up to the mike again, and as the men stopped cheering, he said, "There will be two exceptions, however. I need Lieutenants Morrow and Lloyd to step forward."

The two officers came up to the stage. Tomassi motioned for them to come up. When they did, he produced two small boxes and two envelopes. He opened each of them and said, "Lieutenant Charles Morrow, I have your promotion to lieutenant commander. You'll be getting a new assignment when we get to Mare Island. Congratulations."

Morrow beamed and shook Tomassi's hand as he took the box with the gold oak leaf clusters. "Thank you, sir! Thank you."

"Good luck, Mr. Morrow." He smiled, then turned to Lloyd. "Lieutenant, junior grade Phillip Lloyd, I have your promotion to lieutenant. Your new assignment will be given to you at Mare Island, also. Congratulations." He handed over the box with the pairs of bars.

Lloyd smiled and said, "Thank you, Commander." He turned to the men, "I'll miss you, fellas."

"We'll miss *you*, sir," Chief Watkins said. The men found it in them to cheer again.

CHAPTER FIFTY-NINE
4 APRIL 1944

The *Sea Otter* set sail for the final time on 28 March. She didn't do any diving, since her damage precluded it. This allowed her to fly not only her ensign, and her battle flag, for the final time, but also her Navy Unit Commendation pennant. This pennant was attached to the top of the number one periscope, and was carried aloft by the breeze. Whenever a patrol plane would see this, they would wag their wings, and the men on deck would wave back.

Admiral Lockhart had tried to get a Presidential Unit Citation for the boat, but, as he put it, some Irish guy up the chain managed to get it reduced. Whoever it was also held up Tomassi's Navy Cross. Will bigotry never go away, he thought.

But on this day, no thoughts like this would enter the heads of anyone on the submarine. On this day, they were sailing under the Golden Gate Bridge. Other ships would pass and give them a blast on the horn. The men on deck would wave back.

Finally, the boat made it to Mare Island. They maneuvered the boat around to the dock that had been set aside for them. After they secured their lines, Bergman hesitated for a moment, then called down, "Helm, finished with engines."

"Helm, finished with engines, aye," called back Chastain as he rang it up on the engine telegraph. His hands didn't come down from the handles for a moment, as he realized he wouldn't do that on this boat again. With that, Bergman turned to Tomassi, saying, "Well, sir, looks like this is it."

"That's what it looks like," Tomassi replied. After a moment, he said, "Call the crew to quarters."

"Aye, sir." Bergman got on the squawk box. "Crew to your quarters." His voice actually cracked a bit when he said it. The men obeyed as always, turning out in a minute.

Tomassi and Bergman went down on deck. Bergman did a head count, and told Tomassi, "Sir, crew of the U.S.S. *Sea Otter* ready for your final words."

"Very well. At ease men and gather round." The men broke ranks and moved up to hear their captain. "Well, you men who've been with the boat longest must be the ones really broken up by this. Anyway, we can leave this boat knowing she's done her best to bring us home. We now will have a brand new boat to take us to action. Also, we have the knowledge that we can take anything the Japs could throw at us and come out on top. To Mr. Morrow and Mr. Lloyd, we wish the very best."

"Hear, hear," could be heard from the ranks, as the two officers prepared to take their leave of the crew.

"To you men, I hope you have a good liberty. Get back here safe and in one piece, and not too hung over." Laughter all around on that remark. "Our new boat should be all set for us by the beginning of May. Get your gear, and all your personal belongings out of the boat before you go, and make damn sure you remember it all!" Tomassi turned to Bergman. "Mr. Bergman, dismiss the men."

"Aye, aye, sir. Crew, leave your quarters."

The men broke it up and headed below to gather their gear. Morrow and Lloyd stepped up to Tomassi. Morrow spoke first.

"Sir, I'd just like to shake your hand. It's been an honor to serve with you. I've learned a lot, and I'm going to be proud to tell people I served with you."

"Oh, please, Morrow! You make me blush." The two of them laughed. Tomassi shook Morrow's hand and said, "Thanks, Mr. Morrow. You'll make a great addition to whatever boat they put you on."

"Thank you, sir." With that, Morrow went below to gather his gear.

Lieutenant Lloyd now walked up. He offered his left hand, since his right was still in a sling. "What Morrow said goes for me too, sir. At least when this arm is healed."

Tomassi took Lloyd's hand. "Thanks, Mr. Lloyd. The skipper that gets you is going to get one hell of a fine officer, and don't you forget it."

"Thank you, sir." With that, Lloyd went below also.

"You going to need help," Tomassi called after him.

"Morrow is helping me, sir," Lloyd replied.

All the things that had made this submarine a home were gone after an hour. The men had taken their gear and belongings, their pin up pictures, and their bags, and had gone. All of the other officers had their gear and had gone, also. Tomassi decided that, like any good captain, he should be last off the boat.

The ensign had already come down and was folded up. Bergman would bring it to the yard commander. Maybe they could get it on the new boat. The battle flag, with all the impressive kills, and the goofy looking sea otter on it, were in the hands of Chief Watkins. He'd keep it, since he'd been chief of the boat since she was launched. The Navy Unit Commendation pennant was with Tomassi. He'd keep it. He'd already taken the log book and put it in his suitcase. He'd try to keep it, though maybe Navy regs might not allow it.

Tomassi stepped out onto the deck once more. He ran his hand along the bulkhead that had been dished in by the Japanese depth charge. This piece of steel was what had kept the ocean out of the boat, and the enemy had done his damndest to break it. Right now, Tomassi remembered the day he'd taken over, and saw the *Eel* down the dock from him. He remembered the feeling of seeing the bride he'd had going away. He felt that again on this day. Only this time, it was more like seeing her on her death bed.

He resolved not to look back. He went down the gangplank and kept on going.

He thought of New London.

CHAPTER SIXTY
11 APRIL 1944

Commander Dominic Tomassi put a dime into a pay phone at New London's train station and called the naval base switchboard. It rang once, and then a woman's voice came on. "Naval base switchboard."

"Uh, can I have the Sub School Administration Office?"

"Who's calling, please?"

"Aw, Lily, you don't know my voice? It's Dom."

"Dom! Oh my God! When did you get back in town?"

"About ten minutes ago. Now, can I have that office?"

"Sure, Dom. And welcome home."

"I' m just on leave, but thanks, honey."

Lily got the number and connected Tomassi. A familiar voice picked up. "Submarine School Administration."

"Hey, Irene, it's Dom."

"Dom! Hey, fella, how you been?"

"Oh, getting along. Hey, is Rosa there?"

"Who?"

"Rosa Flaherty, my sister-in-law. You remember her."

"Yeah, I'm just kidding with you. Just a moment."

After a moment, Rosa's voice came on. "Hello?"

"Hi, Rosa, it's Dom."

A gasp came from the other end, then a big yell. "*Dom*! Oh my God, how are you?"

"I'm fine, Rosa. Did you miss me?"

"Oh, hell yeah I missed you! What time is it where you are?"

Tomassi leaned out of the phone booth for a moment to see the clock on the wall. "It's twenty after ten."

"You mean you're here in New London? I thought you'd be calling from Honolulu."

"No. Not even on a commander's pay. No, I just got here from San Francisco. Well, three days on a train anyway."

"Wow, honey. Why didn't you tell me you were coming?"

"I didn't really know until last week. Besides, I wanted to surprise you."

"You sure did! Oh, baby, we gotta have lunch and try to catch up."

"Sure."

"Oh, but it's Meatless Tuesday. That's a shame. I know you love a good steak."

"In a coffee shop, it may be Meatless Tuesday, but not at the officers' club."

"Of course. I'll meet you at the gate."

Tomassi met the sister of his late wife at the gate and drove her to the officers' club. Rosa was also widowed, only it happened during the war. Tomassi had gotten Rosa a job as a civilian typist on the base, which allowed her to use the house he had off-base. She hadn't dated since her husband's death. That included officers, who could have taken her to the club.

The two of them walked in and the chief steward, Chief Jordan, was there to greet them. "Why, Commander Tomassi," the old black man exclaimed, "Ain't seen you in what? Two years?"

"Two and a half. Great to see you, Jordan. How you been?" Tomassi shook hands with Jordan.

"Well, I guess I can't complain. Only big problems I have are keeping this white suit spotless."

"Perils of the naval service, huh?"

Jordan laughed, "I think so, sir. Who's the lady?"

"This is my wife's sister, Rosa."

"How do you do, ma'am?"

Rosa shook hands with Jordan, "I'm fine, thank you, Mr. Jordan."

"It's 'Chief,' ma'am, and I'm fine. We've got a nice table over here, sir."

Jordan took the couple to the table. Tomassi held the seat for Rosa, then sat down himself. "We want two steaks, medium. Also, baked potatoes, with sour cream, and green beans. Plus, a nice red wine."

"I got just the bottle, sir. Coming right up."
Jordan walked away and told another steward what
Tomassi and Rosa had ordered.

"Well," Rosa said, "Where do we start?"

Tomassi looked into her brown eyes. He then
looked at her straight, shiny black hair, her high
cheekbones, and her fine, long nose. "Let me look at
you for a moment, Rosa. I always thought after I met
you, that maybe I might have married the wrong
sister."

Rosa nodded, "I always thought Sophia got a
great deal with you. I mean not just your paycheck.
You've always been a handsome guy."

"The guy you got wasn't bad."

"No, I guess not. I thought he'd get to stay
stateside. But, no, he went over."

"Where did he get it?"

"Salerno."

"Oh. I always thought my brother would go
overseas. But he's got a nice P.O.W. camp in Texas to
run."

"Funny old world, eh?"

Tomassi looked away for a moment, then said,
"I noticed when you got out of the car that you were
showing a bit more leg than usual."

"Yeah. Dresses are shorter now. Fabric
rationing. Means all the girls get to show more leg."

"But in your case, I definitely approve."

"Thanks, Dom." Chief Jordan showed up with
the red wine at this point. He poured a taste for
Tomassi, who nodded his approval. Jordan poured a

glass for each of them and told them lunch would be ready in a few minutes.

"*Salute*," Rosa toasted.

After having a drink, Tomassi said, "I'd love to see the house when we're done."

Rosa unlocked the door and went in with Tomassi right behind. He took in a deep breath. "Ah, nothing like old home," he said. He jumped onto the sofa. He hadn't been on it since before shoving off for Pearl in 1941. "Oh, yeah! Nothing like it."

"I'm glad you approve," Rosa said. She picked up the mail from the floor, near the slot in the door.

"Anything for me?"

"Not for a while. I think people know you're in the service."

Tomassi put his feet up on the coffee table and put his hands behind his head. He then got up again. "I've got to see the bedroom."

"It's your house. You don't need my permission."

He ran up the hallway, then turned at the last door on the left, and jumped onto the bed. He let out a whoop. "Oh, yeah. My own bed."

Rosa walked up to the door. "It's plenty comfy, Dom."

"I should hope so. Sophia picked it out." He got up and dragged Rosa onto it. They both smiled and laughed. They looked into each other's eyes. "You need to be back at work soon," he asked.

She looked at the clock by the bed. "Not for another fifteen minutes."

"Perfect," Tomassi exclaimed.

After they had made love, Rosa and Dom lay still for a minute. Rosa then looked at him and asked, "Did you feel guilty? I mean, the last time, at Thanksgiving of '41?"

Tomassi looked back at her and said, "Yeah, I did. I was married to your sister, and you were engaged to that Mick. So yes, I felt guilty."

"Did you ever do anything about it?"

"Yeah. When I was in Australia, on Thanksgiving of '42. I went to confession. The chaplain had me pray the rosary. You?"

"I went to confession, too. The priest told me to write to Bill. But I never got up the nerve. I was going to sit down and write him, but then the Western Union boy came up with the news that Bill was dead." Rosa laughed, "Maybe if I go to Heaven, I'll get to tell him."

"I'll pray for you to go there."

"And I for you."

"Thanks." Tomassi took a deep breath, then said, "Changing the subject, I'm getting a new boat. It'll be commissioned at the beginning of May."

"Oh, Dom, that's great. Is it your second?"

"Third."

"Well now."

"Anyway, my reason for being here is to ask you to sponsor the boat."

"What would I do?"

"You'd break the champagne bottle on her bow."

"Sure, Dom. I've got vacation coming. I'll go with you."

CHAPTER SIXTY-ONE
1 MAY 1944

Tomassi got some strings pulled, with both Admiral Lockhart and the commandant of the Twelfth Naval District, to get the Secretary of the Navy to invite Rosa to sponsor the new sub. They took the train to San Francisco, and on this morning, sat at the podium, listening to the admiral in charge of the district give a speech at the launching ceremony.

While the admiral was talking, Rosa leaned over to Tomassi and asked, "Dom, what do I say again?"

"Just before you break the bottle on the bow, you say, 'In the name of the United States, I christen thee U.S.S. *Tiburon*.'"

"What the hell's a tiburon?"

"It's like a small shark."

"Then why don't they call her *Shark*?"

"Because last I heard, the *Shark II* is still out there. And, that would make this boat *Shark III*."

"Oh. So we don't like the name *Shark*."

"The Japs don't, anyway."

Rosa nodded. She'd hate for Dom to go down to the sea in a ship with a jinx name.

Tomassi looked out on the men in their dress whites, sitting and listening to the admiral talking. In that sea of faces were some nine or ten new men. This boat would need the extra men, in addition to the five replacements. New radars and new guns on the boat caused this need.

The admiral finally finished, and everyone applauded. He turned to Rosa and said, "I know present the sponsor of this new submarine, Mrs. Rosa Flaherty." More applause.

Rosa got up and stood near the bow of the new sub. When the champagne bottle was broken, the sub would slide, stern first, into the bay. Rosa clenched the bottle by the neck and took a deep breath. She glanced down for a moment at the workmen who were waiting for her. They would knock out the wooden beams holding the sub in place and send her into the water.

"In the name of the United States, I christen thee U.S.S. *Tiburon*." Rosa swung and hit the bow of the sub, shattering the bottle. With that, the workmen knocked out the blocks, causing the sub to slide into the water. Everyone cheered and applauded.

Tomassi walked up to Rosa and kissed her in front of everyone. More cheers from the men.

CHAPTER SIXTY-TWO
3 MAY 1944

The *Tiburon* got commissioned on this day. Tomassi took a chance to get familiar with his new boat. She was of a new type called the *Balao* class. The main differences were internal. She had four of a new type of diesel engine, which could move her some five knots faster than the *Gato* class he'd been on before. She was also built with more reinforcement, to better withstand the kind of pounding which had done in the *Sea Otter*.

She also had more armament up top. Her deck gun was a 5-inch gun, which would have more punch than the 4 incher of the old boats. She also had 40mm guns instead of 20mm on the conning tower. These weapons needed a crew of three instead of two. They had seats for the men who were firing them and packed a greater punch against aircraft and small surface ships.

Best of all, though, was her radar. Tomassi and Bergman were on the bridge when Tomassi got to see the newest innovation.

"What do you think of the new radar, sir," Bergman asked.

"I see a new antenna up there," Tomassi said, pointing to the classic shape of the SS set. It looked just like the radar antennae in the movies.

Bergman smiled. "That's not the best one." He looked down the hatch and said, "Up scope." The periscope started to rise, then Bergman called down, "Stop." He then pointed to the lens.

"What am I looking for," Tomassi asked.

Bergman then pointed at the top of the scope, just above the lens. Above the oblong lens opening, there was a small circle. "That, sir, is the ST radar. We don't have to try to bring the tower above water to use our radar now. We just raise the scope, and the radarmen can find our targets, even at night and in thick fog."

Tomassi beamed. "What'll they think of next?"

That evening, the men and officers of the *Tiburon* gathered at the Fairmount Hotel. Tomassi had invited them to the bar. With everyone there, he announced the drinks were on him for the night.

He knew most of the men but had to familiarize himself with his new officers. His new diving officer was lieutenant, junior grade Jablonski. He was a new man from sub school. Jablonski was in his mid-twenties. He had a wife and a new baby girl.

After talking to Jablonski for a few minutes, Tomassi found the other new officer. He didn't remember the man's name, so he went up to him and introduced himself.

"Hello, Lieutenant."

"Hello, Commander."

"I'm Dominic Tomassi. Whaddaya say?" He held out his hand.

The lieutenant took his hand and answered, "I'm Harold Leighton, Junior. Please to meet you, Commander."

Tomassi dropped his hand, and his mouth came open. "The son of Seaman Harold Leighton?"

"You knew my father?"

"My father kept going on about your father all the time. He was a destroyer man in the last war. He would tell me about your father's Medal of Honor."

Leighton nodded, "Everyone goes on about his Medal of Honor."

"Oh, and you're sick of hearing it."

"Frankly, sir, yes I am. I got to go to Annapolis just on the strength of it, but I'm mighty tired of hearing about him. It's like he follows me, and I last saw him when I was little. I think I was six when he shoved off that final time."

"Well, anyway, I'm glad to have you on my crew. If your half as brave as your old man, we'll make everyone forget him."

Leighton nodded again, "Yeah. Well, everyone does laugh when I tell them I chose the subs."

"My dad did, too. Especially since his job had been to help sink them in the last war. Tell me, what boats have you been on?"

"I'm afraid just a couple of S-boats for training, sir. This will be my first combat assignment. What about you, sir?"

"Well, my first boat was the *R-12*. That was many moons ago."

Leighton's eyes grew big for a moment, then his voice dropped. "Oh. The *R-12*."

"Why do you say it like that?"

"Oh, well, you wouldn't have known. She was lost, about a year ago, off of Key West."

Tomassi's jaw dropped again. "What? Oh, Lord. What happened? Well, first of all, how did you find out?"

"Well, sir, I was the stenographer on the court of inquiry. I had to take all the notes of the hearings."

"What was the verdict?"

"It was an accident. Commander Shelton said he was on the bridge and had ordered a dive. Then, the forward torpedo room called. They had water coming in. He tried to belay the dive, but the water came in too fast. He and the four men on the bridge with him, well, they were left floating on the water. Everyone else drowned, including four Brazilian observers."

Tomassi looked down for a moment. Then he said, "And even after hearing that, you chose the subs?"

"Yes, sir. Anything was better than being stuck in an office."

"What is your specialty, Leighton?"

"I'm your new gunnery officer, sir."

"All right." Tomassi pointed to Bergman. "Well, I don't know if you met Commander Bergman. He's the exec."

"Bergman? Is he a Jew?"

"A what?"

Leighton spoke quickly to be heard over the crowd. "A Jew! A Jew!"

Tomassi pulled out a handkerchief and said, "*Gesundheit.*"

Leighton laughed. "I can't believe I fell for that, sir."

Tomassi nodded, then said, "You sound as crazy as I am. We'll get along just fine."

CHAPTER SIXTY-THREE
9 MAY 1944

The *Tiburon* had shoved off from Mare Island on the 4th. She did her shakedown, and made her trim dives, along the way to Pearl. She also tested her cannons. The 5 incher, and the 40mms, worked just fine.

As they pulled into the sub base, Admiral Lockhart was there, as always. He came aboard and shook hands with Tomassi. "How'd it go, Dom?"

"Fine, sir. Just fine. I'm in love with the boat already, and we haven't even gone after the Japs yet."

"Does all of your crew feel that way?"

"Well, not quite. There's always settling in with new machinery, and all that. I had my chief engineer draw up a list for the repair crew. Plus, I'd love to get the torpedo tubes tested before we go fight."

"That'll happen. Are the new men working out?"

"Yes, sir. I didn't know I'd get the son of a Medal of Honor man."

"I figured Leighton could learn from the best, and what better chance than with a new boat?"

"Fine, sir."

Lockhart turned to his aide, he handed him a small box. "I figured we'd take care of some unfinished business while I'm here, and in front of your men." He nodded to the aide, who opened up a citation paper while the admiral opened the box and produced a Navy Cross.

The aide read the citation. "For action off of Sendai, Japan on 29 February, 1944, Commander Dominic Tomassi, USN, is hereby awarded the Navy Cross. With extreme disregard for his own safety, and with the desire to remove his crew from danger, Commander Tomassi brought his submarine, *Sea Otter*, to the surface against heavy odds, after having his vessel badly damaged by enemy depth charge attack. His brilliant torpedo and gun attacks resulted in the sinking of one Japanese tanker and damage to two enemy warships. His boldness also allowed for his ship to escape from the pursuing enemy. His actions are a great credit, not only to the submarine service, but to the United States Navy in general."

With that, Admiral Lockhart pinned the Navy Cross on Tomassi's chest. He then held out his hand. "Congratulations, Dom."

"Thank you, Admiral." With that, the men cheered and applauded.

After checking the men in at the Royal Hawaiian, Tomassi headed outside and flagged down a taxi. The driver asked him, "Where to, skipper?"

"Sugar's House on River Street."

The cabbie turned around. "Been away a while, have we?"

Tomassi smiled back, "Yeah."

"Well, then, you didn't hear. With the lifting of martial law, the Honolulu vice squad went in and closed down all the houses on River Street."

"What?"

"Yeah. No more happy houses."

Tomassi frowned, "Well, if that ain't new high for gratitude. I go out and bust my ass for this country. I keep these islands safe from the Japs, and this is how they pay me back?"

The cabbie shook his head, "Life's a bitch, ain't it? I'm not happy about it either, skipper. You GI's kept me in business going to River Street. I'm not happy about it, either."

Tomassi nodded, "Yeah. Well, take me to Happy Jack's Bar. We can still drink, right, or have they put Prohibition back?"

"No, we can still drink. Happy Jack's it is, skipper."

CHAPTER SIXTY-FOUR
7 JUNE 1944

For her maiden patrol, the *Tiburon* was sent to hunt in the waters off of Tokyo Bay, in the "Hit Parade" area. As if to underscore the fact that she was only one submarine caught up in a world of war, Sparks had relayed to Tomassi the full news of the invasion of France that had taken place on the 6th, while the Tiburon was assuming her station.

Tomassi and Bergman were on the bridge in the morning twilight as Tomassi read through the report. "Powerful Allied land forces, supported by air and naval forces, made their landing today on the continent of Europe. American and British and other Allied units are pushing their way through strong German resistance. They have secured their beachheads and advancing inland."

Bergman nodded, "That's nice."

"That's how I feel. When are we going to get on with invading Japan? They're the ones who bombed Pearl Harbor, not the Germans."

Bergman nodded again, then said, "You told me once you'd been to Italy before the war."

"That's right."

"Well, did you try and find out about your family?"

"There wasn't much to find out. I already knew my grandfather had come to America in the 1890's. Why?"

"Well, suppose he hadn't made the trip. You'd have been in the Italian Navy."

"So? He did make the trip. And if he hadn't, yeah, I'd be in the Italian Navy. What about you? Where did your grandfather come from?"

"He came to America from Poland."

Tomassi chuckled, "So if he hadn't made the trip, you'd probably be in some concentration camp."

Bergman smiled, "I'd like to think I'd be a guerilla fighter instead. Who knows?"

Radarman Conroe came on over the squawk box. "Bridge, radar. I have a single contact, bearing zero-two-zero relative, range ten thousand yards. Looks like she could be a freighter."

"Very well," Tomassi replied. He turned to Bergman. "A single, unescorted freighter?"

Bergman shrugged. "We'll sink him anyway."

Tomassi turned back to the squawk box. "Helm, right full rudder. Come right to course zero-one-five."

"Helm right full rudder. Coming right to course zero-one-five, sir," came the reply from the helmsman, Chastain.

"Very well. Battle stations, surface." The Bells of St. Mary's rang as the gun crews manned their posts.

After about ten minutes, the enemy ship came into view. She looked to be a medium-sized freighter. The commander and executive officer of the sub looked at her through their binoculars. Tomassi shook his head a little. Bergman noticed this.

"What is it, sir?"

"I can't help but think she looks familiar."

Bergman looked again. "I don't recall her, sir."

"I mean, from one of the manuals. Something is special about her. I'm trying to think of it."

Lt. Leighton called up from the con. "Shall I ready the bow tubes, sir?"

"Hold your horses, Mr. Leighton. We'll give the gun crews a chance first. They need practice."

The range was closing, but the enemy ship didn't seem to run. She wasn't speeding up or zigzagging. What the hell, Tomassi thought. If her lookouts are taking an extra long nap, we'll wake them up with a 5-inch shell.

Tomassi picked up his megaphone and called to the gun crew. "Commence firing."

The 5-inch gun fired. The enemy freighter responded with a salvo of her own guns! The shells fell into the water behind the sub, as the salvo had gone long.

"Oh my God! She's a Q-ship," Tomassi exclaimed. He gave orders in rapid succession. "Secure the guns! Stand by to dive! Make ready all tubes! Lookouts below!"

Another salvo came from the enemy ship. This one fell short. The gun crews had secured their weapons and were tumbling down the hatches. The lookouts had already gone below.

Tomassi saw the enemy ship turn towards him. She was going to ram them if he didn't dive the boat.

"Clear the bridge!" He rang the alarm and yelled, "Dive! Dive!"

As the *Tiburon* submerged, she was shaken by another shell from the enemy hitting the water. "Take her to ninety feet," Tomassi yelled down to the control room.

"Ninety feet, aye sir," Lt. Jablonski answered.

"Sound, what do you read?"

Soundman Messi answered, "She's closing on us fast, sir. We're going to pass under her."

"Stand by stern tubes," Tomassi told the talker, Osborne.

"Stand by stern tubes," Osborne repeated.

The whole crew held their breath as the sound of the enemy ship passing overhead filled their ears. At this depth, if the enemy rolled depth charges, they could by finished in a hurry.

The enemy was passing aft. No splashes were picked up. Tomassi yelled down to Jablonski, "Periscope depth."

"Periscope depth, aye sir."

After a few moments, Osborne reported, "Mark fifty, leveled off."

"Up scope," Tomassi ordered. The periscope came up, and Tomassi swung it around. He began to calm down, and calmly stated, "Angle on the bow, one-hundred-seventy starboard. Bearing, mark."

Bergman called, "One-eight-five."

"Range, mark."

"Two-five-double-oh."

It was time to go back on the hunt. Tomassi called, "Gyro angle five right. Set torpedoes to nine feet. Target speed, eight knots." Leighton fed this data into the TDC. "Open outer doors on stern tubes."

Osborne repeated, "Open outer doors on stern tubes."

Bergman called, "Check."

Leighton replied, "Set."

Tomassi turned to Osborne. "Fire seven."

"Fire seven. Seven's away, sir."

"Fire eight."

"Fire eight. Eight's away, sir."

"Fire nine."

"Fire nine. Nine's away, sir."

"Fire ten."

"Fire ten. Ten's away, sir."

Tomassi looked back through the scope. The enemy was making the turn Tomassi had anticipated.

After a moment, Soundman Messi reported, "All torpedoes running hot, straight, and normal, sir."

Tomassi watched as the tin fish closed in. The enemy couldn't turn fast enough, and the four torpedoes hit. When the smoke had cleared, the enemy was going down fast.

"We got the bastard," Tomassi exclaimed. Everyone in the con cheered. Bergman took a look for himself and smiled.

"I'm still curious," Tomassi said. "Down scope. Stations for battle surface."

"Stations for battle surface," Osborne repeated.

"What about," Bergman asked.

"I'm sure I've seen her before in one of the manuals," replied Tomassi.

After the sub surfaced, Tomassi had her come about and sail through the wreckage. Lifeboats were already seen heading to Japan. Maybe the enemy thought the Americans would shoot them.

From the bridge, Tomassi looked around in the water. He saw a flag floating to starboard. It was mostly red, with a black cross in the upper left corner, with black and white lines forming an off-center cross like a Scandinavian flag, and a swastika where the lines met toward the hoist. It was a German Battle Flag!

Tomassi pointed, "Look, Bergman. She was a Kraut!"

Bergman looked at the Nazi flag and smiled. He shouted to the men on deck. "Hey! Bring up that Kraut flag. I want to wipe my ass with it!"

Tomassi shot him an angry look. "The hell you will!" He turned to the men on deck. "Bring that flag to engineering and have them hose it down. I'm putting it in my collection."

Later that morning, Tomassi looked through the Confidential Raider Supplement that he'd kept from 1942. He did know that ship from somewhere! He pointed out the silhouette to Bergman as they sat in the wardroom.

"I knew it! She's was a German raider." He looked at the data for the German ship. "She was the freighter *Mittelschloss*. Her British designation was 'Raider FE.'"

"How about that," Bergman said. "I got to kill Germans after all."

"And we took out the last German raider! I'm putting this in the log."

Tomassi went back to his cabin and noted in the log, "08:04 hours. Sunk sixty miles south of Yokohama, German raider 'Fox Easy.' Survivors seen in lifeboats heading back to Japan."

CHAPTER SIXTY-FIVE
4 JULY 1944

The *Tiburon* made her grand entrance into Pearl Harbor that Independence Day with a most unusual flourish.

It wasn't that Old Glory was flying from the top of the number one periscope. Some boats did this instead of putting it on the staff at the back of the conning tower. No, that wasn't it.

It wasn't the battle flag that was stretched between the number two periscope and the radar antenna. It had the name of the boat on top, and a small shark, which was what a tiburon was. The fish had a Japanese ship in its jaws, with little stick figure men jumping overboard. Below that silhouette was a German swastika flag, the civilian version familiar to most people, with its red field and black swastika in a white circle. There were also two Japanese flags, signifying the two tankers the *Tiburon* had sunk during her patrol. There was also a pennant with a red meatball in it on the banner, with three hash marks below it, to signify the trawler and two sampans they had sunk using the deck gun and two 40mm guns. But, no, that wasn't the funny thing.

What caught everyone's eyes was that, below Old Glory, was a German Battle Flag, with its big, ugly, crooked cross just off center. As far as could be ascertained, no U.S. sub had ever sailed into port bearing a swastika flag.

Another thing that was eye catching was the broom lashed to the periscope. Tomassi had made patrols where he had sunk every enemy he had engaged. But he'd always neglected to show it off. But, when the *Tiburon* was still at Mare Island, he did finally manage to procure a broom, just for this purpose.

The *Tiburon* made her way to the dock at the sub yard. Admiral Lockhart was there, as usual, to greet a man who was quickly becoming a favorite. He came aboard and shook hands with Tomassi.

"Hi, Dom. I see you gave your boat a good maiden patrol."

"Yes, sir, and thanks."

Lockhart pointed up to the periscope. "How the hell did you manage to get that flag on there?"

"Well, sir, I had them raise to scope a couple of feet and put the Kraut flag on. Then, I slipped on Old Glory above that other flag. Then, they raised it up all the way, so everyone could see."

Lockhart looked at Tomassi for a moment, and then said, "I kind of figured that, Dom. I mean, how the hell did you get that Kraut flag?"

Tomassi laughed, "Oh! Well, we got ourselves a German raider. I looked in the Raider Supplement." Tomassi brought out the page he'd torn from the book out of his shirt pocket. He pointed to the silhouette he'd circled, third from the bottom. "She was raider 'Fox Easy,' the *Mittelschloss*. I had the exec confirm it."

Lockhart turned to Bergman. "Is this true, Commander Bergman?"

"Aye, sir," Bergman replied. "I was happy to confirm it."

Lockhart smiled. "Well, now, Dom. You keep finding a way to surprise me." He handed back the paper to Tomassi. "Maybe I can write you up for a star for your Navy Cross."

Tomassi smiled again. "Oh, Admiral, I'm gonna blush, you talk so nicely about me."

CHAPTER SIXTY-SIX
16 AUGUST 1944

For Tomassi, this patrol had been a bust. Not a glorious string of sinkings as he would have wanted. They had been sent to the "Maru Morgue," the name for the patrol of the Ryuku Islands. For their trouble, they sighted many frigates, and got some depth charges. The war had raged on, of course, and Tomassi had gotten the word from Sparks on the 11th. "Bridge, radio room."

"Captain, aye."

"Urgent incoming message. Captain's ears only."

"OK, Sparks. On my way."

When Tomassi got there, Troilo handed over the first part of the message he had decoded. Tomassi read it out, then thought out loud. "I hope the hunting's better at Saipan. That's where we're going."

Troilo then said, "Not to hunt, sir."

"What?"

Troilo then handed Tomassi the second part of the message. Tomassi read it. He smiled. "We have a base there now! I heard we we're invading it. But now I guess it's secure. Well, thanks Sparks."

Troilo smiled, "My pleasure, sir."

Now, the *Tiburon* was at Saipan, and pulled into the lagoon near the west coast village of Garapan. They had been told to moor alongside the new tender

U.S.S. *Neptune*. When they got there, the gangplank came down, and none other than Admiral Lockhart stepped down onto the sub.

"Permission to come aboard," the admiral asked.

A flabbergasted Tomassi said, "Permission granted, sir."

"Well, Dom, what do you think of this setup?"

Tomassi looked around. Besides the tender, there were other subs, plus patrol craft of various sizes moving in and around the lagoon. Aircraft took off from airfields south and east of the village.

"Most impressive, sir," Tomassi said.

"Well, I have an office here aboard the *Neptune*. I'd like you to report right away, as soon as your boat is secure."

"Aye, aye, sir."

Half an hour later, Tomassi had gone into Admiral Lockhart's office aboard the *Neptune*. He reported in, and Lockhart returned his salute. "Have a seat, Dom."

"Thank you, sir."

After Tomassi was comfortable, Lockhart began. "Dom, the Japs are beginning to move their prisoners of war from Southeast Asia to the Japanese home islands. There are some Americans, but it's mostly British, Dutch, and Australians. What matters to us is that they are being moved by freighter. We've picked up some intelligence on this, as well as picked up survivors from some of these ships. They call them 'hell ships.' Hundreds of men crammed into the holds of the ships, with no food or water for days.

"What is of concern to you, and other sub captains, is that you'll be in a position to rescue them when and if you torpedo the ships they are on. Therefore, starting with your next patrol, and until further notice, you'll have to stand by and search for survivors when you sink a Jap freighter. If you can come up right away, that's fine. If you have to sit for eight hours while being depth charged, you'll do that too. What matters is that our boys get rescued."

"Understood, sir," Tomassi said.

"Also, Dom," Lockhart continued, "you're not going back to Pearl after this patrol. You'll be here, in Saipan. Your boat will be based here, and you'll report to the commander of Submarine Division 55. He's Captain Hartman. I'll take you over in a little while."

"Oh. Nice," Tomassi said. "Well, join the Navy and see the world, right, sir?"

Lockhart smiled, "That's right, Dom. I'd never been to Saipan until this trip. Well, let's go see Hartman." As the two men got up, Lockhart hastened to add, "Oh, Dom, Happy Birthday."

Tomassi smiled, "Thank you, Admiral."

CHAPTER SIXTY-SEVEN
6 SEPTEMBER 1944

The *Tiburon* found herself back in the "Maru Morgue" area, patrolling off the southern end of the Ryuku Islands, near Okinawa. This time, the action came thick and fast.

Radar watch had picked up a convoy coming in from the southwest. It had four merchantmen and three escorts. Tiburon was in a perfect position to intercept it. Tomassi turned the boat southwest to hit them head on at 17:40. By 18:25, they had visual contact. Battle stations, torpedo, were manned.

Some unexpected help came at this point. Radar had picked up another contact due south. Thanks to IFF (Identification, Friend or Foe) signals, the blip was found to be another American sub, their old friend *Garlopa*. Tomassi had a quick chat with *Garlopa*, and it was decided that she would hit the convoy from the rear, while Tiburon struck from ahead.

Tomassi and Bergman stood on the bridge. Tomassi said, "Remember, we also have to check for survivors. I'm thinking of taking out at least one of the *marus*, then we'll deal with an escort, just to give us some time. Maybe the others will turn and run. *Garlopa* can take a bite out of them. Then we can look for the prisoners."

"Understood, sir," Bergman replied.

Tomassi got on the squawk box. "Mr. Leighton, we've got multiple targets. We'll give them to you pretty fast."

"Aye, sir," Leighton replied.

The officers looked through their binoculars, and sighted the frigate in the lead, with two pairs of freighters behind him on either quarter. "We'll take on the freighter to our port, then the frigate," Tomassi said into the squawk box. "Shifting to TBT, bearing coming down." Tomassi pointed at the TBT, and Bergman got on it. After Bergman had pressed the button, Tomassi continued, "Angle on the bow, five port. Gyro angle ten left, set torpedoes to eleven feet. Open outer doors on tubes one and two. Commence firing when set."

"Aye, sir," said Leighton.

"OK, Leighton, shifting targets. Frigate, angle on the bow, five right. Set torpedoes to five feet. Gyro angle ten right, open outer doors on tubes three and four. Bearing coming down on the TBT." Tomassi pointed to Bergman, who swung the large binoculars over, and pressed the button to send the bearing and range down into the con. "Commence firing when set," Tomassi added.

Silence from the other end.

"Mr. Leighton, acknowledge."

"Uh, aye, sir. Tracking second target. Set for first target," Leighton replied. This was followed by the swooshing sound of torpedoes being fired.

Osborne, on the talker watch, reported, "Tubes one and two fired, sir. Sound reports them running hot, straight, and normal."

Just after this, an explosion was heard, and smoke and fire seen aft of the freighters. Bergman said, "I guess the *Garlopa* started shooting."

"I think so. I hope they're getting one of the frigates."

Osborne came on again. "Torpedoes three and four fired, sir. Sound reports them running hot, straight, and normal."

"Very well," Tomassi replied.

The frigate in front of the *Tiburon* started to speed up, and her forward gun mount was turning towards the sub. At this point, the first torpedoes were hitting the freighter. She stopped dead. Tomassi smiled and scratched his whiskers. Just after this, the frigate was hit by torpedoes three and four. Hew bow flew into the air, and the rest of her sailed right down for the deep six at full speed.

This would clear the way for Tomassi to shoot at the other lead freighter. "Helm, right ten degrees rudder. Come right to course two-zero-zero."

Chastain at the helm replied, "Helm, right ten degrees rudder. Coming right to course two-zero-zero, sir."

"Very well. Mr. Leighton, stand by for new target."

"Aye, sir." Leighton didn't sound so sure of himself.

Another explosion and more smoke could be seen in the distance. *Garlopa* was hitting the jackpot, also.

"Steady on new course, sir," Chastain reported.

"Very well. Mr. Leighton, new target. Bearing coming down on the TBT." Bergman pressed the button. Tomassi then spoke, "Gyro angle fifteen left, angle on the bow twenty starboard. Set torpedoes to twelve feet. Open outer doors on tubes five and six. Commence firing when set."

Silence for a moment, then Leighton said, "Aye, sir."

More explosions from the distance. I hope they save me this one, Tomassi thought.

Osborne reported, "Torpedoes five and six away, sir. Sound reports them running hot, straight, and normal."

"Very well." Some twenty seconds later, the target was hit amidships. She stopped dead in the water and listed to starboard. Tomassi did a sweep with his binoculars. There was one freighter untouched, sailing off to Tomassi's right. There were three columns of smoke where the *Garlopa* had struck. "Reload all bow tubes. Helm, all ahead flank."

"Helm, all ahead flank, sir," Chastain replied.

"Helm, right full rudder. Come right to course two-three-five."

"Helm, right full rudder, coming right to course two-three-five, sir."

"Very well."

The sub chased down the fleeing Japanese ship and, with four torpedoes, put an end to her. Tomassi then turned the boat around, back in the direction of *Garlopa*. After a couple minutes of sailing, the lookouts reported people in the water.

Tomassi had drilled the men for this situation. He called for rescue parties to come on deck. "Remember," he called to them, "If you see a Jap, leave him. We only want the whites."

The rescue partied didn't see any Japanese. They did pick up white men who were covered with black oil. They were practically skeletons with flesh on them. The men stripped the survivors of their dirty uniforms and passed them below. The new Pharmacist's Mate, Huffman, was in charge of treating their wounds, and giving them water. They got their water from soaked cloths, a bit at a time. They were put in the after torpedo room, as well as the officer's quarters. They had identified themselves as Australians.

The *Garlopa* had called the *Tiburon* and reported they had picked up sixty-four men. *Tiburon* replied they had picked up some seventy-five men. Tomassi then told Troilo to call back to Saipan, and get at least another boat to the area, immediately.

The good news was how many lives they had saved, plus the fact that the whole convoy, freighters and escorts, had been obliterated. The bad news was that two submarines weren't enough to pick up all the men in the water. A sub with eighty men on it to start just couldn't handle all the survivors.

Later that evening, Tomassi went aft to have a chat with one of the survivors. The man was lying in an empty torpedo rack. He was now clean, except for some ringworm on his face and neck. He also had salt water sores on his body, and chapped lips. What hair he had left was a sandy blond color.

The man tried to sit up. Tomassi put a hand on his shoulder. "No, stay as you are, mate."

"Thank you, sir." The man didn't have much of a voice left.

"So, where you from?"

"Fremantle, sir."

"Really? I was in Fremantle for about ten months with my last boat."

"Really, sir? Well, how about that?"

"How are you feeling?"

"Better than ever, sir."

"What's your name?"

"Private John Stanley, sir."

"I'm Commander Dominic Tomassi. Whaddaya say?" He held out his hand. Stanley shook it.

"I want to thank you, sir, on behalf of my mates, for rescuing us from those bloody Nips."

"Our pleasure. I've never been able to ask this, but what was it like getting torpedoed?"

"Oh. It was bloody madness, sir. The Nips had us in that stinking hold from when we left Singapore. Those torpedoes made an awful racket, and the Japs ran about like crazy trying to save their own arses. I had to use all my strength to get a hatch open and get

354

on deck. The mates followed me, and we got into the water. The Japs were shooting at us, sir. They were bloody mad. I managed to get most of the lads out." Stanley went silent for a moment. A tear ran down his cheek. "I couldn't get them all out."

"Rest easy, Stanley. We'll be in Saipan in a few days. They'll fix you up and get you home."

"Thanks ever so, sir." Stanley held out his hand, and Tomassi shook it.

CHAPTER SIXTY-EIGHT
5 NOVEMBER 1944

After dropping off the Australians, Tomassi put to sea again right away. During September and October, the *Tiburon* patrolled the "Maru Morgue" again. She managed to sink two tankers and two sampans.

On this early November day, Tomassi had gotten the boat back to Saipan and expected to get some rest. Instead, he was called to a conference with Captain Hartman, Commander Submarine Division 55, and the commanders of the other boats.

He got to the wardroom of the *Neptune* just before 09:00. Hartman was already there, with a map on an easel covered with a cloth. Hartman looked up from the papers he was working on. "Hi, Dom."

"Hi, Jim," Tomassi replied. Hartman was the first superior he'd ever had who would insist on being on a first name basis with his men. Hartman himself was nearly fifty years old, about six feet in height, with prematurely gray hair. He had a fair complexion, and blue eyes.

"You might as well have some coffee, Dom."

"OK. I'm early, then?"

Hartman looked at his watch. "A little."

The hatch opened and three other officers, all commanders, stepped in. "Ah, gentlemen, come on in," Hartman said. "I don't think you know each other, do you?"

Tomassi replied, "No, sir. I'm not good with names anyway, so who knows, maybe I did meet them."

Hartman smiled as he got up, "Well, anyway–" he pointed to each man in turn "– this is Bill Christian of the *Garlopa*."

Tomassi shook his hand. "Well, I finally get to meet you." He turned to Hartman. "His boat came to my rescue when I was on the *Sea Otter*."

Christian smiled, "It was a pleasure, and with this last job, too."

Hartman then pointed to the next man, "This is Harold Mendel, of the *Whitefish*."

Tomassi offered his hand, "Hi, Harold. Dom Tomassi. Whaddaya say?"

"Hi ya, Dom. Pleasure."

Hartman finished by saying, "And this is John Cannon of the *Ono*."

"Ah, Cannon. We meet again."

"Yes, Professor Moriarty. We meet again." Cannon and Tomassi didn't shake hands.

"I take it you don't get along," Hartman asked.

"Oh, not since the academy, sir," Cannon replied.

Hartman frowned, "Well, get over it. This is a big job I need you men for." He motioned for the men to sit. When they did, he uncovered the map and told them, "Gentlemen, the Third Fleet is preparing to make a strike against the Japanese mainland. This will be the first carrier air raid on the home islands since Doolittle." The men smiled and looked at each other.

Hartman continued, "The problem is the same one that Doolittle encountered; the one that made him launch early. It's also a problem each of you has had to deal with. It's the Japanese picket boat line." He pointed on the map to a sector of ocean southeast of Kyushu. "The carrier task forces are to come through this sector to make the strike. The Japs would get suspicious if airstrikes or destroyer sweeps were to take out the pickets. We all know there are survivors to every massacre. It's likely that one of those pickets would get to word out, and the carriers would have to fight for their lives with the element of surprise lost.

"What we have planned, instead, is for submarines to attack the pickets. The Japs are used to having subs sink the pickets. We think they wouldn't catch on so fast if you were to do a sweep. Questions so far?"

Tomassi spoke up. "Are we sure four subs would be enough?"

"Actually, there will be another four subs on your right flank, doing the same job as a diversion. If we keep them guessing, and blind, the fleet can get through," Hartman answered.

Cannon now asked, "Whose brainstorm was this, anyway?"

Hartman glared at Cannon and answered, "Admiral Lockhart."

"Oh." Cannon shrank in his seat. Tomassi couldn't help but laugh, prompting Cannon to snap back, "We all know you're his fair-haired boy, Tomassi. Or, should I say, fair-haired dago."

Tomassi had been sipping his coffee. He lowered his cup and shot a glare at Cannon. "I told you before, Cannon, you'd better smile when you say that!"

"At ease, both of you," Hartman snapped. "Whatever problem you two have, save it for another time."

"Oh, no problem, Jim," Tomassi said, "We're one big, happy family."

"All right. You'd better be able to get along. I've checked on who has the seniority among you four. It looks like Dom has, so he's the one to lead this wolf pack."

Cannon rolled his eyes. "We're doomed."

Hartman snapped again, "Enough, John! You don't like it, too damn bad. You're not weaseling out of this. I can't spare another sub for this mission. Work it out between you." He left the compartment.

Tomassi turned to Christian, "So, Bill Christian?"

"Yeah."

"You related to the admiral?"

"He's my father."

Tomassi chuckled, "I'm sorry to hear that."

"I know he didn't have a high opinion of you, but I do."

Cannon laughed, "Your dad is a good judge of character."

Tomassi looked at Christian. "I'm keeping your boat close to mine." He then pointed at Cannon. "And his boat on the other flank!"

"Great," Cannon replied, "It'll keep me upwind of you."

Tomassi bit his thumb at Cannon.

"I hope the Japs get you, dago!"

"The feeling's mutual!"

CHAPTER SIXTY-NINE
15 NOVEMBER 1944

"Dom's Devastators." That was the name of the pack Tomassi had taken out of Saipan on the 10th. He put his boat, *Tiburon*, on the right flank. To his left, he put the *Garlopa*. To the left of her, he put the *Whitefish*. On the left flank, closest to Kyushu, he put his academy nemesis, John Cannon, in the *Ono*.

The subs were spaced out some six miles apart. They would be on station until after Thanksgiving. The airstrike they were supposed to be making way for had been cancelled. But this operation would go on anyway, just to see about its feasibility.

Tomassi had just finished pointing out to Bergman the relative positions of the rest of the wolf pack. Bergman asked, "What was the problem with Cannon?"

"Cannon? Oh, he's your garden variety bigot. If you were anything he could pick on, he would. He didn't like damn near anyone. He probably wouldn't like you."

"What if I called him a Nazi?"

Tomassi grinned, "He'd try to take a piece out of you."

Radarman Sheffield spoke up, "Sir, I have a contact bearing zero-four-zero relative. It's kind of small."

Tomassi and Bergman climbed up from the control room. "What's the range," Tomassi asked.

"I make it out to be seven thousand yards, sir."

"All right. Helm, right ten degrees rudder, come right to course three-five-five."

Chastain replied, "Helm, right ten degrees rudder, coming right to course three-five-five, sir."

"Very well. Battle stations, surface."

Osborne repeated, "Battle stations, surface."

As the Bells of St. Mary's rang, Tomassi and Bergman got their helmets and life vests and headed up to the bridge. They were hit in the face with sea spray. The sub was rolling in a heavy sea. Normally, they would go under and ride that kind of thing out. But their job was to engage the sampans on the picket line. So, literally, come hell or high water, they would ride it out.

The gunners on the 5 incher had to strap themselves in. Waves broke over the boat, but the lookouts didn't let it stop them. One called out, "Small vessel, dead ahead." The officers looked in their binoculars. A three-masted sampan was there, and he very likely had seen the sub.

"Helm, all ahead full."

"Helm, all ahead full, aye."

"Very well." The sampan slowly started to turn away. Tomassi would use the superior speed of the submarine's four diesels to close the gap. Both hunter and hunted bobbed up and down in the rough swells. The ammo passers had to fight to stay upright on the pitching deck.

The range finally closed to within four thousand yards, and Tomassi ordered, "Commence firing." The 5 inch gun let loose. As they got closer, the 40mm guns joined in. Within minutes, the sampan was hit. Her sails were shredded, and what looked like an antenna was blasted away. The sea managed to calm down for a minute, so that the sub could see their target was still afloat, but not for long.

"We're getting close, sir," Bergman said. "Do you think there might be code books on that boat?"

"I don't see why not," Tomassi replied. "Why?"

"Request permission to take a boarding party and look."

Tomassi looked at Bergman as if he were crazy. But Bergman had a pleading look, as if he were a kid wanting to play a new game.

"Oh, all right. But don't go getting killed, OK?"

Bergman smiled, "Aye, sir!"

Tomassi grabbed his megaphone and called, "Cease fire!" The guns stopped firing as the sub got closer to the boat. One or two Japanese were on deck, firing pistols at the sub. A burst from a .50-caliber took care of them.

Bergman had gathered volunteers from below. Even Hawkins, the cook, came along. Only Bergman and Chief Watkins carried the Tommy Guns. The other men had pistols.

Tomassi asked for a carbine and determined to keep watch while his men were on the enemy boat. The engines were stopped as they came alongside, and with Bergman's men on deck, Tomassi gave the order that harkened back to the days of sail.

"Away boarders!"

Bergman and his party jumped over to the sampan and started to go below. Tomassi heard shooting from the Tommy Guns. A Japanese sailor ran out on deck, and Tomassi took aim. He cut loose with the carbine, emptying the clip into the enemy. Just as the last round came out, the Japanese sailor hit the deck, groaning. Tomassi threw the carbine at him, then ran to one of the .50-caliber guns, and fired it. That killed the bad guy.

A few minutes later, Bergman came out of the pilothouse. He waved a codebook and said, "I've got it, sir."

Tomassi grabbed his megaphone again and called, "Does she look like she's sinking?"

"No, sir. We didn't hit her right."

"Is everyone dead below?"

"Yes, sir."

"Did you make sure?"

Hawkins replied with a grin, "I did, sir."

"Good man, Hawkins." Tomassi thought for a moment, then called on the squawk box, "Bring up one of the scuttling charges. We'll use it on the sampan."

A minute later, one of the blocks on TNT was brought up. "Pass it over to Mr. Bergman," Tomassi ordered. He then got back on his megaphone, "Set that thing for two minutes and get the hell back here!"

"Aye, sir."

Bergman handed the charge to Watkins, who went below with it. He came back up a few seconds later. With that, the boarding party jumped back onto the Tiburon. Tomassi ordered, "Helm, all astern full."

The sub back away for a minute, then made a turn to port, and full speed ahead. As she took her new course, the charge on the sampan went off like the Fourth of July.

"I hope the other boats can do that," Tomassi said. Then he ordered, "Secure from battle stations."

CHAPTER SEVENTY
30 NOVEMBER 1944

The *Tiburon* made it into port behind the *Garlopa* and the *Whitefish*. No one had heard from the *Ono* since the 17th, when she reported sinking a sampan, then was diving to evade a destroyer. The grand total for "Dom's Devastators" was four Japanese sampans sunk, and one American sub "overdue, presumed lost."

For himself, Tomassi had little to be proud of. Even though he and John Cannon had no love lost between them, losing a sub under his command made Tomassi feel low. The fact that Admiral Lockhart's aide met him as they pulled up alongside the *Neptune* didn't make him feel any better. He was sure he would end up being busted for it. He thought he'd probably sit out the war in some recruiting station in Kansas, or something like it.

The aide led Tomassi and Bergman up into the admiral's office aboard the tender. Tomassi turned to Bergman, and said, "I bet it'll be some recruiting station for me."

"Oh, bull, sir. Don't think the worst."

The aide knocked on the admiral's door. "Enter," came the voice from within.

"Commanders Tomassi and Bergman, sir," the aide said as he opened the door.

"Show them in."

The two sub officers went in. As they saluted, Tomassi said, "Admiral, Commander Tomassi and Lt. Commander Bergman of the *Tiburon* reporting."

Lockhart told them, "Stand at ease."

"Thank you, sir."

"Relax, Dom."

"I don't understand, sir."

"You think I'm here to chew you out."

"Well, sir, I was expecting to be greeted by Captain Hartman."

"Hartman is dead."

Tomassi gasped, "What?"

Lockhart continued, "He had a heart attack the day after you shoved off. His exec was running things while you and your wolf pack were out. He's too green, though. Can't handle it."

"Oh. All right, sir."

Lockhart opened a drawer to his right. As he reached into it, he said, "He would need a good, qualified man above him to guide him." The admiral put two manila envelopes on his desk, in front of the two officers. "Plus, you need a break from sea duty. Two years, command of three boats, and a lot of frayed nerves. This operation could have gone completely haywire with anyone in charge. Cannon got himself killed, presumably, because he got careless. That could have happened even if I led the wolf pack.

"Besides, this type of operation had never been tried. It's likely, due to the attention you drew, and all the depth charges your boats had to endure, that we may never try it again. Now, go ahead and open the envelopes."

Tomassi reached for the envelope in front of him. As he opened it, he could hear Bergman tear into his. As Bergman's envelope came open, he grabbed two silver oak leaf clusters. He smiled as he held them up.

"All right, Bergman! Good show," Tomassi said. As he opened his envelope, his found in his hand a pair of silver eagles.

Bergman now smiled. "Captain! Congratulations, Dom."

"Now it's Dom?"

"Sure. And you can call me 'Myron.'"

The two men smiled as the shook hands. They dropped their orders on the deck. Lockhart spoke up. "OK, Dom. Starting tomorrow, you'll be in command of Submarine Division 55. Congratulations, and to you, Commander Bergman."

They both looked at the admiral and said, "Thank you, sir!"

CHAPTER SEVENTY-ONE
1 DECEMBER 1944

"From, Commander, Submarines Pacific, to, Captain Dominic Tomassi, USN. Subject, relief of command. You are ordered as of 1 December, 1944, to relinquish command of the U.S.S. *Tiburon* to Commander Myron Bergman and immediately assume command of Submarine Division 55, with your flag aboard U.S.S. *Neptune* at Saipan. Signed, C.A. Lockhart, Vice Admiral, USN." Tomassi folded up his orders and faced Bergman.

Bergman saluted and said, "I relieve you, Captain."

Tomassi returned the salute and said, "I stand relieved." He then turned to the crew assembled on the foredeck. "Well, I leave you men in very good hands. You all know I wouldn't trade you, willingly, for anything. Any command I get from here on will pale compared to the time I spent with you, both on the *Sea Otter*, and here on the *Tiburon*." He stood for a moment, then said, "I'll look forward to seeing you guys coming into this harbor, with that broom lashed to the periscope every time. Understood?"

The men laughed and nodded, and Bergman said, "Aye, aye, sir."

"This goodbye isn't permanent. Any boat that is based here comes under my command, as division leader. Mostly, that means I'll be getting you supplies, ammo, new men. All that good stuff. If there are special orders, they'll come from the admiral through me. I'll make sure you guys get the really fun ones." More laughs from the men.

"Does the captain wish to give one final inspection to the ship's company," Bergman asked.

"Yes."

Tomassi turned first to Bergman, shaking his hand and saying, "Well, I'll see you whenever you come back to port."

"Aye, sir. Maybe we can have a drink at the officers' club."

"Yeah."

Tomassi next went to the newly minted exec, Lt. Commander Leighton. "See you around, Leighton."

"See you later, sir."

Tomassi then went over to Chief Watkins. "See you, Chief."

Watkins shook Tomassi's hand. "So long, sir. We'll look forward to those fun orders."

"Sure, Chief." He then went to Chief Engineman's Mate Rampone. "So long, Chief."

"So long, Captain."

"Keep those diesels running."

"One hundred percent, sir."

The next man Tomassi spoke to was Troilo. "So long, Sparks."

"So long, sir. Been a pleasure."

"Thanks."

Tomassi next talked to Hawkins, the cook. "See you, Hawkins."

"Good bye, sir."

"Next time you make applejack, save me a glass."

Hawkins smiled, "You've got it, sir."

"Was it worth losing your liberty that time?"

"Yes, sir."

Tomassi shook hands with each man, all seventy-nine of the ship's company. He then went to the gangplank, and turning around once more, said, "*Arrivederci.*"

CHAPTER SEVENTY-TWO
17 JULY 1945

Captain Dominic Tomassi was going nuts. The eight months he spent as Commander, Submarine Division 55, were limited to the tender *Neptune* and the island of Saipan. With his rank, in the submarine service, he could only go on patrol if there something really big going on; something that would require him to coordinate several subs.

But, that sort of operation belonged to times past. The big invasions of this war, that had required such things, looked less and less likely to happen again. It hadn't been needed at Iwo Jima, or at Okinawa. The fight for Okinawa raged on while Tomassi sent out boats to hunt for less and less Japanese shipping.

If he were a surface sailor, he could have gotten a cruiser, a transport, a battleship, or even a carrier. But, no, I had to be a submariner, he thought. So, here I am. I'm stuck in this office, with only a porthole to see out of, not a periscope.

He got to watch the boats go out, and watch them come back, with more added to their battle flags. More ships sunk, more sampans sunk, more fliers rescued. The *Garlopa* had managed to pick up two entire B-29 crews last week, and safely bring them back to Saipan to rejoin their buddies. The *Dugong II* picked up seven Navy fliers from one carrier. All

Tomassi got to do was congratulate them and get them more fuel for their next lifeguard mission.

The *Tiburon* also managed to pick up some fliers. They had provided lifeguard support for the airstrike of the Third Fleet on Osaka. Bergman and his men saved an amazing number of fifteen aviators.

That was four weeks ago, and after they came back, they went right out again. Today, the *Tiburon* would come back again. Tomassi went on deck and looked through his binoculars. She was there, flying her battle flag from the periscope shears, as always. Soon, she was close enough for Tomassi to make out that she'd sunk another merchantman, and another sampan. She'd also made another rescue of a flier. Lucky them, he thought. At least for them, the scenery changed a bit.

Half an hour later, Tomassi was back at his desk. Someone knocked on his door. "Enter," he said.

The door opened. It was his new exec, Commander Mathers. "Commander Bergman is here, sir."

"Show him in."

Mathers stepped aside, Bergman came in, and Mathers closed the door. Bergman saluted. "Sir, Commander Bergman of the *Tiburon* reporting."

Tomassi got up. "At ease, Myron. Welcome back." They shook hands.

"Thanks, Dom. Got a smoke?"

Tomassi opened his box of cigars and Bergman took one. Bergman got out his lighter and lit up the smoke.

"Had a good patrol?"

"Yes, Dom. Got a tanker, some 6,000 tons. Also, we sank a sampan with gunfire, and rescued a Navy flier near the Bungo Straits."

"Good job." Tomassi sat back behind his desk and sighed.

Bergman pulled up a chair and sat opposite him. "Something wrong?"

"Hmm? Well … I guess I'm just jealous. You get to have the adventure out there, and I get to fill out requisitions. The most pressing problem I had after you went out this last time was getting more toilet paper for the *Needlefish*. Do you believe that?"

"My most pressing problem was dodging a Jap tin can in a hundred feet of water last Monday."

"See? I'd gladly trade you. I miss the action."

"Not to change the subject, Dom, but what happened to your last exec? And also, that redheaded yeoman that was out there in the front office? She was really hot stuff."

"They're both dead."

Bergman nearly dropped his cigar. "What?"

"Well, they'd gone up into the hills to do some sightseeing. Strictly platonic, of course." Tomassi winked.

"Of course."

"Well, when they didn't come back, I asked the Marines to find them. Turns out, there were some

Jap stragglers in the hills. They found the bodies. She'd been raped, and they'd both been shot."

"Damn!"

"So, after they brought the bodies back, the Marines went after the Japs. They came back a week later and presented me with seven severed Jap heads. They told me one of them was a lieutenant, and the rest were enlisted men."

Bergman shook his head, "Wow. And you complain about no action?"

"I mean out there." Tomassi pointed out the porthole. "I wish I were back out there. I've dated all the Army nurses, and the Navy ones are all frigid. I've run up a big tab at the officers' club. I'm getting stir crazy on this damn tender."

"What do you want, Dom?"

"I want to come with you on your next patrol. I'll send you someplace where there's bound to be shipping. Maybe Nagasaki. I'm sure I can get away with it. Like the time Admiral Lockhart hitched a ride."

"When was that?"

"Oh, in early '43. He got on one of the outbound subs, and it was a day before the skipper realized he was there!" Tomassi laughed. "He got off at Midway, though, and took a plane back to Pearl."

Bergman leaned back and took a drag from his cigar. He then said, "You're welcome anytime, Dom."

CHAPTER SEVENTY-THREE
9 AUGUST 1945

How great not to have to shave every day. What a strange thing to think, but it's what Tomassi was thinking. Every day he spent in his office on the tender, he'd have to shave. But, since putting to sea back on July 31st, he didn't shave.

Sure, it was a little cramped in the *Tiburon*. The extra body, his, meant having to double up with Lt. Jablonski. But it was OK. Tomassi felt alive again back at sea. He'd gotten Bergman the patrol area he said he would. Nagasaki still had some life to it, even at this late stage in the war. Shipping was coming in from Korea, and Bergman had sunk a freighter on the 6th. Also, on the 6th, they had gotten word of an air raid on Hiroshima. The town was totally destroyed. The strange part was that the total destruction came, not from a whole group of B-29's, but from one plane, carrying one bomb.

On this morning, before diving the boat, Sparks relayed a message from headquarters. "Bridge, radio room."

Bergman answered, "Bridge, aye."

"Sir, we've got a report that the Russians have declared war on Japan and have launched an invasion of Manchuria."

Bergman and Tomassi looked at each other and shrugged. "Very well, Sparks. Thanks," Bergman answered. He took his finger off the button, and said to Tomassi, "What do you think, Dom?"

Tomassi scratched his whiskers and said, "Well, I guess the Japs will try to evacuate Korea if the Russians are coming. That means more for you to sink, and for me to 'observe.'"

"Yes. How do you like what you've been observing, Dom?"

"I'm so glad," Tomassi smiled, "that you got this boat. Nothing could make me happier than to see our crew still running so well."

"Thanks, Dom."

With that, the lookouts were ordered below, and the boat dived. That was at about 06:30. As the morning progressed, the *Tiburon* proceeded on to Nagasaki harbor. She cruised in from the East China Sea, passing Takashima Island. She kept on silent running to evade the patrol craft that they came across.

They proceeded between Iojima and Koyagi Islands, then along the northern side of Koyagi, heading northeast. The fact that the fans were turned off made this creeping along unbearable. Everyone had a soaked shirt.

Tomassi looked over at Lt. Commander Leighton. He recalled in the reports Bergman made that he didn't think Leighton was really fit for combat. He was slow in his reactions, and if something should happen to Bergman, he might not know how to handle himself. Well, Tomassi thought, it looked like the war would be over soon. Hopefully, there wouldn't be a problem.

"Helm, what's our course," Bergman asked.

Chastain answered, "Course zero-five-zero, sir."

"Sound, do you have anything?"

Soundman Messi did a sweep, and answered, "Some faint screws in the distance, bearing three-five-five relative."

"All right," Bergman said. "Up scope." The periscope was raised, and Bergman began to look in the direction of Nagasaki.

Tomassi glanced at his watch. It was two minutes past eleven. Suddenly, Bergman screamed in terror and pain. He fell to the deck, clutching his right eye. Tomassi rushed up to him. "What is it?"

"Sudden flash! Brightest light I ever saw! Oh, God, I'm blind!"

Tomassi thought that maybe a destroyer had shined a light at the scope, and blinded Bergman with it. But it's late morning. No tin can would have a searchlight going now. What was it? Tomassi rushed up to the periscope and looked.

A giant cloud, shaped like a mushroom, was forming in Tomassi's line of sight. It looked like Nagasaki was going to disappear into this cloud. He slowly backed away from the periscope and muttered, "Oh, Lord."

Leighton stepped up. "What is it, Captain?"

Tomassi stepped back and pointed. Leighton looked into the scope and opened his mouth in disbelief. "What in the world is that, sir?"

"You remember that message the other day? The one about Hiroshima?"

"Yes, sir."

"That must be what happened just now."

Bergman was rolling on the deck, moaning and clutching his eye. Tomassi looked at him, then at Leighton. Leighton just stood there, staring. Tomassi couldn't just let him do that.

"Mr. Leighton!"

Leighton looked up. "Sir?"

Tomassi looked at him for a moment, then when Leighton did nothing, dashed to the squawk box. "Pharmacist's Mate to the conning tower, on the double." He turned to Leighton and said, "Come on, boy! What do you do?"

Leighton froze.

"Sir, high speed screws bearing three-five-zero, relative. Sounds like a destroyer," Messi said.

Tomassi looked at Leighton. The young commander stood there, scared and motionless. The periscope was still up.

"Down scope," Tomassi yelled. Lieutenant Prince, the OOD, pushed the handles up and lowered the periscope. Tomassi then went to the hatch leading below. At this point, Pharmacist's Mate Huffman came up. "Doc, take Mr. Bergman below and check his eye. He saw a blinding flash."

"Aye, sir," Huffman said before he took Bergman below.

Tomassi then called down to the control room. "Mr. Jablonski, take her down to eighty feet."

"Eighty feet, aye."

"Helm, right full rudder, come right to course one-seven-zero."

"Helm, right full rudder, coming right to course one-seven-zero, sir," Chastain answered.

"Very well."

All this time, Leighton stood like a statue. Tomassi could only shake his head.

Everyone looked up nervously as the Japanese destroyer passed over. Hopefully she wasn't listening. She probably was, since other subs had penetrated Nagasaki harbor before. It seemed she was going so slowly. No one could even dare to speak, lest someone on the tin can hear them and start a depth charging.

After about five minutes of this, the enemy was gone. He'd turned back into the harbor. No doubt they, too, were amazed at the sight that had greeted Tomassi, Bergman, and Leighton in the periscope.

When it seemed the Japanese destroyer was finally gone, Tomassi turned to the talker, Osborne, and said, "Secure from silent running."

"Secure from silent running," Osborne repeated.

"Who's the OOD?"

Lieutenant Prince spoke up, "I am, sir. Lieutenant Prince."

"Mr. Prince, you have the con." Tomassi turned to Leighton and wiggled his finger, saying, "Come with me, Mr. Leighton."

Tomassi and Leighton went below, then up the passage to the wardroom. After they entered it, Tomassi turned and said, "What the hell is wrong with you? You commander goes down with an injury, sound reports an enemy ship approaching, and you stand there with your thumb up your ass! I want to know what's wrong with you."

Leighton shot back, "I didn't want this! I shouldn't have listened to everyone. I didn't think that fast, and I don't belong."

"Well, you're here anyway. Plus, you're the son of a Medal of Honor winner. People expect something more from you."

"I don't care what they think, sir."

"You'd damn well better, mister. The lives of eighty men depend on you. Who knows if Mr. Bergman can resume his duties? He might be hurt enough to require you to take the boat home. But, to do that, you have to keep that boat, and all of us, in one piece."

The cook, Hawkins, entered at this point to look at the coffee machine.

Tomassi continued, "You've got to pull yourself together, mister. We need you to –"

"Fuck you," Leighton yelled. Then he slapped Tomassi.

Tomassi and Hawkins stood there in disbelief. Tomassi contemplated taking a swing at Leighton for this, and clenched his fist, but thought the better of it. He turned to Hawkins. "Hawkins, did you see and hear what just happened?"

"Yes I did, sir," Hawkins nodded.

Tomassi took in a breath, then said, "Hawkins, I want you to fetch Chief Watkins, then when you've got him here, stand by."

"Aye, sir," Hawkins said before leaving the compartment.

"Mister, do you realize what you just did?"

Leighton nodded, "Yes, sir. I don't care. I've had enough. I want to get out of the sub service. I am just not cut out for this."

"You couldn't just ask for a transfer, could you? You went and struck a superior officer, and in front of an enlisted man, to boot. Not only would that get you out of subs, but into the brig. Is that what you want?"

"That's what I've got, sir."

"You're damn right."

At this point, Chief Watkins entered the compartment, with Hawkins behind him. "You sent for me, sir?"

"Yes, Chief. Mister Leighton just swore at me and slapped me. Hawkins saw it."

Watkins turned to Hawkins. "Is that true?"

"Yes, Chief, it is."

"Chief," Tomassi said, "Mr. Leighton is under arrest. Take him up to the con to tell the OOD. Then, take him to his cabin and keep him there under 24-hour guard. We're going back to Saipan. Unless and until Mr. Bergman takes charge again, I'll be in command, and Lt. Prince will be the exec. Is that clear, Chief?"

"Aye, sir," Watkins replied.

"You're dismissed, Hawkins."

"Aye, sir." Hawkins turned and left the wardroom.

Chief Watkins then turned to Leighton. "Sir, after you." Leightonturned and left.

After about an hour, Tomassi went to Bergman's cabin. Huffman was with him, checking his right eye.

"Well, Doc, how does it look," Tomassi asked.

Huffman turned to Tomassi, "I think his eye is better, sir. The flash he saw, whatever it was, only blinded him temporarily."

"What about his pain?"

"Well, sir, the back of the eye doesn't have pain receptors. What he felt was psychosomatic."

"Will he be able to resume his duties?"

"Anytime, sir."

"OK Doc, thanks. That's all."

"Aye, sir," Huffman said as he left.

"Hear that, Myron? Anytime you want, you can get back on that bridge."

Bergman shook his head. "Did I hear right, sir? Leighton really hit you?"

"He slapped me. I think my whiskers kept it from being serious." Both of them laughed.

"I didn't think he'd crack like this, Dom. It's beyond my belief. What did you say to him?"

"Oh, making this *my* fault? I just wanted to know why he was just standing there when a Jap tin can was barreling down on us."

"Well, I thought he was shaky, Dom. I just never figured him for the type to strike a superior officer. I mean, his dad was –"

"It doesn't matter what his dad was. He's the one who couldn't take it when everyone's lives were at risk."

"Anyway, I hear we're going back to Saipan."

"Yeah. But hey, I'm sure with these atom bombs and the Russkies finally in it, there won't be much left to sink anyway."

"I wondered if this would be the only patrol where I didn't sink anything," Bergman said. "Glad I was wrong."

CHAPTER SEVENTY-FOUR
15 AUGUST 1945

Ceasefire! That was the glorious word that Radioman Troilo was able to give the crew of the *Tiburon* before they sailed into Garapan harbor. The Japanese had finally quit the war. *Tiburon* may not have gotten the last sinking of the war, but she'd gotten in plenty of hits.

Captain Dominic Tomassi stood on the bridge of the sub, with Bergman beside him, and Lieutenant Prince ready to guide the boat in. Lt. Commander Leighton would go into the brig of the tender *Neptune* as soon as they were alongside. Regardless of it being the end of the war, striking a superior warranted punishment. This was one thing Tomassi didn't look forward to.

All hands were on deck on the *Neptune*, waving like mad and cheering the incoming boats. The *Garlopa* had also come home to Saipan on this glorious day. She had two sinkings to the *Tiburon's* one. No matter. The time for racking up kills was over.

Tomassi turned to Bergman. "How's the eye, Myron?"

"Fine, sir. Just fine. Doc wants me to get checked out anyway, with the doctor on the tender."

"Good idea."

"Dom?"

"Yeah?"

"Do you think it's time to look for a wife?"

"I think so. I think I'll put in for retirement."

"A captain's pension should be good bait, right, Dom?"

"I'm thinking, if Admiral Lockhart puts in a good word for me, I might get to be a 'Tombstone Admiral.'"

"What's that?"

"It's when a captain has enough friends in high places, that he can get a last minute promotion to rear admiral. He won't have had a task force to command, or whatever, but he gets the pension of a rear admiral, and it says it on his tombstone."

Bergman smiled, "Think I could get one of those?"

Tomassi looked at him for a moment, shook his head, and said, "Nah! You'll be a 'Tombstone Captain,' just watch."

Bergman shook his head and laughed, "I'll remember this when I go to the synagogue, Dom."

Tomassi laughed, "I'll put in a good word for you when we get to Pearl, Myron. Maybe there'll be room for two 'Tombstone Admirals.' Who knows, you could be the first one to jump *over* captain right to rear admiral."

"That's better, Dom."

As the *Tiburon* pulled up alongside the *Neptune,* Dominic Tomassi thought of New London again, and of Rosa.

Lightning Source UK Ltd.
Milton Keynes UK
UKHW012349210421
382415UK00001B/92